A

DESTINY

OF

CARNAGE

MALLORY FOX

Mallory Fox

A DESTINY OF CARNAGE
(A VIOLENT AGENDA BOOK FOUR)

Copyright © Jul 2022 by Mallory Fox

Published in the United Kingdom by
Black Jade Publishing Ltd.

Cover Design by Vicious Desires Design

To J.
Thank you for being the light to my darkness. Sorry for all the times I get stabby with you. Just know there's a bit of Jude, Lorcan, Dino, and even Dante in you that I adore and love. Though you will never, ever read this book, so I'm safe and can write what the hell I like.
Love me. x

MALLORY FOX

A Destiny of Carnage

Death isn't the end. Surrender is overrated.
Killing for love is the only cure…

I fear nothing, no one.

Not even the boys who loved me that I lost. **Dead**. Buried. Gone.
One by one. I am alone.
I need to be stronger. I have to evolve If I'm to survive. If I'm
going to save us all.

Jude is my rock. Lorcan is my faith. Dante is my blade. Dino *was*
the light to my darkness.

And me…I'm the monster who comes in the night. I'm the bitch
back from hell to make you weep. My father will know it when I
slice him and every last one of his sinners into pretty ribbons for
what they did to me…
To *my* family.

And in the end, they will beg.
Love, honor, and obey.
Not f*cking likely.

I'd rather slaughter them all.

AUTHOR'S NOTE

A Destiny of Carnage is a serial killer romance intended for mature audiences. Some scenes contain graphic violence and potentially triggering moments. A list of all triggers can be found at malloryfoxauthor.com. Please read at your own discretion.

Love & All Things Dark,
Mallory

GLOSSARY

The Organization a.k.a. 'The Five'

Lorcan James Duke *(formerly Joseph Duke)*

Albert Marques

Royden Earlshore

Kristian Vice *(formerly Liam 'Minotaur' Vice)*

Graham 'Griffin' Baron

The Harper-Black Family

(in Order of Inheritance)

Adrien Harper-Black *(married to Rebecca Hawkes)*

Viola Hawkes

Lily Hawkes *(daughter of Alex Hawkes)*

The Duke Family

(in Order of Inheritance)

Gordon 'Grandaddy' Duke *(married to Francesca 'Frankie' Gainsborough)*

Joseph Duke *(married to Katia Jayne Roweport)*

Tatiana Duke‡ *(married to Carl Marques)*

Byron Saint Marques† *(son of Tatiana Duke)*

Lorcan James Duke*

London Alaric Marques *(son of Tatiana Duke)*

Saskia Evelyn Duke*

The Marques Family

(in Order of Inheritance)

Albert 'Old Boy' Marques *(married to Fiona Grayson)*

~~Carl Marques~~ *(married to Tatiana Duke)*,

Jake Marques‡ *(married to Polly Leigh)*

~~Byron Saint Marques†~~

Jude Luther Marques *(son of Jake Marques)*

London Alaric Marques

Cecilia 'Cece' Grace Marques

~~Aurora May Marques~~

The Earlshore Family

(in Order of Inheritance)

Royden Earlshore *(married to Melissa 'Mimi' Derby)*

Carlotta Earlshore

The Vice Family

(in Order of Inheritance)

~~Harry Vice~~ *(married to Lola 'Birdie' Donovan)*

Kristian Vice *(married to ~~Nancy Haines~~)*

Kardinal 'Dino' Vice

Sorrow Vice *(daughter of Zeta Donovan)*

The Baron Family

(in Order of Inheritance)

Graham 'Griffin' Baron *(remarried to Lettie Knightly)*

~~Kenneth 'Midas' Baron†~~ *(divorced from Dahlia Donovan)*

Bea Baron‡ *(divorced from Charlie Havemeyer)*

Jackie Baron‡ *(married to Orion Montford)*

Finlay Baron *(son of Kenneth Baron)*

Royce Montford *(son of Jackie Baron)*

Pascal Havemeyer *(daughter of Bea Baron)*

† missing or presumed dead, * adopted, ‡ inheritance skipped or repudiated

ONE

VIOLA

HOW OFTEN HAVE *you thought about blood in the past week?*

I smile at the man in the inoffensive gray slacks and a sky blue shirt asking me that question. Blood. I'm always thinking about it. It haunts my nightmares and stalks my dreams. It stains the walls. It seeps through my skin and whispers in my ear. I see crimson, ruby, scarlet, carnelian, and vermillion reds everywhere. Never cardinal, though.

That color is gone.

I keep my smile in place and cock my head, letting him see in my eyes what I'd love to do to the prick assessing me today. It's become a ritual—Dr. Shalpert and I discussing my obsession with slaughter. It was fun at first. Now it's just tedious.

"Every second," I finally answer him.

His frown deepens as he glances down to scribble in his notebook. He uses a mechanical pencil with a 0.5mm lead. It means he likes to be precise. It also means he's not heavy-handed and won't easily snap the lead when pressing down to take notes. I take that and add it to all the other partial bits of information I know about him, storing it away for another day. From the clothes he wears, the steel-rimmed glasses on his face, and the wedding band on his finger—Dr. Shalpert takes his job seriously even though he is not a bad man.

But he is the one person I need to convince of my insanity.

"Are you still seeing things, hearing voices?"

I stare at him, unblinking. I don't fidget or look away, which is what the average person would do. "All the time."

I smile, letting him see the crazy.

The drugs they found in my system when they arrested me will help paint a pretty picture of a history of mental illness. I made sure the ones I used to coat my lips, and that ingested when I kissed Dino's brother, had the right cocktail known for hallucinations in users with underlying psychiatric or personality disorders.

There's a soft knock on the door, and an orderly pokes their head into the room. "Miss Hartridge's lawyer is here to see her."

If you're mentally capable, a visit from your lawyer trumps everything. Dr. Shalpert puts his canary yellow legal pad down, letting me see a glimpse of short-hand notes he's already accumulated from our session and waves me away.

"We'll finish this later," says Dr. Shalpert.

I suppress the irritation at having to delay my diagnosis. Since this is a private facility, the doctors here don't really care if their patients get the help they need, though they appear to go through the motions. I have no idea if he'll recommend transferring me across or not, but I need him to. I've been in St Michael's for a couple of weeks now, and it's apparent Jude is not here. He's not in this part of the facility anyway—where the juvenile delinquents, degenerates, and murderers are.

No.

He's on the other side.

Where the mentally unstable ones are.

The orderly takes me to a lounge room with soft yellow walls, like every wall in this place, and fake plants—no hard edges, thick, shatter-proof plastic as windows set into the stonework, an aquarium sealed into the wall, and muted paintings all around. Two flowery sofas face each other, and an imitation fireplace sits in the middle of the external wall.

Lorcan's lawyer, Carver, is waiting for me, and next to him, posing as his colleague, if his security tag is anything to go by, is Lorcan himself.

The lawyer runs a hand through his hair as he stands up, offering me his other hand to shake. My eyes flick to Lorcan's as he stands to do the same.

Deep, vermillion green eyes shrouded by dark, thick lashes, devoid of any emotion that I can interpret, take me in. Lorcan leans slightly in as I take his palm in mine. His grip is firm, and his skin is warm. He smells of citrus and bergamot, of all things rich, sexy, and opulent.

It makes the itch under my skin, constant since I got here, subside.

Just a little.

"Are you okay?" Lorcan's words are hushed, but I still hear him, as close as he is.

"I'm fine," I say softly, meaning it. I was never scared of being caught by the authorities. I'm not a wilting flower needing to be saved. I never was. I let that shine in my eyes as I sit across from Carver and Lorcan.

Lorcan frowns but takes his place next to his lawyer, now mine.

"We want to take you through some of the required paperwork," Carver says, leaning forward to pass me a file. There is no paperwork. It's code for Lorcan and me to have an open line of communication while I'm in here. I flip through the file and pretend to read as the orderly leaves. Once we're alone and the light on the camera in the corner of the room switches off, Carver gets up and walks to the reinforced window to look out, minding his own fucking business as he gets paid to do.

Lorcan gets to his feet, eyes narrowed as he looks over me from top to toe, as has become his routine every time he visits.

Then he pulls me to him, crushing my body to his chest, kissing the life out of me until my breath belongs to him. The scent of him wraps around me. Nothing matters but his lips, his tongue plunging inside, and his arms holding me to him as though he will never let me go. Without thinking or caring, I reach for where his cock is straining against his trousers and run my hand over the rich fabric, making him groan into my mouth.

After losing myself a few seconds, I push Lorcan away, breaking contact.

"V," he says, using the nickname I told him to use. One—because I change my name so often. And two—he can't call me Viola in here. "You ruin me every fucking time I come in here," he says in a hoarse voice.

His eyes are dark orbs, absorbing every part of me as his nostrils flare and his breathing is hard. But he steps back to give me space, his gaze switching back and forth over my face as though searing every detail into his skull so he doesn't forget.

My breaths are short, and my hair feels in disarray. I ignore fixing myself. *We don't have time.*

The last message I ever sent him from Pascal's phone was a list of what I needed to get into this place and out again when the time comes.

Lorcan came good, quickly getting Quinn to ensure I was Verity Hawthorne in the system and that she was the one they arrested, not Viola Hawkes. I'm twenty-three, but Verity Hawthorne is seventeen. She can do time in a young offender facility instead of a women's prison. I can't.

Of course, there was confusion when my prints came back with a different name once they'd booked me. But with Lorcan's lawyer on board, threatening to sue, it seemed like a minor mix-up. Someone must have taken the name down wrong.

In all the chaos, the murders and attempted murder, and my anonymous tip to the police naming Kristian's fiancée as the person responsible for his death, they eventually believed that was what happened. Systems and databases don't lie. And Quinn is that good.

The last part of my final message to Lorcan from Pascal's phone was to get me in St Michael's. I didn't want a women's detention center, and I didn't want bail. Not many murderers pleading guilty get bail anyway.

The rest is fucking history....

Or it will be when I find Jude and get us both out of here. Jude going missing *is* the only reason I let myself get arrested.

There's no other reason.

None.

The familiar buzz, the monster creeping under my skin, thinks differently.

I ignore it because it's wrong.

Dark red flickers at the edges of my vision.

Liar.

"V," Lorcan says again.

"What?" I snap back to reality, seeing Lorcan in front of me and no one else.

"Please tell me you found him." His green eyes bore into mine, desperately needing something. *Anything.*

I rub my brow and let out a sigh. "There is a Jude Marques in solitary, but it's not our Jude. It's some kid with a tendency to stare at walls. I have a hunch he's borrowed the kid's name as a way to get into the more secure part of the facility."

Lorcan's eyes narrow. "Is that where Byron is?"

"Supposedly," I say, giving the barest movement to my shoulders.

"What about Griffin's guys? Do they know? Can they help?"

I give a shake of my head. "Bunch of whining bitches," I say under my breath, rolling my eyes. The ones I have encountered have been trying their hardest to hurt me for killing Griffin. Even though I didn't pull the trigger and Kristian did.

Lorcan takes hold of my chin gently, too gently for my liking, and turns my face toward him. "You need them. You can't do this alone."

Fuck em. "I don't need anyone," is all I say. My words sound hollow even to me. I'm tired and cranky at all this extra mask-wearing I have to do. Why couldn't Jude have stayed put? Why did he have to disappear?

Because they all leave in the end.

"Did you bring what I need?" I add.

He nods and indicates to Carver, who is planting a failsafe for me just in case I ever need it. My fingers itch to take what's mine now, but I don't. I can't take it with me. They have metal detectors just shy of the inner security doors, the ones I have to walk through when they escort me back into the main part of the detention center. I leave the lawyer to begrudgingly hide my plan b in the stitching of the sofa armrest and then glance back at Lorcan, the unspoken question hanging in the air between us.

I should ask about Dante, but I won't.

That fucker doesn't deserve any more of my headspace.

After I turned myself in, he went dark and disappeared. Of course, he did. This is Dante. He was never going to risk me pointing the finger at him. Lorcan still has the USB drive in a safe somewhere, containing everything I gathered together to frame Dante when he was stalking me. I know because Lor told me where it was when it was clear Dante had abandoned me again.

I'd forgotten all about it. I must be losing my touch.

"You've always got me," Lorcan's smooth voice cuts through my shitty thoughts, knowing exactly what I'm thinking.

I clench my jaw and stare into his green orbs as he scans my face, eyes hungry for whatever I can give him. Even as withdrawn as I look now, he's drinking the very sight of me, warts and all, up. I haven't seen him in weeks. Fuck knows what I look like. The only time he was allowed to visit was right before I was remanded to St Michael's to wait for my summons to Youth Court. I was surprised to see him with Carver. After what I did to Dino, I assumed he'd drop me too.

But he didn't.

He stayed.

He's the only one who has. I've no idea what that says about him.

What does that say about you, V?

Lorcan mustn't like what he sees because he frowns.

"Fuck Dante, the bastard," he hisses, assuming the reason for the darkness peeking through my mask. "Forget about him."

"I can't yet," I say. Dante knows too much, and I'm vulnerable just being in here. If he has left me to rot, which is the most likely possibility, I still need to be aware that he can make it so that I don't survive another night. Especially if he thought I would rat on him. I don't say that out loud, not when Lorcan never trusted Dante. Paranoia comes with the territory of what I do. I don't need Lorcan freaking out along with me.

"I still don't know why you're putting yourself through this," Lor says, eyes clouding over with fears and demons of his own.

I blink at him, not bothering to answer that. When I don't move or say anything, Lorcan sighs and tilts his head, drawing me into his arms. I let him hold me. It's more for him than for me. When he asked me that question before, and I looked into his eyes, allowing him to see what I rarely let anyone see—that I'm cold, dead, and empty inside, he held me like he's holding me now. Squeezing until I can't fucking breathe.

Lorcan needs this. He craves touch, always needing to reach for me unawares whenever he's stressed or upset. And he's upset now because he knows the answer to his question.

He already knows *why*.

Dino.

After what I did...how easy was it to take the fall for shooting Kristian? Even though Dino's prints were on the gun, so were mine. Dino used *my* gun to kill his brother. When I gave myself up, I admitted guilt for everything, for Dino, for Kristian, and pleaded temporary insanity through the use of hallucinogenic narcotics, which I had overloaded myself with just before they took me in.

I was supposed to protect *him*. Keep *him* safe. I promised Lorcan I would. Taking the fall is what the boys would do for me. It's what Jude has done for me.

But I wasn't thinking clearly that night, and I'm still not. Getting arrested was an instinctive move. It meant my father couldn't get to me easily, but I could get to Jude. Though now I'm in here, I don't plan on staying, and I certainly don't plan on letting Adrien live.

But Lorcan continues to hold me, his heart beating where my jaw rests on his chest. I stay there for a minute or two, thinking of everything I need to do, until he says the words I've been dreading.

"We haven't been able to find him." His voice is strained and hushed as he kisses my hair.

Something dark twists in my gut.

Him—he means Dino.

After I was arrested, none of the boys could get back into the hospital. Then there was the funeral—a closed casket affair for one of Lola Vice's sons, which I couldn't attend. No one was invited, and it wasn't announced anywhere which son was being buried.

"He's alive," I say firmly, ignoring the darkness surging within me, wanting to lash out at Lorcan. I hold it in check, breathing hard. All this while Lorcan holds me.

It's a delicate balance.

When Carver clears his throat, I know our time is up.

Lorcan says nothing but presses me to him tighter. I let him crush me to his body one last time, and then I extract myself from his iron grip. I look into his haunted green eyes just as the orderly returns and Lorcan and Carver go to take their leave.

I *know* it was Kristian. He was stone cold dead when I was dragged away from his body in the church.

Dino made sure of that by shooting him in the head.

"Make friends, V. You need allies," Lorcan says under his breath as he shakes my hand goodbye.

I stare at him, knowing he's right, as red stains the corners of my vision, forcing me to blink it away.

He's right because he sounds just like bloody Dante.

TWO

VIOLA

BY THE NEXT DAY, Dr. Shalpert hasn't made any indication my answers have swayed him into believing I'm clinically unstable. That's fine. It just means I'll have to take matters into my own hands.

One of the orderlies takes me to the dining room for breakfast. The residents, that's what they call us here, are already sitting down to eat or are lined up at the serving hatch to get their food. I already know the utensils are plastic, as are the trays and tables. Nothing is breakable or can be made into a weapon.

Unless you know what to look for.

Once the orderly who escorted me has taken his place on the far side of the wall, I line up, grab some food, and then head over to my table.

The girl with braids in her hair, dark gray eyes, and pale skin, known as Raine to everyone in here, shoves me forward as she walks past with her tray. Killing Griffin has started a chain reaction of hostility within the ranks of his crew.

"Watch where you're fucking going, stupid bitch," Raine snipes, even though she's the one who veered into me.

I don't react. I calmly wait until she's sitting at her table with a bunch of guys. I get to my feet and make my way to the self-serve counter where residents can pour themselves a hot drink. There is a dispenser with boiling water in it and a row of cups with teabags or coffee granules. I palm a few sugar packets while filling a cup of hot water and then empty the packets into the water.

Lorcan was the one who suggested I try and recruit Griffin's old crew in here, but he's not the one getting dark, dead-girl-walking looks. I've been here for two weeks, mostly in isolation until now, just waiting for them to make their move.

They'll want revenge. *I would.*

So I need to show them I'm not to be messed with.

I head back to my table, taking the route back that brings me behind Raine's chair. She doesn't move fast enough. I chuck the hot water at the back of her neck. The sugar acts as an acid, eating into her skin.

"What the fu—" She screeches, clawing at her neck. The guys at her table don't waste time getting to their feet. One of them lunges for me; the one built like a tank. I shove my palm into his face, arm ramrod straight, breaking his nose with a delicious sounding crush. I kick him in the balls, and he joins Raine on the floor, who is still whimpering and rolling around like she's on fire.

Someone pounces on me from behind, pinning my arms in a bear hug. "I've got her!" The one holding me shouts, while the toned, floppy-haired guy with slitted eyes produces a shiv from somewhere hidden and stalks up in my face. I hook my foot around his leg as the one holding me tries to pick me up. He tightens his grip around my body in response.

"Jordan, gut the bitch," Raine, clutching the back of her neck, trying to get to her feet, hisses at the floppy-haired guy with the sharpened bit of plastic in his hand advancing on me.

"I'm going to hurt you for what you did to Grif," Jordan promises, a shitty smile easing onto his lips.

I'm a seething ball of rage when he gets within spitting distance. The darkness waiting to erupt, to be let loose, seethes under my skin.

"Do it," I taunt, allowing twisted insanity to slide onto my face. It's not the first time I've wanted one of these fucktards to hurt me. My darkness wants to feel something other than this. "Gut me, go on."

He hesitates at that.

Interesting. He might be a gang leader in here, but he's a reluctant one. I can always tell the ones with morals.

"Kill me if you have the balls," I snarl.

Jordan snorts and pockets his makeshift weapon instead, slamming a blow into the side of my head. Pain explodes across my cheek, and eye socket as my head snaps to the side. My vision falters. Blood fills my mouth where my teeth clamped down on my tongue.

"You're lucky. He wants you alive," he growls.

I flash an insane grin at him, licking my lips, whispering something inaudible.

He frowns and steps closer. *Good.* "What the fuck did you say?"

I say it louder for the kids in the back. And because he's close enough. "Not as lucky as you will be."

There's a shout as the orderlies finally get their asses in gear to stop the fight. Jordan's gaze slides to them approaching as the rest of his crew and the crowd of teenagers watching disperses.

"Fuck, they're here," says the guy behind me, relaxing ever so slightly. *Now.*

I throw my head back, elbows wide enough to force him to let go. Then I launch myself at Jordan, and we both hit the floor. Like a switch, I let the darkness out to play. He grapples with me, trying to hold me back. I scream and bite. There's blood in my mouth, soft flesh between my teeth, and nothing but rage consuming me from within. It takes several of the orderlies to pull me off and haul me away, screaming and spitting blood that I'm going to kill them all.

If that doesn't get me sent to the other side, fuck knows what will…

It doesn't.

But the warden sends me solitary for the rest of the week, which suits me fine. I'm in no mood to be around the masses. No one bothers to give me anything to clean the blood off, so I'm left with the taste of copper in my mouth and black shit under my clipped nails as I sit on the thin mattress, enjoying the old throbbing in my wrist from where it used to be broken.

Getting into the segregation unit where I know Jude is, is proving harder than I thought. *How do I convince the people running this shitty facility that I'm a threat if scarring one resident and biting a hole in the neck of another one isn't bloody enough?*

Annoyingly, Lorcan is right.

I need allies.

"Hey, psycho," one of Jordan's crew, a guy with short black hair, dark brown eyes, and brown skin, calls out. "Jordan wants a word."

I'm barely five seconds out of solitary and on my way to the communal common area when I'm being summoned. I give him a visceral look.

"He just wants to talk." He stares me out, his gaze callous and full of hostility until I suck in a breath and shrug. Griffin's guy may want to talk, but I'm itching for a fight after a week of seeing no one but the orderly who brings my meals. Still, Lor's request to smooth things over for the sake of finding Jude is not lost on me. I've no idea if Jordan is working for my father now or if he's going it alone now that Griffin is gone. Maybe it's time I found out.

The guy grunts for me to follow him, so I do, down the hallway toward the rooms at the rear of the building that seem to have much better views.

24

He catches me staring.

"Residents who have been here longer get the nice rooms."

I glance at him. "Is that so?"

I don't plan on staying here for a second longer than I have to.

Raine is leaning against the wall outside one of the rooms. She practically vibrates with malice when she sees me.

"I don't care that we're meant to keep you alive. I'm going to stab your pretty eyes out for what you did to me," she grits out.

Although the back of her neck would have hurt more when I doused her with the boiling liquid, she's lucky I didn't scar her face with it."Raine, move out the way. Jordan wants to talk to her," says the guy leading me to see Jordan.

She glances at him. "She's a fucking psycho, Cal. There's no talking to bitches like her."

"That's not your call to make," Cal intones.

After a few seconds, she moves out the way, bristling at me. I don't bother to acknowledge her as I walk past. She's like a rabid dog, demanding attention. She reminds me of Kristian in that way.

And look what happened to him.

Jordan, light brown hair flopping over into his face, tattoos everywhere, smirks as I walk in. He's lounging on an actual sofa. On the right side is a single bed, neatly made. His room is twice the size of mine and actually has windows, even though there are bars that run vertically over the entire frame.

"V, is that what they call you?" When I make no move to indicate yes or no, he cocks his head. "Alright, no foreplay. Take a pew." He indicates to the bed.

I'd rather stand, given I'm now trapped inside this room with a guy who has promised to kill me. The excitement of the whole situation has my body crawling with adrenaline. I like walking on the edge. It's the only thing that keeps me feeling alive.

And the darkness at bay.

"I understand now why you took Griffin out. Your boy, Duke

25

—he visited me while you were in lockdown. Pascal is a sweet girl. She didn't deserve that." I cock my head, waiting for him to continue. He sighs when he doesn't get a response. "You're looking for the gorilla?"

My brows raise.

"Jude," he snorts.

Okay, that's got my attention. I shift my stance, gaze flitting to Raine as she peers around the door and then back to Jordan. "You know where he is?"

"That motherfucker caused all kinds of fucked up shit in here."

I slit my eyes. "Sounds like Jude. Where is he?"

"The bastard's safe as houses where he is."

"In segregation?"

He gives me an evil-looking grin.

I have to stop myself from storming over to Jordan and beating the answer out of him. The guy loves the sound of his voice way too much, but that also means he won't like being rushed. I force myself to stay where I am, jaw clenching as I give him a dark smile. "Are you going to tell me how I get to him, or do I have to pry it from you with my teeth?"

Raine, from her doorway position, hisses while Jordan chuckles. "You're hilarious," he says.

"Glad you think so, but I wasn't joking."

"She's fucking nuts," Raine growls out. "This is a mistake, Jord, and you know it."

"Of course, she's fucking nuts. She's Adrien's daughter, for christ's sake," he snaps back.

"That's exactly why you can't trust her."

"Shut the fuck up, Raine."

I wait for Jordan to tell me what I want to know. Their bickering is getting old. Why do I always end up surrounded by teenagers?

"Jordan, stop stalling," I say to him, eyes narrowed. I'm

losing my patience. Any minute now, I'll give in to the voice in my head to hurt him. *And then where will we be?*

"Hold your horses. Our assistance doesn't come free. Your gorilla knew that and was able to give us a copy of a USB with a lot of valuable information on it."

I tilt my head. "Ah, I see, so this is a negotiation?"

He shakes his head. "Nope. I already negotiated with Duke. He agreed to give me what I want, but I need you to agree too."

"Agree to what?"

He smirks, "To take out the trash once you get to the other side."

I listen while Jordan tells me who he wants me to kill and why. Bateman is one of the newer orderlies, a transfer from another detention center with a weakness for young girls strapped to beds who can't fight him off. Any complaints made against him get ignored. Jordan doesn't tolerate men in power taking advantage of defenseless, helpless women. And neither do I.

Maybe we'll get along great.

"You forget one thing. I'm not on the other side."

"There's a one-way ticket into segregation if you know the right buttons to push."

"I've been doing just that."

He shakes his head. "Nah. You've been hurting other residents. That doesn't count here, or haven't you noticed? You need to become a danger to yourself, so they're afraid you'll top yourself."

"I can do that."

"You sure?"

I give him a blank look that makes him laugh.

"Maybe you can," he says, eyes roving over me. "Although, you don't look like the kamikaze type."

"I'll do whatever it takes," I say with a shrug.

"Or we can help you get in and out again, and no one needs to know any different."

Okay, I'll bite. I cock my head at him. "How?"

"One of our guys on staff will switch you with one of the permanents over there during visiting hours, which is tomorrow night. It's the only time the doors between both sides have foot traffic. There's a girl who looks just like you in a straitjacket. Brunette, though, you'll have to dye your hair. She comes here, and you go over there. My guy makes a few adjustments to the system. No one is none the wiser."

"You said it was a return ticket?"

"After a week or so, we switch you back. If it helps, we made your boy the same deal. That's how he got into Hades."

"Hades?"

"Hades. The other side. The underworld. Let's just say the place you're so keen to get to has a certain reputation." He grins.

I frown at him. "If you have that reach here, why can't you take the trash out yourself?"

"I'm up for review, and so is Raine. One wrong step, and we're dying of old age in this shithole. But I heard you don't give a fuck. And if you already have a death wish…."

If he's trying to scare me, it's not working. "Fine."

"Just to be clear, Bateman needs to be gone before we let you back out."

"He's as good as dead."

"Good. It looks like we have a deal. Raine will get you the hair dye." He looks over at Cal, who walks into the small toilet cubicle attached to the room. Cal comes out a minute later with a wet plastic bag and hands it to Jordan.

"What's that?"

He opens the bag, revealing a huge stash of pills of all colors. "Every day, we're given drugs to keep us happy. The residents sell those drugs to me for protection, among other things. Anti-depressants, antipsychotics, tranquilizers, mood stabilizers, and even good old sleeping pills." He starts separating the blues from the pinks, whites, and yellows.

"And you're showing me because?"

"Because…" He picks up a handful of the blue pills with an imprint I recognize on them. "These are your ticket in."

I raise a brow. "Trancs?"

Eyes shining, Jordan smirks at me. "You know your narcotics. Even better. I don't need to convince you I'm not poisoning you." He offers them to me. I look at them but don't take them.

"Why do I need those?" My gaze is shuttered, guarded even as I say it.

"My guy likes to keep his identity secret. He'll only move patients who are drugged. You'll need to take these an hour before he comes for you."

I blink at him. "Dye my hair and drug myself. That's a pretty fucking big ask." I do know what the pills are. But that doesn't mean they aren't tampered with. Any mark can be counterfeited. And tomorrow was when Lorcan would visit and update me about Dino. If I engage with this plan, I won't have time to tell him, but if I wait another week, that is a week too fucking long. And I can guarantee Lor will try and stop me.

He shrugs and leans back. "What other choice do you have?"

Jaw clenched, I look him in the eyes as he stares back at me. Then, I glance at Raine leaning against the door frame, watching the exchange outside Jordan's room. She's not happy, that much I can tell. Anger radiates off her in waves. On the other hand, Cal has schooled his features into a neutral mask. All while Jordan looks positively gleeful.

I breathe and go with my gut, holding a palm out for the drugs.

What other choice do I have?

THREE

VIOLA

"HELLO, BEAUTIFUL."

Sweet words, soft and seductive, pierce the cloudiness of my brain. I bolt awake, eyes blinking painfully open. It's like my lids are glued shut. I pry them apart, forcing myself to look around, and at the person staring down at me.

Jude, sexy Jude...

Fucking finally.

Blond hair messy and in disarray, twinkling hazel eyes, he smirks. "I want to ask what the fuck you're doing here, but I think I know the answer."

"Ju..." I slur. Saliva dribbles down the side of my mouth. *Fuck I can't talk. I can't move. What the hell did they give me?* My brain kicks in. I took the trancs as directed, enough to knock me out about an hour before visiting hours. Adrenaline surges, as well as panic, making my heart thud noisily in my chest. I move my gaze about the room, trying to work out where I am. I'm laid on a single bed in a small rectangle-shaped room. There's nothing else in the room, but I note that the walls are sky blue, not eggnog yellow. *I must be in the non-sectional psych ward.* There's a door behind Jude that's closed over. We're alone.

Jude is here, and we're alone.

I try to sit up, but it's like I've been zapped of all my energy. Jude smirks again, pushing me back down onto the bed with ease.

"Nah, don't try to move or talk. If it's the same shit Jordan loaded me up with, it's a bitch if you're not prepared. Just chill. Let me stare at you some more." He runs his eyes over me as he sits on the bed, dragging a hand through his unkempt hair.

"Fuck, I must be dreaming. You can't be real. Can you?" A dark light fills his eyes as he takes me in. "I need to know if you're real."

My throat is raw and parched, and my tongue feels thick and rough, like sandpaper in my mouth. I want to say, 'kiss me and find out the fuck out', but I can't make my lips move. I blink my heavy eyelids at him instead.

"I'm going to take that as yes, beautiful," he drawls, leaning down to run his tongue over my lips, teasing softly with his teeth as he explores my unusually pliant mouth.

I give a soft moan.

Eventually, he pulls back, the lust in his gaze now blazing.

I stare at him. *How did he know I would be here? How is he even here?*

"Jordan got word to me, and I bribed an orderly to smuggle me into your room," he says, reading my mind. "What were you thinking? You can't stay here, babe. You look nothing like Dahlia." He must see my confusion because he adds, "The girl they switched you with." He shakes his head. "Someone is going to fucking notice you're not her."

I can't do anything but lie there and look at him, allowing myself to drink him in for once—the square of his stubbled jaw, the slope of his broad shoulders, and the corded muscle in his arms as he towers above me on the bed. Then I gaze back into his eyes...eyes that raze over me. Anyone else but Jude, this close while I'm vulnerable and weak, would have my body reacting to escape.

But I feel…

Calm.

Safe.

Slowly, he reaches forward to graze a knuckle over my cheek, down my neck, tracing lightly over my breasts. My lips part. My breath catches. His hand wanders down my stomach to my thighs. I'm still wearing the jeans and t-shirt from earlier when I took the pills, but his touch lights me on fire, even over the denim. That I can't move makes this whole situation unbearable and hot as hell.

As his luscious mouth curves into a dark smile, my body responds, clenching and fluttering awake.

"If I weren't such a fucking gentleman, I'd fuck you raw right now," he chuckles.

My usual mask is gone. Vulnerable and exposed, unable to fight it or hide it like I usually would, I give off a tight moan between breaths. It's barely a whisper and a nod, but he gets it. What else can I do?

"Are you sure? You're fairly out of it right now."

My eyes flash with a feral look as I try to lift a heavy hand and grab onto his collar with every ounce of effort in my bones. Desire roars to life behind his eyes as he climbs onto the bed and on top of me, kissing me desperately. I want to respond, but my body is lead. Still, the sensation of his hands everywhere, mauling at my clothes and then under them, rough palms searing my skin, fingers digging into my flesh, is enough.

Jude isn't gentle, and I don't want him to be.

I'm where I finally belong.

My jeans are wrenched off, and the cooling air on my skin sends shivers down my spine. Jude's mouth and tongue are on my collar bone, neck, and bare breasts as he hauls my top over my head to devour them.

"You don't know how long I've fucking waited to do this," he growls in my ear.

"Jude." At least I can say his name now. My lips and tongue work now, though it's still an effort.

He rips off my panties, tearing the thin material from my body, until I'm completely naked under him. He eye fucks me like a starved man and then kisses me savagely, running his hands all over me until I'm lost in his kiss.

"You can't fucking know how much I've wanted to do this," he whispers in my ear. "Needed to. You drive me insane, Viola. I've dreamt of this fucking moment for so long."

He glides a hand over my wet pussy. I know I'm soaking. I can feel my heat running down my thighs and all over his hands as he holds me possessively, claiming me.

As he looks into my eyes, burning the insanity of this moment into my brain, igniting the need until it's burning me up from the inside, I look right back. My body might be heavily sedated, but my mind is furiously awake and in the moment.

It can't be anywhere else. Not around Jude.

"Tell me it's the same for you?"

"It is," I hiss.

He smirks and shoves three fingers inside. "Tell me how much you fucking want me."

"Want you," I grit out.

He pumps me harder, stretching my relaxed pussy until my body feels like it's falling apart.

Jude is still fully dressed, much to my annoyance, but there's nothing I can do. I don't have the energy to undress him or fight him. All I can do is lie there and let the exploding sensations sweep over me as he fucks me repeatedly with his fingers.

"Fuck me," I pant.

He chuckles. "You want my cock in you? Is that it?"

I give a jerky nod, trembling as he strokes me long and hard.

"Greedy bitch," he snorts. "Always getting what you want." I eye him greedily as he strips off. His body is angular, hard, and sculpted as ever. Knowing Jude, he hasn't stopped working out in here. My eyes are drawn to the thick length of him between his legs. He catches me looking. "Like what you see? It's all yours, beautiful." He leans down over me, returning the heat that left when he sat up to undress. "It's always been fucking yours," he rumbles in my ear as he licks my neck.

He nudges my weak legs easily apart with his knees, and he eases in. Even though I'm relaxed, he's still too big to fit all the way the first time. "Fuck, you're tight." But that doesn't stop him. He lifts my leg, adjusts his hips, and rams all the way in. There's a flood of pleasure through my core, rippling all the way down to my goddamn toes.

I moan in response, letting Jude use me the way he needs to.

"Ah fuck, I'm not going to be able to hold back," he pants between strokes.

My eyes blaze as he starts to slow down. I manage a stilted shake of my head. I don't want him to take this slowly. I need him hard and fast. It's been so long. I need him to consume me, so I don't carve someone up too soon.

"Hurt me, Jude." My voice is barely a whisper.

His gaze darkens as he increases the pace, hands digging into my flesh where he holds me down on the bed. Every punch of his cock soothes the ragged edges of my soul. He breaks me apart, puts me back together in a heartbeat, and then does it all over again until my weak legs are shaking and my lower half is a quivering mess.

He comes with a groan, and I feel him release, hot and messy, deep inside me. My eyes flutter closed as the explosion of ecstasy overtakes everything else. His lips are on mine as I shudder beneath him, invading my mouth with his tongue just as he claims the rest of me.

· · ·

Later, after we're spent, tangled in sheets, limbs wrapped around each other, pressed against every part of each other, I open my eyes to see him looking right at me.

My initial reaction is to jerk away, but the drugs are still in my system. Moving is still an effort, although it's less like I'm dead from the waist down and more like moving underwater.

"I should drug you more often," Jude teases, stroking my hair from my face.

"Fuck you," but I say it lightly.

"Baby, you just did." His eyes sparkle with amusement, full of longing, lust, and a look that flits across his features for a split second. It reminds me of a puppy dog.

I manage to turn away from him to lie on my back, breaking the connection. It's not awful to look at Jude that way. It's just too intense. I'm reminded of Dino. He used to look at me like that. Stare at him long enough, and he's peeling away the layers to the core of my soul.

He can penetrate my insides with his cock, but I draw the line at his eyes. I don't want him under my skin, seeing the darkest, deepest parts of me.

Why the hell is Jude looking at me like that?

I shift uncomfortably as he drapes an arm over my lower half possessively so I can't easily escape.

"Viola," he says.

I ignore him.

"Viola, look at me."

I flick my eyes up and then shoot him a glance, shuttering my features. "There. I'm looking at you."

His lips curl up in a twisted smile. "I'm so fucking happy to see you...you have no idea."

I scowl at him. "I thought you were the one who didn't have feelings."

"Who the fuck said that? I'm a moody bastard, or haven't you realized? Now, tell me—why are you in here? How did you even get in here? I'm over the fucking moon you are, but this is the last place I wanted you to end up."

That's right, Jude has no idea what's been happening on the outside. I give him the condensed version of the events. He was informed right up until the boys attended my father's party at his estate. As I enlighten him, he watches me intently the whole time, not even flinching when I tell him what Kristian did to me and then what I did to Dino. He only frowns when I get to the part about turning myself in. But his brow smoothes when I reveal that I'm here under a false name.

"Okay, I get all that, but why the fuck are you here?"

I frown at him. "You disappeared. I had to come and find you."

He shakes his head. "Nah, you don't get to do that. This isn't my fucking fault."

I turn toward him, eyes narrowed. "What do you mean?"

"You didn't come in here to find me."

I shift his arm off me so I can sit up. I'm tired of lying down. The world spins as I right myself, glaring at him. "That's exactly why I did it."

Jude shifts, too, leaning back to sit against the headboard. "You're deluding yourself, babe. Admit it. You let them cage you because of what happened to Sinner. It's eating you up inside, and this is the only way to ease some of the pain. You want someone to take away your choices and make it easy on you for once. No lies, no games. Just surviving."

There's a flash of something behind his eyes that I can't decipher.

"That's not what this is."

He shrugs. "Fine, keep telling yourself that. Tell Lorcan and the rest so that they don't start to worry. But you and I both know that's bullshit."

I give him a look. "It's you, isn't it?"

"What is?"

I cock my head at him. "You're talking about yourself."

He snorts and looks away but doesn't correct me.

"Is that why you missed your transfer window with Jordan?"

His hazel eyes, darker now, cut back to me. "They've got my cousin drugged up to the eyeballs. I've been interfering with his meds, trying to wean him off that shit." He lifts his shoulders into a shrug. "It's taking longer than I expected because even without the drugs, he's a mess."

I nod my head. Keep someone in one of these places long enough; the drugs alone will erode whatever is left of a person. I should know—it happened to my mother.

"So, what's the plan?" When he winces, flatting his lips in a smile that doesn't reach the eyes. He reaches up to run a hand through his hair. I don't miss the slight tremor to his hand as he does. I close my own eyes and open them.

From what I know, Jude is an addict. This place must be like a candy store to him.

"What are they giving you?"

He narrows his eyes. "What do you mean?"

"Your hand. It's shaking. You need a fix of something. What is it?"

He gives me a dubious look, making one hand into a fist and palming it in the other. "You're fucking seeing things. It's been a long time since I had a fight, that's all." He looks me dead in the eyes. "You, of all people, should know what that's like."

He's half right. I know what it feels like to have the itch to slice someone's carotid open, spilling their life to the ground. I know what it feels like to be angry enough that my whole body shakes. I'm not so weak that I can't control my limbs. Having a tremor is terrible for your aim. I do everything in my power not to have one.

I don't say any of this. I'm tired, and I don't want to argue.

But I understand why Jude hasn't left this place.

He doesn't have school anymore and failed to protect his cousins. Lorcan is the one who gets to inherit the Duke family fortune. Dino is the one who has his family business to continue, if not reluctantly. Jude has nothing and no one.

He doesn't even have me because he's not stupid.

I always planned to leave.

Only Dino assumed I would stay.

I let out a breath. "Do you still have that USB? Did you manage to get it open?" When he first came in here, Lorcan and I smuggled him in some leverage—a digital lockbox with all the dirt we could get on every staff member.

"You have no fucking faith. Of course, I did. How did you think I got in here?"

"Who the fuck knows," I snap.

He sighs. "There's a computer in the dispensary. I complained of migraines, and the nurse took pity on me. I had to…to make a copy to give to Jordan." I raise both brows, and he grins at me. "Don't get mad. I didn't screw her. I just asked nicely if I could sleep it off in one of the sick bays."

I'm unaware of the claw of jealousy gripping my insides ever so tightly until he admits nothing happened. "I don't give a fuck if you screw her or not," I snap.

He flashes a smile and hauls me towards him. He smells of soap and drugs, but underneath it all, he smells like Jude. The kiss is invasive and hungry. I let him devour me until he pushes me back down onto the bed and climbs on top.

I don't stop him.

I'll interrogate him later about his addiction. For now, I don't want to talk or think.

I just want to be destroyed from the inside out.

FOUR

JUDE

I'M FUCKING DREAMING. Viola can't be here.

And yet she is.

Like some kind of creep, I watch her sleeping, unable to take my eyes off her. I'm still in shock over what she told me about Sinner. No one fucking told me. What did I expect? I cut off all ties with Duke's lawyer and even my grandfather. I had to, or someone would figure out that the guy in solitary that I switched with wasn't me.

But Sinner. *Fuck.*

He's got to be alive.

He's the best of the three of us, constantly harping on about my bad habits and cleaning up after me. It can't fucking end like this. He can't be dead, or why the hell did I take the rap for this shit? Maybe coming in here was a mistake?

I let out a breath and run my hand through my hair. My nerves are shot to pieces, making my fingers tremble, reminding me just how much of a mistake it was to let them lock me away. They pump me so full of shit, somedays, I can't see straight, never mind save Byron. Because the whole reason I'm here is to find him and get him out.

No one deserves to be in this hellhole.

Viola frowns in her sleep, her brow furrowing in a way that is too fucking cute. She might be a crazy killer, but that doesn't mean she deserves to be here. Her father made her that way, and it rips my heartstrings to see her like this.

She moans, making me instantly hard again.

This girl will be the death of me.

I wait for her to settle and then bang on the door. From what I can see, it's dark outside through the tiny, barred window in Viola's room. Roberts is waiting to let me out. I told him to give me twenty-four hours, and he did, the cocksucker. He had no choice, given the dirt I have on him.

He doesn't escort me back to my room. He takes me to the dispensary, where I have a stash of what I need from Jordan waiting for me to collect. I give Roberts half, which he accepts with a grunt, and then I take the rest back to my room. I should go back to Viola, but I need a time out. I've been so used to being on my own these last few months that I just need a minute and a few chill pills to get my head straight. The effect of the drugs isn't as good as it once was, and it takes longer. So I take a few more than I should. Suddenly, the calm and relaxed feeling starts to melt my bones, pulling me into a state of immense pleasure. Finally, I drift off into a damn good night's sleep.

"So this is what you're hooked on?" I crank open my eyes to see a pissed-off brown-haired Viola glowering down at me. She's got her hair in a ponytail, and she's wearing scrubs, just like everyone else in here, totally different from what I found her in yesterday.

"How did you know where to find me?" I smack my lips a few times, mouth dry as fuck, as I sit up and take her in. The brown hair doesn't suit her. Already I miss the blonde. And where did she get those fucking scrubs?

She rolls her eyes in her head. "Don't insult me." She perches on the end of the bed, making the thin mattress shift with the extra weight. These beds are so shit, but at least they're clean. She tosses something small and blue at me. I know what it is before I've even caught it. She found my stash of benzos.

"What the fuck, Jude?" she hisses.

"Who gave you the pajamas?" I say, slipping the benzo into my pocket, changing the fucking subject.

"One of the nurses came in this morning. She knew who I was. I'm assuming Jordan has her on his payroll too?"

I nod at her. "Most likely. He has fucking almost everyone."

"If he's that connected, why is he still in here?"

"Griffin didn't want him out. There was some kind of disagreement between Jordan and Griffin's brother, Midas, before he died."

"Midas was Finn's dad, right?"

I nod at her. "With Graham gone, Finn moves up to take his seat as one of The Five."

She scowls. "Is that why Lorcan is pissed that I killed Griffin?"

"Kristian killed Griffin." I correct her.

"I ask him to. The fucker deserved to die."

"Fucking Amen to that," I intone.

She gives me a look. "You're not annoyed?"

"Why would I be annoyed? As you said, the fucker deserved to die."

She blinks at me with her huge, brown eyes and then empties the air from her lungs. "You're the easiest out of them all, you know."

I furrow my brow at her, but I can't help the slight fucking grin easing onto my lips. One little bit of praise, and I'm lapping it up.

Fuck, I'm whipped.

Like a goddamn pussy.

Viola leaves me to shower and put on some new scrubs. I fucking miss clothes. On the other side, you can wear whatever the fuck you like, within reason. When I go to check my stash, it's fucking gone. The bitch must have taken it. What the fuck?! Why the fuck would she do that? I'm seething by the time I find her in the main common room. She's sitting at one of the craft tables with her back to the wall, watching everyone. I can almost hear her brain ticking over as she takes in each resident and categorically puts them in a mental box of useful to not. She leans back in her chair when she sees me approaching.

I stalk over to her and lean down until my eyes are level with hers, placing my hands on either side of the chair arms she's sitting in.

"Where the fuck are they?" I say in a low voice.

"Careful," she says softly, eyes flashing with a warning.

I don't want to be fucking careful. I want my stash back. Why the fuck would she take it? I let my anger show in my eyes, but she just smirks, glancing down.

I follow her gaze.

The bitch has a ballpoint pen in her hand. I've no idea how she got that, but the threat is clear. She will stab me with it if I don't back off.

I swallow my anger, snarling as I run my hands through my still-damp hair.

"Now, back the fuck away and sit down."

I take a step back and collapse into the empty seat opposite her.

"There's a good boy," she says under her breath.

I blink at her, wrangling my temper back into its fucking box. *For fuck's sake. What am I doing?* Viola is still watching me, face unreadable. But her hand is clenched around the pen as though her life depends on it. She has every right to shove that piece of plastic through my fucking eye. I'm acting like a complete tosser.

I drag a lungful of air into my lungs, closing my eyes for a minute.

Chill the fuck out, you prick. You're scaring her.

I snort a laugh at that. As if I could scare her, she's the fucking Terminator on steroids.

"What's so funny?" her sweet voice asks.

I open my eyes and stare at her. "I'm a complete prick for getting wound up about the pills."

She raises a brow. "You can't even sit still, can you?"

I look where her gaze rests on my right hand, clawing at the chair arm material. Fucking hell. I white knuckle my hand to make it stop and then stare at her.

"I just…need it to help me sleep. That's all."

She shakes her head. "I know addiction when I see it." She tilts her head, studying me like she can figure me out. "I have the same thing."

That pulls me out of my own fucking ass. I cast my eyes over her, aware that we're in a psych ward and being watched, but not in the least bothered. It's her and me, and that's all there is. No other fucker exists.

"Explain," I say.

She doesn't get to because a nurse comes over with a tray of little cups with pills and hands us one with a chaser of water.

Viola watches me intently as I knock it back. The nurse has already fucked off, so I needn't have eaten the drugs, but if that's all I'm getting tonight, I'll take everything I can.

She chuffs and pockets hers when the nurse is turned away.

'If you don't want yours, I'll have them," I say.

She gives me a look and then shakes her head. "You have one day to get your act together, or I'm moving without you."

I glare at her. "Moving to do what?"

"What you couldn't."

With that, she walks off.

FIVE

JUDE

I FIND her in her room a little later during recreation, sitting at the desk, grinding my pills into blue dust using the base of a plastic cup.

"Do I even want to know?"

"Jordan wants me to kill Bateman."

I raise my brows and lean against the wall by the door, jamming my hands into my pockets to stop them from fidgeting. "You're going back." It's more a statement than a question.

She lifts her gaze to me mid-grind. "We're both going back. I came in here to get you. I'm not leaving you here."

I say nothing. I don't want to argue with her. Seeing her fucking up my stash like that has me licking my lips. I want more than anything to go over there and take them back. I also want to grab her and fuck her brains out on that damn desk, but I hold myself in check. I'm not a fucking savage.

"So that's your price with Jordan, killing Bateman?"

She turns back to her task, nodding. "I'll have it done by Friday, so I would get what you need from your cousin by then if I were you."

"He won't talk to me," I say. "But he might talk to you."

She stops crushing pills to look my way. "Is the almighty Jude asking for my help?" There's a slight smirk on her lips as she says it.

"Bitch," I tease her with a smile on my lips. I can't stay mad at her, no matter what she fucking does to me. I've never met a girl like her—cold and distant but burning hot at the same time —an ice planet with a molten core, like Uranus. I let out a chuckle at that, suddenly thinking of Viola's pretty, little anus.

She tilts her head, a bemused look on her face. "What's so funny?"

In answer to her, I stalk over to where she is and place my hands on her shoulders, massaging the knots of tension I find there away. She stiffens at first but then relaxes, closing her eyes and leaning back, becoming putty in my hands. I take the opportunity to stroke my fingers over her neck and down the front of her top to her pert breasts.

She's definitely a fucking heavenly body.

And every time, I gravitate toward her. I can't keep away.

I bend down until my mouth is in line with her ear.

"Strip and get on the fucking bed," I growl at her, kneading her breasts.

"You're trying to distract me," she says, opening her eyes.

"Too right, I am. But I also want to fuck that tight, little ass."

She reaches her arm up behind her, cupping her palm around the back of my neck, turning around to put her lips on mine. Her tongue darts inside. She smells of the shampoo they use here— mint and citrus. She tastes of toothpaste...and like fucking coming home.

It doesn't last. Her fingers, latched onto my neck, dig in as she bites down. A flash of pain. The sharp tang of blood. She's punishing me with a vicious kiss. I let her hurt me because I deserve it. I take everything she has, wrap my hands around her upper body, and haul her to her feet. She spins around and growls as I sink my teeth into her lower lip, fighting back. She pushes against me. I walk back, my legs hitting the edge of the bed as I fall onto it.

Then, she's on top of me in a heartbeat. She straddles me, climbing onto my chest, and entwining her legs through mine. I can't buck her off. I'm not sure I want to. Even when her fist curls in my hair and she yanks at my head to shove the end of the biro against the exposed part of my neck.

"You only get to fuck my tight, little ass when I say you can." She pushes the pen harder, nearly choking me. "Got it?"

"I get it," I say lazily, unflinching, staring deep into her angry, glittering orbs. I let her jab the pen as far as she can without sticking it in my goddamn carotid. She's pissed at me and frustrated. Even I can tell she needs to hurt someone, and she needs to do it soon.

If it needs to be me, then fuck it.

Bring it.

I stare her out until she blinks a few times, drops her hands from my hair roots, and removes the pen from my throat.

"You're not trying to stop me," she breathes out. "You're as bad a fucking Dino."

"He gets it, and so does Lor," I say in response. When she doesn't answer, I prop myself up on my elbows. "Sometimes, you need an outlet." I cock my head. "We've got you."

"What you have is a fucking death wish," she sneers, head shaking as she climbs off me, concealing the pen away somewhere as she does. "I almost killed him."

"But you didn't," I say, keeping my voice light and my eyes on her as she starts pacing the tiny, white room.

She stops pacing and looks at her hands. After a few seconds, she snaps back from wherever she disappeared to inside her head and scowls at me. "Only because Dante stopped me."

"You would have stopped."

She walks over to the ground-up drugs on the table and starts scraping the powder onto a torn-off piece of the bag. Once it's full, she twists the ends and pockets it. Her hands are stained blue by the time she's finished. She dusts away the excess and heads to the sink in her room to wash her hands.

When she's finished, Viola heads to the door and opens it. There's a lot of commotion in the hallway as we step into it. Just like the central part of the facility, residents are allowed to come and go from their rooms to the common areas as they please until late in the evening, when we're supposed to retreat to our rooms. We're not in prison, or so we keep getting reminded.

"Where is everyone going?" She looks up and down the corridor.

"To eat. It's dinner time."

"Then we do the opposite," she says. "Take me to Byron."

My cousin is the same as the last time I saw him. Even with probing the nurses and orderlies to no longer give him any sedatives, he's still pretty much catatonic.

Viola walks right up to him, snapping her fingers in his face. He doesn't even flinch.

"See, he's gone."

She looks over her shoulder at me. "You're just going to give up?"

"Look at him. He's a living, breathing corpse."

"Just roll him over," she says, giving me a death look.

"What? Why?"

"Because you're going to shove some of your pills up his asshole," she says sweetly, fluttering her eyelashes."

I stare at her. "You're fucking kidding me. Why?" I say again.

"Because benzodiazepines are the only thing that can wake your cousin up, and he needs it in large doses absorbed into the bloodstream quickly. I have nothing here to dissolve them in or inject him with. Hopefully, he has a tight, little anus for you to enjoy."

The look I give her is dark, bordering on bloody murderous.

She holds up a handful of pills. "The faster you do this, the quicker we can go and eat."

I close my eyes and count to five, and then open them. Nope, she's still fucking there, causing my life to be a fucking misery. I have half a mind to take the pills and lock myself in my room, but I know she'll hunt me down and hurt me in places I never knew existed if I did that.

"Fucking fine," I snap. "Just give me the damn things and get out."

She hands me the drugs but then crosses her arms in front of her chest. "I'm not going anywhere." Her lips are twitching as she says it. She's fucking loving this.

"You fucking bitch," I say, half meaning it, half wanting to grab her and kiss that smirk right off her beautiful face.

Byron is light as a feather, so it's easy for me to lean him against my shoulder, yank his scrubs down, and shove the pills into God knows fucking where. Then he's back in his chair with his pants where they should be, and I'm scrubbing my hands in the sink.

When I turn my attention to Viola, she's watching me with an amused look.

"You're so getting it up the bum for that,"

She snorts. "That turn you on, did it?"

"I could be tempted." I give her a Jude special—twisted grin, deviant fucking eyes. "Three-ways are still a gift of mine, babe."

She rolls her eyes and walks out of the room.

I catch her in the corridor, wrapping an arm around her waist. One of the nurses is watching us as she heads to Byron's room. I give her something to look at, drag Viola's annoyed face toward me by her chin, and lick away the snarl from her lips.

"They're watching," she hisses.

"I don't give a fuck," I answer back. And I don't. This place is a joke. No one fucking cares.

To prove a point, I drag Viola into my room with the nurse frowning but doing nothing to stop us.

. . .

The next day, while I stand behind Viola as she gets her breakfast, the nurse is still watching us, and so is fucking Bateman. The pervert has had a hard-on for her since he saw her. It's why I didn't leave her side once when she was vulnerable and drugged up to her eyeballs. I won't shed a tear if she kills him.

"So, what now?" I tell her as we sit with our trays loaded with bacon and eggs.

"You need to do what you did to Byron another five more days," she says, popping her juice carton with a straw with more force than necessary.

I glare at her. "You left that part out, didn't you?"

She ignores my comment and starts spearing the egg yolk with her plastic fork. "Today is Monday. He should wake up on Friday."

"You're meant to switch back on Friday," I remind her.

"*We* are switching back. You're not staying here."

"We'll see about that," I grind out, pushing my food around my plate. I'm not hungry. My head is starting to pound, and my mouth is dry as fuck. I knock back my juice, emptying the carton in one go. Then I get to my feet.

Viola's gaze follows me up. "Where are you going?"

"Fucking anywhere. I need to get the hell out of here."

I leave Viola to her meal and head to the dispensary. The redhead nurse who usually sorts me out isn't on today, so I just stand there staring at the fucking door until I realize how obvious I look.

Fuck this shit. How dare she come in here and ruin fucking everything.

I go to the only place I know that might have what I need— Viola's room. I search high and fucking low, tearing the bed sheets off, emptying the bin, even living loose fucking floorboards. It's not here, which means she has it on her.

I run my hands through my hair, chewing my lip as I survey

the mess I've made. I don't hear her come in, but I sense her near after a dozen ragged breathes.

"How bad is it?" Her voice has no worry or sympathy, just a cold, hard question. I'm grateful for it. It makes it easier to look at her when I turn around.

Her face is unreadable. Fuck knows what she's thinking.

I shake my head, rubbing my hands through my hair, trying to calm my manic heart.

"I can't do this," I say to her, honestly.

She narrows her eyes. "What will help?"

"Nothing, nothing will fucking help," I snort. After a few seconds, I sit on the floor, leaning back against the bed frame.

Viola comes over and does the same. She doesn't try to touch me or talk to me. She just sits next to me and sighs out loud. I'm sweating profusely now, feeling like I'm about to have a heart attack. *Great. Here it fucking goes. Get ready to have the ride of your damn life Marques.*

"Well, this is fucking boring," she says after a minute of me breathing hard.

The laugh sticks in my throat. It is. It's fucking boring, and I never wanted to show this amazing, beautiful, deadly girl, this pathetic, screwed-up side of me.

But what choice do I have?

"Distract me," I say to her after a minute.

"We're not doing anal without lube," she says as a matter of fact.

I give her a smirk. "I can't believe I'm saying this, but that's the last thing I want to do."

She glances over and nods like she understands, eyes practically fucking glowing. "Then how about we kill someone?"

SIX

VIOLA

ABOUT FOURTEEN HOURS into his withdrawal, Jude
looks like shit. He stayed the night until it was apparent that
none of us would get any sleep, and then I kicked him out. Sleep
is one of the most important requirements before a job. If you're
not getting any rest, you may end up fucking dead. And as much
as Jude looks to be in pain, I draw the line at losing valuable
shut-eye, so I made him go back to his room where he can toss
and turn to his heart's desire.

I'm not very good at being sympathetic.

But I'm good at doing my job, so I'll be fine if I see Jude as
just that. He won't know that I just want to punch his face for
fucking his body up or that I'm itching to tie him to a bed and
leave him there to get the poison out of his system.

What he won't know won't hurt him.

"How are you going to do it?" Jude asks as soon as he turns
up to my room during personal time.

I don't answer him, so he comes and sits in my room as I get
ready. He asks me again as we walk to the cafeteria for breakfast.
Jude looks nauseated at seeing what's on offer—sloppy scram-

bled eggs, toast, and lukewarm tea. But just like sleep, I also need fuel. I'll eat whatever they put in front of me.

When I have a full tray, I glance at Jude, who is still behind me, as I edge my way around the other residents in the cafeteria. Occasionally, one of them touches me, and I have to quell the urge to break limbs.

I find a seat at the back where I can see the whole room without worrying about someone behind. The darkness inside me is starving, throbbing in time with the ache in my wrist. My last kill was two months ago. Granted, it started gloriously. I practically bathed in his blood. But then it was snatched away from me at the last second. I *need* to see the light behind their eyes fade because of me—no one else.

And now, every time I think of the color of Kristian's blood, I see Dino's.

The itch under my skin was subdued, and the hum in my bones was quiet for a long time. But it doesn't last. It never lasts.

Jordan didn't even have to offer me anything to kill Bateman. I would have done it for free and will do it the way I want it done.

Jude has taken a seat opposite me. His face is puffy, his eyes are bloodshot red, and he's as restless as fuck—obviously not coping with his body's reaction to going cold turkey straight away.

I could have let him wean off slowly. Oh, but where's the fun in that? Why would I give him a break? He was the one who got himself in this mess. I didn't tell him the pills he needs to give to Byron daily can be dissolved under the tongue, either.

As if sensing my thoughts, Jude glares at me, mouth open as though he's talking. Oh, he is talking. "—do I even bother," he finishes as I catch the end of his words.

"What did you say?" I ask, in all innocence.

"Fuck, Viola, you're annoying. You're deliberately not answering my questions." He huffs like a teenage girl. "I asked why do I fucking bother?"

I give him a level look. "That nurse is watching us again."

Jude's eyes flit to the petite brunette. "I've not seen her before. She must be new."

"New?" I repeat.

"Yes, fucking new. Why does that matter? So she's fucking watching. Let her," Jude rages on.

I wait until he's looking back at me to speak to him slowly, so he'll understand. "Control your mood. You're being more irritable than usual. It's making you careless." *Fucking hell, I sound like Dante.*

Jude doesn't notice that I do. He just clenches his jaw, grinding his teeth. The sound sends ugly, unwelcome shivers down my spine. He was doing it all last night in my fucking ear too.

His addictions are becoming an issue. He needs to get himself under control.

"I need to know Bateman's schedule," I say after a minute of silence when he's calmed down.

He looks up and narrows his eyes at me. Finally, he nods. "I can get you that."

"Good, because planning is everything."

Jude steals me a staff schedule, and I work out what shifts Bateman has. He's like every other predator I know—unassuming and unremarkable with his dirty, mouse-colored hair and small, beady eyes. Since I've been so consumed with Jude, I wasn't aware of the monster lurking beneath Bateman's pasty skin, but now I'm stalking the creep. I can't miss the occasional hunger surfacing whenever one of the younger girls walks past.

I know his type—he likes the innocent ones, the weak ones— the ones who can't fight back. It makes me see red, so much so that I want him covered in it from head to toe.

The following week, I study my prey when he doesn't think anyone is watching. I take note when he comes out to check on us in the yard for physical activity. I'm aware of his skulking around the common area during our mandatory study time. And he's there against the wall, watching, waiting, every breakfast, lunch, dinner, and break.

I also watch Jude while his body goes through a physical and mental breakdown. Of all the boys, Jude is the easiest to deal with, but he's also the worst at helping me. *It would be a completely different game if Dino were in here with me.*

At the thought of the redhead, my insides become knotted and twisted, and the darkness tries its hardest to surface. It's a torment I've come to dread. But I can't lose focus. I'm on the job. So, I shut down all thoughts about him and think only of the task at hand.

"We need to get him alone," I say to Jude after a few days of studying Bateman. I do have the drugs all powdered up. It would be easy to spike his coffee, but what if he collapses in the middle of the day?

"Not if he's on the night shift," Jude offers when I say this to him.

That could work.

"Have you been dosing Byron, as I asked?" Giving Jude the pills was a test. If he's taken them himself, we have a problem.

"What do you take me for?" he snaps, then sighs, scrubbing his face with his hand. "How did you know they would work on him?"

"My father used to induce the same state in me." I've been there, in that place where your body is unable to move, but your brain is in overdrive, many times. I was always aware of what he did to get me out of it, even if I couldn't administer it myself.

Jude's face is a picture of horror.

We finally decide to wait until Thursday night to kill Bateman. It's risky. Leaving it so late means we have more time to plan and less time for things to go wrong. But it also means I only have one shot at this. Jude is grumpier and rattier as the days go by, which makes me change my mind about him being the easiest—Lorcan is easier to deal with than Jude any day of the bloody week.

But dwelling on the boys who aren't here doesn't help matters.

And I, point blank, refuse to think of Dante at all.

Thursday comes around in the blink of an eye, something to be said for all the days rolling into one. Jude pretty much retreated to his room at the start of the week and hasn't yet emerged.

I knock on his door and listen to the sound of him moving about. Eventually, the door creaks open enough for me to see a withdrawn and sullen-looking Jude. His jaw is covered in stubble, and his eyes are dull and red.

He needs a goddamn shower.

"It's time," I say through the crack.

"Fuck, already? I'm still fucking dying here."

I suck in a breath and shake my head. This is not how I expected things to go. I'm so very disappointed. Jude blinks a few times, hazel eyes bleary and bloodshot as he takes me in.

"Give me ten minutes. I need to go to the communal bathroom."

I nod at him. "I'll wait in the TV room."

Fifteen minutes later, Jude appears. His hair is damp and hanging over his face, and his eyes are still puffed. But at least he's in fresh scrubs, and he's not hurling his guts up, which is the indication I got the first time I came to find him a couple of days ago.

"Can you do this?" I ask him as he sits with me at the table behind the sofa. There's no one in the TV room because it's pizza night, and most kids are in the canteen getting their fill of pepperoni and cheese. There's a game show on TV that I turned the volume up on before Jude showed.

"I'm here, aren't I?" he rasps, drinking a carton of juice he must have picked up on the way. "I would give fucking anything for a nice cold beer, right about now," he snorts.

I forget how long Jude has been stuck inside. I give him a level look. "Lor said he could get you out." I shrug.

Jude looks over at me. "I wanted to see if you'd come to rescue me," he says, but he doesn't laugh or smirk. It's like he's empty inside. *Dead.*

Like Dino.

I shove that poisonous thought away and grimace at Jude. "Are you sure you're okay because I can do this alone?" *I don't need anyone.*

He grunts, finishing his juice in one go. "Just tell me what the plan is."

"Bateman does the rounds at ten, then grabs a coffee in the kitchens. I'll distract him. You put this"—I slide the plastic wrap of powdered drugs over to Jude—"in his coffee when he's not looking."

He stares at the baggie with desperate eyes. For a second, I think he will snatch it and inhale the goddamn thing there and then, but his features harden. He takes it from me gingerly instead, as though it might bite, and shoves it into his pocket.

"Jude," I say. His red-rimmed eyes dart to me. "Don't fuck this up."

His jaw clenches, then he nods, letting out a breath with a curl to his lips that has him looking like his old self. "I've got this, babe. Don't fucking sweat it."

We spend the next few hours grabbing some food from the canteen and then watching bad TV. Most evenings tail off the day's activities with recreation time, so we can pretty much do what we like.

"Movie time," one of the orderlies calls out.

I glance at the clock on the wall as teenagers shuffle into the TV room—it's 9 p.m. We stay in our seats as the room fills up, the lights go out, and the movie starts.

I am too busy taking in who is here and who is missing to

notice Jude reaching across. The first inkling I have of him being soppy as fuck, is his hand in mine under the table we're sitting at. His hand is warm and firm, reminding me of his strength. This guy who hated me, who I hated at first, is here with me, holding my fucking hand.

I glare at him in the dark.

He grins and adds with a shrug. "You're not letting go."

"Shut the fuck up," someone hisses at him.

I don't know who it is, but I consider shoving my pen through their ear canal so they never have to worry about someone talking during a movie again. But Jude's fingers stroke over my palm, and I lose interest in anyone else.

A little later, a glance at the clock says it's almost half-past.

I extract my palm from Jude's and get out of my seat. One of the nurses, who's been eyeing us all week, frowns as I do.

"I think she knows you're not supposed to be here," Jude says under his breath.

"I don't care what she thinks; we'll be gone by tomorrow."

I walk out, leaving Jude to follow me later. I don't need the cameras to see us together.

The kitchens are empty apart from Bateman making a hot drink. He looks up as I approach, and I immediately switch my facial expression to one that blends a tremendous amount of innocence and a small tease of allure. Bateman likes the weaker ones. I can't be anything but submissive right now.

"Sir, can you help me with my bed?" I walk right into the kitchen and stare up at the orderly.

He frowns down at me. "Your bed?"

"Yes, Sir," I breathe out. "I'm trying to move it to the other side of the room."

He frowns. "Did you get permission for that?"

It's my turn to frown. "My father is paying a lot of money for me to be here. I want my bed on the other side of the room." I bite my lower lip. "I won't tell anyone you helped me." I place my hand on his arm.

Bateman looks me over, a sick light behind his eyes coming on as he takes in my skimpy scrubs and swiped-back ponytail hair. He must like what he sees because he agrees to help me. I can already hear the cogs turning in his brain. I'm a rich brat who needs to be taught a lesson.

Bateman follows me to my room, where there are no cameras. Out of the corner of my eye, I see Jude coming up a side corridor. He gives the barest nod at the signal I give him.

I leave the door to my room open while Bateman helps me move my bed to the other side. His eyes are darting everywhere when he's done, checking the door to see if anyone is coming, checking me out to see if I'm worth it.

But Bateman isn't a predator. He's a scavenger.

And Jude is going to come by in a few minutes.

"Okay, thank you," I say to the older man, edging him toward the door. He peers around the doorframe into the corridor. There's no sign of Jude or anyone for that matter.

Where the fuck is he?

Bateman turns to me, eyes shining as he closes the door. "Since I helped you, maybe you can help me," he says quietly.

"Help you with what?" I ask as adrenaline surges. I take a step back.

Where the hell is Jude.

As the pervert locks the door to my room with his key, giving me a creepy smile, I glance around my room for a weapon. *Fuck drugging him. I'll gut him here and now.*

But the room is stark empty the way it's always been. I eye Bateman and take another step back. In the pocket of my scrubs is the ballpoint pen I stole from one of the nurses.

If this disgusting pig, *I refuse to call him a man,* touches me….
I'll kill him.

"Viola!" There's hammering on the door. It's only fucking Jude, minutes too late.

"It's locked," I call out to him as Bateman looks at me and then back at the door.

"Did you plan this," the pig hisses at me.

I show him my dangerous smile, the one I like to show before I bury my blade in someone. "Oh, I plan fucking everything," I say softly, dangerously.

Bateman has enough time to run toward the door before I'm on him, launching myself onto his back. I lock an arm around his throat as he shouts, holding on, stabbing him in the neck with the pointed end of the pen. It's precise enough that blood sprays out in a beautiful arc. His scream turns into a gurgle, his throat filling up with blood. Then he collapses to the floor.

I get to my feet, stepping over the widening pool of blood.

"Viola, what the fuck is going on in there?" Jude yells at me through the door. He's pounding now like he's trying to break it down.

"Shut the fuck up," I snap at him, nabbing the keys from Bateman's belt. I don't have long. I shove the keys under the door gap and then dash to the bed, stripping the bottom sheet. I'm using it to mop up the blood as Jude storms into the room. His eyes whip to me and then to the dead body.

He actually facepalms.

"Just help me clean this up."

"How, Viola? How are we going to clean this up? You were going to OD him and let someone find him dead of a heart attack. This is a little bit different, don't you think?"

"Have you quite finished?" I glower at him.

"Yes." His jaw clenches as he says it. "Yes, I have."

"Then help me. I need bleach, and I need more sheets. Go to laundry. Get me one of those big laundry bags."

"There are cameras in the hallways." As if I need reminding.

"Yes, I know. You said they're never checked."

He gives me a dark look. "I'm sure if an orderly goes fucking missing, they'll check them."

"If he goes missing," I snap.

Jude grimaces, blinking hard, and then stalks off to get what I need muttering about needing the guys to come and sort me out.

I need Dante. That's who I need.

Or Dino.

As soon as Jude leaves and the door closes behind him, I carry on mopping up the blood. There's the sound of the door opening again. *Fucking Jude. What now?*

I tear my gaze away to look at the door.

The brunette nurse with the permanent frown from earlier is staring at me, eyes bugging out of her head. There are a few seconds where no one moves. She's in shock, taking me in on all fours, blood flowing like a river around my hands and knees. The whites of her eyes are showing as she whips her gaze between me and the dead body. Then she screams.

And it's fucking loud.

I scrabble in the mess to get to her, but she's gone, hurrying down the hallway before I can even make it to the bloody door.

Jude appears at the end of the hall, arms loaded with sheets, just as the alarm sounds.

I give a sharp shake of my head. *No.*

Oblivious, he drops the sheets and storms over. He grabs my hand, taking no notice of the blood staining it, and drags me down the hall. "Come on."

"Where are we going?"

He doesn't say anything, his mouth set in a grim line.

"Jude," I growl. "Let fucking go of me." His grip is like iron around my wrist. Even if I pull back or pry his fingers off, I'm not strong enough. I'm too lightweight against his bulk.

The alarm overhead is flashing all kinds of warnings at us. Jude ignores it and continues dragging me all the way to his room, then tosses me inside. "Stay there," he glares as I snarl at him, lunging straight for him.

He slams the door in my face.

Rage comes roaring through my body. But it's too late. I hear the lock click shut as I batter the door and scream at the dickhead through the wood. But the fucker is gone.

He fucking left me.

Rawness screams through every part of me until I'm breathing hard, and every part of me hurts...and just fucking hurts. Eventually, I stop thrashing and slide down the door to sit and wait.

The old injury in my wrist is pulsing, and my throat feels like it's been ripped apart from all the screaming. So I sit and hold my wrist and wait.

He'd better come fucking back.

SEVEN

VIOLA

WHEN I WAKE UP, I'm strapped to a bed with a sore throat, ragged from screaming, and banging headache. I've no idea what day it is.

Or where Jude is, for that matter.

"Where's Jude," I croak as the memories come crashing back. After the alarm sounded off, they came to Jude's room to get me. It took three of them to pump my veins full of sedatives to stop me from tearing them all apart and burning the place down to find him.

The nurse, a silver-haired older woman this time, purses her lips as she shoves another needle full of shit into my arm. She doesn't look at me once.

Darkness, heavy and suffocating, sucks me under again. When I open my eyes later, the orderly who switched me, the one working for Jordan—Roberts—is wheeling my bed down the corridor.

"Where is Jude?"

Roberts eyes me warily like I'm a dangerous animal. He needn't worry. I'm strapped to the bed.

"Jude is in solitary."

"Why?"

He glares at me. "You know why. He killed Bateman."

I clench my teeth together before I can correct him. It's obvious. *Jude took the fall for me.* There are no cameras in the rooms, so it's Jude's word against mine. He must have convinced them he killed Bateman, and I was just caught in the middle. I don't know how I feel about that, but I can't blindly charge in without knowing the facts.

Where are they taking me?

I close my eyes to block out the overhead lights burning my retinas off. Then I drag them open again, twisting my head to look behind me. The walls are pea green with white doors on either side. There are no cameras. I don't recognize the corridor. We're some other part of the facility.

"Where are you taking me?" I look back at Roberts, who sighs.

"Jordan wants you switched, so we're doing it before it's too late."

"No." I shake my head. "I'm not leaving Jude."

Roberts gives me a sympathetic look. "There's nothing you can do for him now. He's gone."

No. Don't you fucking say that.

I strain, somewhat hopelessly, against the 4-point hold on the gurney I'm tied to. There's no way to escape from them. I know this. Dante drilled into me every single form of restraining someone; how they do it in hospitals is where he got his inspiration.

"They will reduce you to nothing in their attempt to control you and use everything in their means to do so. If you ever get caught and can't escape physically, use anything to get free, V. I won't be there to get you out all the time."

Dante's words echo in my mind. I don't just have my body. I also have my mind. If Roberts takes me back to the central part of the facility, I'll lose my only connection to Jude. I'll never see him again.

They'll bury him here.

The rage grips my chest like a vice, making my heart hammer and breathing ratchet up a notch. I struggle again. It's no use. These restraints are made to hold down someone a lot bigger than me. I just don't have the physical strength. Behind me, I can see the connecting doorway approaching. We're almost there.

"I can pay you," I say to Roberts. He looks down at me, eyes narrowed.

"What?"

"How much?" A grit out. Everyone has a price. Even Roberts. "Just tell me a price, and I'll ensure you get it."

He grimaces and stops rolling the gurney. "A hundred thousand."

"Done," I hiss. "Now, take me back to my room."

"Your room is a crime scene."

"Then whatever room they had me in."

He grimaces at that and turns the bed around. The muscles in my body only start to relax once we get to the blue hallways. As we pass the windows, it's dark outside. It must be the middle of the night.

"What time and day is it?" I ask him.

Roberts grunts as he forces the bed into one of the rooms. "It's 2 a.m. Saturday morning."

I nod. I've lost a day and a half. Not as much as I thought.

The room he's wheeled me into is much like the one I was in before, except the desk is on the back wall, and the bed is on the right. Roberts wheels me in but doesn't uncuff me. Instead, he reaches for his phone.

"Who am I calling?"

I glare at him. He wants a number for someone to call to make the transaction—clever, clever guy. I reel off Lorcan's number. Roberts dials it.

"Let me speak to him," I demand. When he doesn't make a move to do that, I add, "He won't talk to you."

Roberts's mouth becomes a grim line as he comes over to where my head is and places the phone to my ear.

"Hello? Who the fuck is this?" Lor's voice seethes down the phone. It's music to my ears after all this time.

"Is that any way to greet your girlfriend?"

"V?"

"Yes, it's me."

"Oh, thank fucking God. Where the hell have you been?"

"With Jude." There's no time to explain, so that's all I'm giving him for now.

I hear him let out a breath. "I thought….fuck, I'm glad you're okay. Do not disappear like that ever again, you hear me?"

Roberts is scowling at me, mouthing at me to hurry up. I shoot a shitty look at him and carry on with what I have to say to lor.

"No time to talk. I need one hundred—"

"Two hundred," Roberts says, tilting his head. He has me where he wants me, so all I can do is glower back and correct my request to Lorcan.

"—two hundred thousand pounds in this guy's account. Can you do that?"

"Is he blackmailing you?" Lor spits.

"No, I'm bribing him."

There's another long, drawn-out sigh from the other end of the line. "Fine, let me grab my laptop."

There's a rustling sound as Lorcan does just that. He must be in bed. My mind flies to who with, but immediately I shut it down. Lorcan needs someone to spoon him in bed at night, or he can't sleep. That means there's someone there with him, and for some fucking reason, I'm rabid at the thought.

"Okay, I've got it. I'm just logging into the offshore account now."

"Switch on Quinn's rerouting software," I say to Lorcan, efficiently resisting the need to interrogate him on his sleeping arrangements these days.

"I already have done."

"Good," I snap. I switch my blank gaze to Roberts. "Now untie me, and then you can give him your details."

He frowns and moves slowly to undo the velcro binds around my wrists and ankles. Then, after a nod from me, he reels off some numbers down the phone. I wait, massaging my wrists and ankles.

Finally, Roberts shakes his head, handing me the phone. "Your boyfriend wants to talk to you."

I take it, just in time to hear Lorcan ask, "Is that it?"

"Is what it?" I retort.

"You call me up in the middle of the night to ask for money, and that's all I get—good?" I roll my eyes, appealing to Roberts to take the phone away, but he doesn't. "Viola? Are you hearing me? I'm not some ATM you can just hit up whenever you feel like it? At least tell me you're okay…." He trails off. "And that Jude is okay."

"I'm kind of busy right now," I say down the phone, eyes never leaving Roberts. "Give me a week. Then you can visit me."

There's a huff and then, "Fine. Just fucking fine." A pause, and then afterward, "Just be careful. Check your emails if you can."

After Lorcan hangs up, Roberts puts his phone away and starts toward the door.

"I need you to do the switch in three days."

He nods at me, and then he's gone, locking the room with me inside for the rest of the night.

I spend the next day trying to find where they've taken Jude. I don't have long. I need to find him by Monday night when Roberts is back. Between the study period, group therapy sessions, and physical activities, we're pretty much left to our own devices, so I use that time to wander the hallways looking for the separation rooms that Roberts mentioned.

The only difference, from before Jude was taken to now, is that I'm watched like a hawk. And the brunette nurse is gone. My name, or should I say Dahlia's name, is also on the clinical assessment board. I have a session with the doctor in the afternoon.

That doesn't worry me; it just means I need to find Jude soon. Though, if the doctor is Dr. Shalpert, I'm screwed.

During my wanderings, I happen to see Byron in one of the common areas looking more alert than he was the last time I saw him.

The drugs we were giving him must have broken through his catatonia. One of the nurses looks up as I enter. I give her a vicious smile, causing her brow to furrow, as I make a beeline toward Jude's cousin.

"Hello, Byron," I say, crouching in front of his wheelchair.

The skinny kid looks straight at me, light-colored hair and eyes pale blue, reminding me of someone. Probably his dead sister, Aurora. He leans back, suddenly wary.

"You recognize me?" I keep my voice low, hoping he will do the same.

He nods. "You were with Jude," he says softly, eyes fitting to the nurse watching us and then back to me. He moistens his lips. "You told Jude to give me those pills that fixed me."

Nodding my head, I give him a sweet smile, putting on my best *I'm-not-here-to-hurt-you* act. It works because Byron smiles back, imitating me a little.

"I'm a friend of your cousin."

"Where is Jude? No one will tell me where he is."

"They took him away for a while. But don't worry, I'm going to get him back."

That seems to appease him. He gives me a shy look from under his lashes. "You look a bit like Aury."

I look nothing like his dead sister, but I don't say that. I need to keep Byron sweet. He's just a kid. Fourteen years old. Jude told me that Aurora was meant to be watching him when he supposedly died. She woke up, and her car was in the lake. Byron was gone. They found his body later, already dead and bloated from drowning.

Only there was no open casket at the funeral.

But Byron, dying, suddenly put the entire Duke's fortune in Joseph's lap. Lorcan was already in line to inherit half. Even though he was adopted, his grandfather made an exception. Why would Joseph go to all this trouble to hide his nephew just for more money?

It doesn't add up.

When I see Lor, I'll tell him he needs to get Byron out of here. The kid doesn't deserve to be locked up. No one fucking does.

Except for me.

"Do you know why you're here?" I ask him. It's a long shot, but it would explain why he was drugged into such a state that he couldn't talk. He *knows* something.

He blinks at me. "I'm not allowed to say."

"I'm Jude's friend. You can tell me."

He narrows his eyes, wary again all of a sudden. But he's not looking at me. I glance over my shoulder at the blonde nurse walking toward us. "I'll speak to you later, Byron," I say, getting to my feet.

Then I'm walking out of the common area before she can catch up to me.

I search every part of the facility but find no rooms that aren't accounted for, so I take a detour just before the start of study time. The corridors are filled with residents on their way to one of the few classes held in the group meeting room. I hate being touched, but I hate losing even more, so I force myself to push through the teenagers to Jude's room. It isn't locked, so it's easy to enter quickly before anyone sees. Jude said he still had the

USB with all the data on St Michael's that Quinn was able to get for him. He must be storing it in his room on this side, just in case he needs it.

I need to find it.

I search everywhere that I would hide the damn thing, eventually locating it inside a loose pipe connected to his basin, wrapped in plastic to keep it dry. I pocket it, still sealed in the plastic, and make my way to the dispensary.

There's one lone computer at the back of the clinic and a single nurse behind the counter.

She looks up at me as I approach. "You shouldn't be here," she says, brow furrowed.

I read her tag. *Paige*, it says. "One of the others said you let him check his emails."

Paige purses her lips. "I don't do that anymore." I take in her appearance as fast as I can—she's got bags under her eyes and a milk stain on her top. There's a wedding band tan line, but no band. And on her desk is a worn paperback with a couple entwined in each other on the front.

Single mother.

Divorced or separated.

Romantic at heart.

"It'll only take a second. My boyfriend said he sent me a love poem." She stares at me. "I miss him so much," I add, giving her wounded kitten eyes.

Her eyes soften slightly at that as she looks toward the door. "Fine. You have five minutes." Reaching behind her, she presses a buzzer and indicates the entrance.

Best not wait for her to change her mind. I head to the back of the room, where the computer is already logged in. There's a fake email account that I share with the boys that Quinn set up for us. I log in and see there are two unread drafts—both from Lorcan.

While the nurse has her back turned, I discreetly slot in the drive and access that first since I came here to do that. At the same time, I open a window with Lorcan's email.

> Do not blame yourself for Dino,
> I know that what you feel inside is
> Tearing you apart. But know, I still
> Love you. And will for as long as you're alive.

> —Lore

It's a shit poem, but the message gets across. The last word of every line is the actual message. *Dino is still alive.* I have no idea why Lorcan insists on sending me messages this way. The email account and software are Quinn's creations—untraceable and unhackable. There's a reason I keep her around.

But Lorcan is a paranoid fuck.

I add my reply after his name, which I know will infuriate him, but sometimes it's the little things.

> *Good.*

> *—V*

Dino is still alive. I knew he was. I felt it in my stained soul. But seeing it in black and white makes me want to be done with this shitty place so that I can find him. I need to get out of here. Soon.

I quickly open the USB window, hunt for the floor plans, and note where everything is mentally in my head. There's only one part that looks unfamiliar. I just need to work out how to get there.

"Your five minutes are up," Paige calls over.

"Okay, I'm done," I say, studying the layout and where it's different, before closing the window. I log out and shut everything down, wiping the history. Even if someone goes to the website where the emails are hosted, they wouldn't be able to log in. Quinn changes the password and portal address every time we log in from a public computer. Ever since I started working with her, I've memorized the next few codes, just in case. Forgetting them is not an option. Dante drilled it into me not to be sloppy or leave trails for anyone to follow—unless you want to be found.

That's how I know Dante is gone.

He's left me nothing.

No breadcrumb. No sweet poem.

He's just gone.

"Thank you," I say to Paige as I push the door open to the other side of the glass. She looks up from her desk.

"Of course. I know what it's like to lose contact with loved ones." I don't miss her tearful look at the photo on her desk showing a smiling family.

Widowed.

I take that and tuck it away for later.

EIGHT

JUDE

SHE'S HAUNTING ME. Every time I close my eyes, Aurora is there. She's either bleeding on the floor or pleading with me to help her while Lorcan stabs her in the heart.

And when I open my eyes, she is still fucking there.

Except for this time, she's covered in blood.

"Jude," she snarls, coming closer. "You need to snap out of it."

"Get the fuck away from me," I grit out, trying to get free of the bed they've strapped me to. But Aurora doesn't stop coming. She reaches out, hand dripping with blood, eyes filled with insanity. "Don't touch me," I shout at her.

"Jude, wake the fuck up. It's me," Aurora says.

I glare at her. "I know who you are. I let him kill you."

"You let who kill me?" she hisses.

I close my eyes so I don't have to look at her as she touches me. Her hands are ice cold. My chest constricts, and I can't breathe. I need to get away.

I let Lorcan kill you.

Aurora unties the bed restraints. I stay stock-still while she does, hoping the fucking bitch will just disappear, but she doesn't. My heart is hammering in my chest when I open my eyes again. She reaches for me, her eyes dark and empty.

She's going to kill me.

No, you fucking don't.

As soon as my arm's free, I sit up and wrap it around her throat. I squeeze until her eyes bulge out of her head. She tries to claw at my arm, but I yank the bitch closer, making her stumble.

"I tried to save you, but you wouldn't listen. I told you to stay away from him."

"Jude, stop, or I'll have to…" she croaks out, tailing off, her voice barely a whisper. There's no fear, though. The cunt is still looking at me with dead eyes, void of emotion.

"You made me do this," I snarl at her. "Now, leave me the fuck alone." Something hot and wet slides down my face. Fuck, I'm crying.

She grabs around my fingers, her brown eyes staring into mine….

Brown eyes?

And yanks, bending my front two fingers back.

The crack is loud in my ears.

The pain—fucking excruciating.

"FUCK," I drop her like a sack of potatoes, clutching my hand.

And then I see her, sprawled on the floor, eyes dark and demonic, looking like she might do more than snap my fingers off. She looks like she wants to kill me.

"You fucking dick." She kicks the base of the bed, and it collapses with me fucking still strapped to it. I fall back, banging my head on the back of the frame. In seconds, she's behind me, with me in some kind of choke hold.

"How do you like to be strangled, eh?"

"Vi—" Is all I manage.

"It's not fucking nice, is it?" she sneers as the room darkens around me, and I lose consciousness again.

. . .

When I wake up, Viola is sitting against the wall, glaring at me. Her neck is covered in red handprints—my red handprints.

I'm still strapped to the bed. And my hand is throbbing like a bitch.

"First," I say, trying to sit up and failing. "Are you okay?"

"Second, what the fuck are you doing here?" As far as I can tell, I'm still in the segregation unit that the fuckers put me in after I confessed to killing Bateman. They deemed me too dangerous to be with the other residents, so they pumped me full of shit and left me here to rot.

She cocks her head. "I got Roberts to smuggle me in here after threatening to cut his dick off. There are no cameras in here."

I flash a grin at her. "That's my girl."

She lets a ghost of a smile stray over her lips. "You were hallucinating?"

"I thought you were Aurora….come back to haunt me."

She sighs and gets to her feet. "And who am I now?"

"The one and only, Viola," I say. She smirks and comes to where I'm restrained, looking down at me. The bed is still set to the lowest position. "Can you let me out now?"

She nods. "We don't have much time. They check on restrained patients every six hours. We've got about an hour left before they come back."

"How do you know that?" I ask her as she bends down to undo the straps holding my wrists and then my ankles.

"I asked one of the nurses out of curiosity. Paige is super helpful."

I snort and sit up, noticing the splint made out of a plastic bag on my fingers as I do. The splintering pain brings a grimace to my lips. "I didn't dream you breaking my fucking fingers then?"

"Nope," her smile is pure evil.

"Bitch," I say as I drag her to me with my good hand and kiss her mouth like a man dying of thirst, and she's the fucking oasis.

"Asshole," she retorts, moaning lightly as I massage the back of her neck where I hurt her. The noise has my cock springing to fucking life.

"I don't suppose we have time—"

"No, we fucking don't. Come on," she says, tossing what looks like an orderly uniform at me."

I stand up and hold it out in front of me. It's miles too fucking small. "Where the fuck did you get this?"

"Laundry. Just put it on. You're going to walk out of here," she says, helping me into the jumpsuit because I've only got one hand.

"This is fucking insane," I say. "It'll never work."

"Oh, it will," she says, pulling me toward the exit just as the fire alarm goes off.

"What the fuck—"

"Jordan," she mouths.

The door to the segregation unit opens, and the sprinklers turn on. Roberts pokes his head around the door, drenched and pissed off. "Hurry the fuck up, now."

I follow Viola through the door and straight into pure carnage. The hallways are filled with bodies of people trying to get out of the building. No one looks twice at us. Fuck, we're going to get out of here.

Everyone filters outside. I'm forced to separate from Viola as the staff stands on one side of the parking lot, the residents on the other.

The last I see of her is a flash of dark brown hair as Robert drags me to the side of the building away from the headcount that's happening.

"Wait, I lost Viola."

"She'll meet you outside," he rumbles at me.

"Meet me where?" I snap, fighting him to go back.

He shakes his head. "I don't get paid enough for this shit."

He shoves me back, making me stumble, wincing at the pain slicing through my broken fingers. "You need to go now, or they'll notice they have one too many on staff today."

"Wait—" I snarl.

Someone grabs my uniform from behind and hauls me through the hedge backward. On the other side of the bush, I turn on whoever the fuck has their hands on me.

"Jude, come on. We need to go." It's the Asian girl—Quinn—from the bar a lifetime ago. She just cocks her head at me when I shake her off and glare her way.

"I'm not leaving without her." I'm practically bristling.

She raises her palms. "I'm just trying to get you in the car."

Over in the road, a yellow Mclaren sits idling its engine, thunderously fucking loud. I lift my hand to cover my eyes, squinting to see who it is, although I already know. *Not fucking obvious.* A guy with messy dark hair and a permanent-looking frown sits in the driver's seat.

Lorcan *fucking* Duke.

"Is your sorry-looking ass going to get in, or are you expecting fucking door-to-door service, mate?" is his response to me flipping him the finger on my good hand. When I don't make a move, he revs the engine. "Hurry the fuck up, Viola's waiting."

"You fucking wanker," I mutter under my breath, striding toward the heap of junk called a car.

Quinn climbs in the middle seat, and I get into the passenger side. I realize there's no room for Viola in this car.

None whatsoever.

NINE

VIOLA

WITH JUDE TAKEN CARE OF, I can do what he came here to do. And it doesn't take me long to find Byron in his room after we've all been allowed back into St Michael's. There's a lot of chaos after Jude's disappearance, but the best part about him escaping is that no one is looking for Jude. They're looking for the guy he switched months ago when Jordan got him into Hades.

I'll leave the rest for Lorcan to sort out. Because…

I don't do red tape.

I burn it.

"Byron," He looks up at me as I approach him in his larger-than-usual room. "Do you remember me?"

He nods. Of course, he does. It's been less than twenty-four hours. No nurse is watching me today. I get right to it, crouching down so I'm not a threat. "We got interrupted yesterday. But I need you to tell me what you are not supposed to tell anyone."

He sucks in a breath. "Everyone is always asking me."

"Well, it'll be our secret. I won't tell a soul you told me."

He tilts his head, eyes solemn, looking every bit like Aurora.

He lets the air out of his lungs and nods. "I just overheard them say that his parents gave him away to cover a scandal."

"Who did you hear?"

"My uncle…Joseph, and another man."

"Do you know who they were talking about?"

He shakes his head.

"That's fine. I think I know who it was."

Lorcan. They were talking about Lorcan.

Byron's eyes widen as he looks behind me.

"He's over there," says a voice. I glance behind to see an orderly pointing at us, leading two heavy-set men to us both. I get to my feet, adrenaline kicking in, as I recognize them and who they work for.

They're my father's men.

They don't see me straight away. They're too engrossed in heading straight for Jude's cousin. The hospital must have called my father the moment Byron woke up. *But why?*

Their eyes connect with mine as they approach, and recognition flares even with my hair dyed this bland color. I have two choices. I can run, although to where is anyone's guess as I'm stuck in this hospital until Lorcan gets me out, or I can stand my ground and face Adrien.

I choose the latter, staring them both down as they approach.

"Your father has been looking for you, Miss Hawkes," one of them says, the shorter one. Little Phil, his name is, if I remember correctly. I don't know the other one, who walks over to Byron's chair and stands behind it.

I sniff at Paul, shaking him off as he tries to put a hand on me. "I can walk by myself," I snap, following him toward the door. The nurse has already fucked off.

"Where are you taking her?" Byron asks. I turn to look back at him. He's watching us go, frowning at Paul, his brow creased, lips pulled in a grim, straight line.

"Jude will come and get you soon." I shoot a look at the guy holding the handles of Byron's wheelchair, getting ready to take

Byron God knows where. "Touch a hair on his head, and I'll skin you alive with my fingernails."

The guy just blinks at me.

My father's reach is apparent as we walk through the halls. No one questions Paul as we go through the blue corridors to the security door. Someone even opens it for us, no questions asked, allowing us into the central part of the detention center. Paul escorts me to the waiting room where I used to meet Lorcan and leaves me there, closing and even locking the door. And then I'm alone.

I sit on one of the sofas to wait, but I don't have to for long. Twenty minutes later, the lock clicks, and the door swings open. Paul is back, this time with my father and a rather miserable-looking Gigi.

I don't bother to get up.

Adrien takes a seat. He doesn't take off his coat. Gigi takes up position behind my father's chair, and Paul stands by the door.

No one gets in. No one gets out.

My father sighs. "Such a disappointment you've turned out to be, Viola, my dear." I stare at him as his words wash over me. "I had such plans for you. You don't know the half of it."

"Selling me to Kristian wasn't enough?" I say, calm on the outside, raging beast just beneath the cool, collected surface on the inside.

He narrows his eyes. "We've all made sacrifices. We all have to do our part for the family. Anyway, Kristian is dead. I'm sure you know that."

I can't read my father very well, so I've no idea if he's joking or serious. Or if he has no idea about what went down in the church. I wait him out.

He cocks his head after I say nothing for a few stilted minutes. The smile is ugly as sin. "You did well. Better than I imagined you would."

The muscle in my jaw twinges. "You wanted him dead?"

He grins. "No, but I had a hunch you might react that way.

You're just like me. Alive or dead, it doesn't matter. There's more than one way to skin a cat."

I shake my head, hand gripping the arm of the sofa as I take in his words. The last time he said that, he took my mother's cat and did just that. I don't have any soft, furry feelings inside for animals, but one day I will peel layers off of him just like he did to Rebecca's beloved Bronte.

He carries on. "What you did to Kardinal was a bonus of sorts—"

"He's not dead," I cut over him. *Dino is still alive.* "Where is he?"

My father's smile broadens like he knows he has me. "No, he is not. Thankfully. He's safe, for now. I've agreed that you're to marry him in his brother's place. The union with Vice is too important to be wasted. As long as you do, he'll be fine."

I glare at him. "You sick fuck."

"You chose right. Kristian was a bomb waiting to go off. The younger one is weaker, more malleable," he says. "Nothing at all like his brother…." He looks at me with empty eyes, leaning back. *Eyes like mine.* "You will be able to control this one."

"Control? Is that what this is about? You want control of Vice's operation?" It's so apparent. My whole life has been one extensive manipulation to get to this point. He played me. And he played Dante. That much is evident.

"Viola, dear, it's always been about control." Adrien shrugs. "Griffin is dead. Earlshore defers to me. You will marry Vice. And as soon as Duke is dead, I'll have everything."

Everything my father is saying screams inside my head. I grip the armrest harder until the material tears and gives way. "What do you mean….'As soon as Duke is dead'. What are you going to do to him?"

"I have someone I trust doing what I should have done long ago."

Inside the arm of the sofa is my failsafe. I reach my fingers around the cold metal. I knew my father would want to see me in here. I knew this was the room he'd choose. It's the nicest room that doesn't feel like you're a facility at all with the paintings and fireplace. It's like a stately home.

"And this is something I should have done a long time ago," I spit out, ripping my blade from its hiding place.

Adrien smiles as I launch myself at him.

Paul is running for me, and Gigi is drawing her weapon, but I don't care. I aim for Adrien's throat because I want him to suffer and be alive when I slice his jugular open and pull his spine through his throat.

My father grabs my hand and twists it, drawing it away from his face. And in one smooth motion shoves a needle into my neck. Then he lays me down on the chair as he gets up.

I can't move.

The muscle relaxant he's giving me is fast-acting.

"You forget, Viola, dear, who trained Dante." I didn't forget. I just hoped his age would have made him slow. But he's just as fast and deadly as when he was the head assassin at the agency. "Good, but not good enough." He smoothes my brow and then pockets my blade.

I rage at him behind my eyes, letting him see how much I hate him.

Adrien looks at Gigi. "Keep her here but make her comfortable. She has a wedding to go to soon."

I watch him leave, taking my blade with him.

One day, very soon, I will kill that motherfucker.

Gigi calls some of the orderlies. They strap me to a bed and wheel me back into the rear of the facility. I know I'm back in Hades because the walls are blue. They take me to a room like the one I found Jude in, a segregation unit designed to cut off all mental stimulation.

They drug me some more and leave me strapped to the gurney in the dark as they kick in. And soon, I can't tell if it's hours or days, morning or night. I don't even know if I'm dreaming or awake. I must be mostly dreaming, though, because the boys often visit me between the nurses coming to change my IVs and sheets. Lorcan is there, telling me he's done with me. Jude turns up and screams at me for ruining his life. And also Dino, who is covered in blood. He just stares. He doesn't say a word.

I drift in and out of it, telling the fucktards to leave me alone and get out of my head. But they never leave me alone. They love tormenting me.

Assholes.

Even their dream selves are absolute pricks.

Dante showing up one day is the worst because he just frowns, and then he tries to get me to stand up. I snarl at him and try to scratch his eyes out, but he easily holds me down.

"I hate you," I slur at him.

"I know you do," is all he says back.

Dream Dante is a pussy. He picks me up and carries me off, away from the darkness. I lean into him, listening to the thud of his chest, inhaling the chemicals and petrol that make up his unique cologne.

"You're very real for a fucking dream," I say to him, allowing my eyelids to close as the overhead lights burn the backs of my retinas.

"And you're a mess. Is this what happens when I leave you alone? Fucking hell, V, I taught you better than this."

A smirk tugs at my lips. Finally, dream Dante is being an asshole.

Of course, it's just a dream. Why would it be anything else?

Now I can bloody sleep.

TEN

DANTE

VIOLA MAKES A NOISE.

I glance at her sleeping it off, whatever they pumped her full off. Occasionally, she frowns but doesn't wake up. She's on my couch at the clinic. Getting a post as the new resident doctor was easy enough. It comes with all the perks. I get a room with a view and a couch. I also get special privileges with what patients I take an interest in.

V has always been my special interest.

She moans again, reminding me why I came back. Leaving her in the first place was not my choice. There are things Viola isn't privy to and doesn't need to know about. Not everything revolves around her, no matter how often I tell her. It was one of Adrien's men, bragging about where they were keeping Viola, that had me coming back. That bastard didn't live long.

I'm surprised she stayed in here as long as she did. But maybe she knows deep down that she needs help. I should have seen it coming. She had been losing it for weeks. There was always going to be a messy fallout that only I could clean up— no one else.

She needs me.

What the hell am I going to do with her?

My phone buzzes. It's one of her puppy dogs. With a sigh, I answer it because if I don't, they'll come here and start interfering, which will get them killed.

"Duke," I say.

"Where the fuck is she? You said you'd get her out! It's been six hours."

"She has a lot of drugs in her system," I say in response. "She needs to rest." The last thing we need is Viola, high on whatever shit they gave her, out for blood.

I can almost hear him bristling down the phone. "Fucking fine."

I put the phone down.

"So, it really is you?" I look up to see V sitting up, her face void of emotion. Her tells are going off like red flags—drumming her fingers, shifting in her chair like she can't sit still. There's also a slight tilt to her head, and her chin is jutted. She does that when she doesn't want anyone to know how uneasy she is, faking confidence.

Interesting.

Why are you faking being easy around me, V?

I take her in, really take her in, wanting to grimace. She's lost weight, and she's exhausted mentally and emotionally. She put herself through hell and back, and for what?

Nothing.

If I ever had less respect for her, it's right now.

I lean back in my chair, arms folded, waiting.

"A doctor, really?" she snorts after a few minutes of us just staring at each other, taking each other in. Her body twitches again, reminding me that the drugs aren't entirely out of her system yet.

I raise a brow. I meant what I said to Lorcan. Keeping her here with me is best for now.

"The white coat suits you," she says again, filling the void.

This is not the V I know. *And love.*

This is a shell of what she was. This place has eroded her training and ability to focus clean away. I warned her this would happen. I fucking warned her.

She needs a good fuck. That's what she needs.

I drag in a breath and rub the back of my neck. I have tells too, but usually, they're deliberate, especially around V. I want her to know I'm exasperated because she's useless at reading emotions in others.

"You left," she says finally, getting to the root of her issue with me. V is easy to manipulate if you know how; she's a cat with claws that often needs someone to sharpen them on. You take that away from her, and she breaks down, saying whatever comes into her head until the real V shines through.

Her last question I deem valid enough to answer.

"I had work to straighten out. You had your plan. I had mine." I shrug. "Are we joined at the hip? Because if we are, I wasn't aware of it."

She glares, not liking my answer because I'm right. Breaking eye contact, she then looks around the room. I don't continue to press. You have to be patient with V.

"I needed you," she says eventually, looking back.

"You need no one. How many times do I have to keep reminding you of that." Needing anyone in this life guarantees a quick death.

"Why are you such a fucking asshole?" she scowls.

My mouth twitches at the corners, but I suppress it. "I should have come sooner." That's as much as I'm willing to relent on this topic.

"A lot sooner," she says, letting the air out of her lungs, lifting her eyes to the ceiling as she blinks. "But you're right. I screwed up," she says as she drops her gaze back to me.

Fucking finally.

Getting V to admit she's wrong is not a walk in the park.

Training her, mentoring her, I was constantly fighting her damn ego. But I wouldn't change her for the world.

She's damn perfect.

"What now," she asks when I pull her file onto my desk and flip through it.

"We get you out of this dump," I say, taking the physical file and chucking it in the shredder. There's a digital copy which I'll have to get to before we leave here. Quinn couldn't hack the files, not even with the virus she installed on the USB drive. That's why it took so damn long for me to get her. There's a protocol even I have to follow to get the necessary security clearance for this job.

"I just need to freshen up," she says, eyeing the connected private bathroom.

"Knock yourself out."

Ten minutes go by, and there's no noise from the bathroom anymore. I go over to the bathroom door and knock on it. "V?" There are no windows in the bathroom, I checked, so I can only assume that she's passed out in there.

I wait a few seconds and then take a step back and kick the door hard, placing my foot right to the left of the lock where the wood is softer and more hollow. There's a thud as the door swings through.

V doesn't wait.

She jabs me in the gut with the shower pole. It knocks the wind out of me, but I recover quickly and grab hold of it, yanking it toward me, pulling her with it. She stumbles forward, weighing nothing and out of shape. I easily grab her wrist, her recently injured one, and bend it sharply. She hisses in pain.

"You fucking bastard," she seethes.

I pull her close and lock her arm under mine, forcing her to the floor, immobilizing her pretty quickly. "This is the wrist you broke, right?" I say, putting pressure on it. "I can very easily break it again."

"Fuck you," she snarls as I hold her in place with one hand

on the side of her head, holding her down and the other twisting her arm behind her back. "I know you're working for Adrien."

That makes me pause. V can be an absolute bitch when she's paranoid, which is most of the time. But after everything I've done....

I give a harsh laugh. "Is that what you think?"

"You turn up just after he does. Do you think I'm stupid?"

"I think you're delusional and scared."

"I'm not scared of you."

"Then why is your pulse racing?"

She shifts to look back at me, panting hard, eyes gleaming with rage. There's no fear there.

Only hate.

"It's not," she lies.

I can feel it under my fingers, throbbing under her skin. Her fear is palatable. I can practically taste it. It's the first thing that's excited me in a very long time. We glare into each other's eyes, a stalemate, until...she relaxes slightly, breathing deeper.

Her hair is over her face. She blows over her top lip to get the strands out of her eyes—eyes that are slightly less hostile now.

I wonder....

I shift slightly, loosening my grip on her wrist and removing my weight from her body. She rolls onto her back until she's directly under me, though my hand is still on her neck and my other is on her waist. As she stares up at me, her hips squirm.

I'm fucking hard, straining in my trousers as she does.

The scrubs she's wearing are thin, and I know by the feel of her body against my hand and forearm that she's not wearing anything under them.

"Are you going to fuck me?" she asks, eyes intense and dark as her gaze sweeps down to my groin and then back up again. She licks her lips. Her throat bobs under my palm.

She's toxic—a problem I need to fix. But maybe I will do that another day. Everything about V makes me want to destroy the system I was born into just to be with her.

Right now, I fucking want to destroy her.

In every way possible.

"Is that what you need? A good seeing to?"

I don't wait for an answer. I release her throat and grab a handful of her hair, wrapping my hand around it as I lower myself down, claiming her mouth with my tongue.

She moans and attacks me with her kiss. Lips, teeth, and tongue bruising for a fight. I shut her up by squeezing her breast hard under her soft cotton top with my other hand, pressing my lower half against her body so she can feel what she does to me.

"Asshole," she hisses, between breaths and the tonguing, angling her hips up to meet mine. "You don't get to be the one to give it to me." I ram my tongue into her mouth to shut her up.

She jerks against me, mewling like a greedy kitten. She tries to claw me, but someone cut her nails. I miss her claws and her curves, but this more lean version of Viola is still undeniably attractive to me. I sweep one hand under the small of her back, down and under the waistband of her loose cotton trousers. There, I knead her bare ass.

She yelps as I dig my fingers into her flesh and bite her neck. Her hands move from around my neck down to the outline of my cock.

"Take this out, and I'll rip it off," she promises.

"How will you do that when it's balls deep inside you?" I ask her.

"Then, I'll rip off your balls."

I grip her hair and kiss her jaw and collarbone. She hisses and grabs me through the material. "I mean it, Dante." But her eyes are glazed, and her lips are parted as I lick a line all the way down to her breastbone.

She rewards me with another moan when my other hand stops playing with her ass and skims around to the front. And as I pull back slightly, stroking the wetness between her legs, she gives a soft pant allowing a smile to ease onto my lips.

She's still gripping my cock like her life depends on it.

Her cotton trousers easily fall off her hips as I yank them down.

Her eyes blaze open, and she goes to sit up, but I shove her back down and hold her there.

"Where do you think you're going?" I say dangerously.

"Don't make me hurt you," she threatens, but she makes no move to run away again.

I finished pulling her trousers down and experimentally run a hand between her legs. Wherever I touch her has her almost thrusting into me. She's soaked, dripping wet, so ready for my cock.

I keep her pinned to the floor as I undo my trousers and shrug out of them. Using my knees, I push her thighs, opening her up to me.

She grabs me, wrapping a hand around my shaft. "I warned you," she teases, stroking me, driving me fucking crazy with the way she's looking at me.

"I'm still going to fuck you," I say as she carries on stroking me, staring into my eyes as I lean down to kiss her mouth. She's not ready for the four fingers I shove inside her. There's a soft gasp as she consumes me back. She's tight and deliciously wet. I'm going to enjoy taking her like this.

She says no, but she hasn't tried to stop me.

I pump her a few more times, making her pant. I break the kiss to trace my fingers, soaked with her juices, over her lips. Her tongue darts out, so I shove a couple of fingers into her mouth. She sucks them greedily while still teasing me with her hands.

"Put my cock inside you," I say in a low voice.

When she doesn't, I slide my hand back to her throat. That gets her moving. She smiles darkly, obeying, lining the tip of me with her warmth.

"Now wrap your legs around me and fill yourself up completely."

Her eyes shine with lust and something else as she wraps her legs around my hips, one hand locked around my neck, climbing me, impaling herself on my cock. Once I'm all the way in, she sighs and thrusts me deeper. With every jerk of her hips, she consumes me in an entirely different way, giving herself to me—heaven and hell all wrapped up in one fucking amazing package.

And I'm giving her some control back.

Maybe.

I shift my hips, lowering them down to make it easier for her, my hand still closed over her throat. And then I take back what I never gave her in the first place. I lift one of her legs over my shoulder, angling deeper, and then bury my cock so far inside her that she says 'fuck' at the invasion.

"You're mine, V," I say with every thrust, watching her come apart beneath me. She always has been. I let her think she could escape. I allowed her to believe she could be free. But all this time, she was mine.

"Say it," I grit out.

Her eyes are locked onto mine, full of darkness, as she fists the shirt I'm still wearing as I fuck her harder than I should. "I'm yours," she growls.

"Good girl." I kiss her lips, and she bites back.

"Just make me come so I can forget everything for a moment."

"I'll do more than that," I promise her. I'm going to ruin her for anyone else.

Because she's all mine.

ELEVEN

VIOLA

DANTE FUCKS LIKE HE KILLS—PRECISELY, effortlessly, and without mercy. He never stops looking into my eyes, not once. He sees me, the real me, and claims it for himself. Every thrust inside, every stroke, has me shuddering beneath him, shaking all over.

He invades all of my senses. Every taste and touch, every scent is him. I'm lost in the feel of him fucking me on the floor of his office. Not once has he changed rhythm or relented pressure.

I hate him, but I also *need* him.

The need is stronger; ever since I've tasted him thoroughly, I need more. It's like I'm addicted, and there's nothing I can do but give in to the dark, devious temptation that is Dante Black.

"Just make me come so I can forget everything for a moment," I hiss at him as he draws back from the kiss to look at me again.

"I'll do more than that," he says, a slight curl to his lips annoying me more than anything.

I told him not to fuck me, but I couldn't help myself. And now he's going to boast all the way fucking home.

Still, it was worth it.

I close my eyes, enjoying the feel of him. Every time he slams into me, I lose a little bit of the rage eating me up from the inside out. He smirks and pushes into me again. Deeper. Harder. I let out a moan. I'm holding onto him, gripping his shirt like it's all I have.

I wasn't ready to let him go.

Even when I thought he'd left me.

He did leave.

Why do you still trust him?

I fucking don't. Dante is gorgeous, sexy, and powerful, and I don't trust him as far as I could throw him. And that isn't far.

The heat has been building between my legs until I'm at the edge, a delicious warmth that sends tingles through every part of my body. I'm drowning in the intense pleasure, getting lost on the waves of it as Dante uses me, abusing my body.

I feel like I'm bloody dreaming, yet I still could be.

I still have no idea how he got here.

If he's working for my father....

I'll kill him.

Dante groans as I clench around him. I'm close. I'm so very fucking close.

"Come inside me," I say, opening my eyes and looking into his arctic blue ones. I want to feel something, anything, and the thought of him emptying inside me, marking me, filling me with his cum, has my entire body raging.

There is a flash of something behind his eyes, but then it's gone. Instead, he blinks at me, tightening his fingers over my delicate neck as he fucks me.

"No." The way he says it is absolute.

"Why not?" I grit out between his raw strokes. My lower half is unable to move anymore. It takes a lot to reach down and grab his balls.

"Viola," he replies, a warning, but I can tell he's fighting not to come. I slide my leg from his shoulder and wrap myself around him, one arm and legs locking him in again, so he can't back out. As the pleasure climaxes and finally tips me over the edge into oblivion. I grip his balls tighter. I orgasm hard. He tenses, too, trying to pull out. But I've got him. He's got me. When he realizes, he stops fighting me and closes my airway instead, taking away my breath.

The dark look on his face is worth it.

"Bitch," he grits out as his hips jerk and shudders, straining despite himself. He's still got his hand tight around my throat. I know why he's not keen. Dante doesn't like leaving evidence anywhere, including leaving part of himself inside me. It's against his nature, so that makes it even more delicious to win against him, to watch his icy gaze lock on mine as I force him to do just that.

I've got you.

I wait him out, not struggling, seeing this through to the end. And just when I think he's not going to let go, he gives in to me. His hips thrust one last time, and his savage gaze flares with something akin to hate as he releases deep inside me against his will. I give him a lustful, dark smile as he fills me up.

"I'm not one of your schoolboys," he says, holding me, squeezing my throat as he finishes, staring into my eyes as I stare back into his.

"No, but you needed a good seeing to," I grit out against his grip, echoing his words from earlier. "Isn't cumming inside me so much better?"

He smirks. "It's certainly cleaner."

Abruptly, he pulls out, and I let him go. His cum is leaking out of me onto the floor. I lie there, soaking up that maybe I finally got one over on Dante.

It's been a long time coming.

He looks at me with shuttered eyes before getting to his feet. But he's not happy. I've never seen him unsettled like this.

"You can't get me pregnant if that's what you're worried about." I may as well put him out of his misery. The facility here makes you take contraception. The last thing they want is pregnant teenagers.

"That's not what I'm worried about," he says in a flippant voice as he tucks himself back into his trousers.

I sit up, leaning back on my elbows. "Then what are you crying about?"

He snorts a headshake at me. The anger swirling around inside of me confuses the hell out of me as he walks away. *What did I want? A fucking cuddle?* I'm used to the boys wanting some validation, seeking to hold me or have me hold them.

I'm not used to this.

I lie back, closing my eyes, trying to keep the fleeting feeling of bliss from vanishing. But it's already gone. Fuck him.

I reach down with my hand between my legs, feeling Dante's cum still warm and wet, and use it to make myself come again. I'm panting, letting all the fucking rage dissipate with the quickening of my fingers.

"When you've finished, please clean up. We can't leave any evidence behind here."

My hard-on dies a small death at that.

Bastard.

I sit up, staring at him until I see what he's doing, sitting at his desk, clicking file after file open, and then taking out a flash drive and inserting it. He's making copies of everything before wiping it clean with Quinn's unique software, removing all and any traces of a file from the computer. No one will be able to recover them.

He's erasing me from the system.

Fine. I'm done here too. I want to go home.

Getting out of St Michael's is easier than it should be. No one says anything as Dante rolls me out in a wheelchair. He flashes some transfer papers, and the staff barely registers them before waving us through security. And just like that, I'm free.

Dante's car isn't the Mustang. It's a sleek-looking Lexus with big comfy seats and all the flashy gadgets.

"Where's the shit brown one?" I ask him as I nestle into the butter-soft leather of the passenger side seat.

"I'm on the job. Where do you think?"

I sigh as he starts the engine and slowly pulls out of the parking lot. At this rate, we'll never get anywhere. The itching is back under my skin. I drum my fingers on the door panel just to alleviate it somewhat. "How is—"

"Jude's fine," Dante cuts me off. "He's been out for weeks."

"That wasn't what I was going to ask."

"How about you stop asking questions and just enjoy the ride for once?"

I give him a blank look. He's still in some mood with me, and I have no idea how to coax him out of it. For the longest time, we've been colleagues—mentor and mentee—but we've never been lovers. I don't know how to navigate the Dante relationship track. And I'm not sure I want to know how.

We sit in silence all the way to Sacred Heart.

"Nothing's changed in the two months since I left then?" I ask, just to annoy Dante further.

He shoots me a sterile look. "Everything's changed." As we park next to the Mustang, I don't know what to make of that. A few more cars are in the lot, including Lorcan's canary yellow Mclaren and Jude's battered Aston. Even Dino's bike is there waiting for its owner to come back.

I need a car.

As Dante gets out, I quickly unbuckle and follow him. "I need a car," I say to him as we head to the boarding house.

"Use mine."

"No, I want my own car."

"Anything else, Princess?" His gaze flicks to me as we go through the steel-enforced double doors. *Steel-enforced?*

"I'll think of something." I muse.

He doesn't deem that with a response.

Quinn is the first person to grab me into a hug when I walk through the door. "Oh my God, Viola." She smells of coconut and vanilla shampoo, and her loungewear tracksuit is plush and soft. I push her away after the appropriate amount of time. After she's checked me over from top to bottom, I glance around. The place is empty. Dante has already fucked off. The others are nowhere to be seen.

"Where's everyone?"

"Rebecca is at that place I told you about. I'll take you to see her tomorrow if you like. Pascal went back to her mother's. Lily went to her dad's."

"Where's Lor and Jude?"

Quinn's lips flatten into a straight line. "They're trying to get a meeting with Lola Vice."

I frown. "Lola Vice? Dino's mother? Why?"

Quinn guides me into her office and hands me a cream card invitation. I take it from her and read what it says, written in beautiful italic script.

The pleasure of your company is requested at the marriage, uniting

Viola Harper-Black
and
Kardinal Vice

Sunday, the seventh of May
at six o'clock in the evening
Harper Black Estate
34 Americas Hill, London, UK

Reception to follow

"The boys got one a few days ago," says Quinn, watching my face for a reaction. "I take it you already know about this?"

I nod. "Has anyone seen Dino?"

Quinn shakes her head. "No, and they won't let anyone see him. That's another reason the boys went to Lola. They're still trying to find him. They're hoping his mother would know."

I take all this in and then hand the card back to Quinn. Marrying Dino isn't the worst thing in the world. He's alive and not dead, so I didn't kill him. But I never want to marry anyone. After what happened to my mother, marriage seems like an empty set of promises—ones I can't keep.

The wedding means nothing. It changes nothing. I have three people to kill, and then I can sleep—Gigi, my father, and possibly Dante if he is indeed working with Adrien, and this is all an act. I may have let him fuck me, but that was an itch to scratch, nothing more.

"Are you going ahead with it?" Quinn asks as she walks around the back of her desk, taking a seat in her chair.

"Of course not. I'm going to need your help."

"Oh?"

I look around the office and back at the door, checking we're alone. I sit down, facing her desk, when it's apparent that Dante is not in earshot.

"Do you remember I asked you for an untraceable identity?"

"I remember," Quinn says slowly. "You want it for you and Rebecca, right?"

"I need to take my mother far away from this mess."

"And the boys?"

"I can't take them with me."

Quinn gives me a look. "So, you're just going to keep on running?"

"I can kill Gigi and my father. Just give me the opportunity. But I don't know if I can kill Dante," I tell her honestly.

"I thought that might be the case. You've let him get too close, haven't you?"

I grit my jaw at her words. Even Quinn can see he's not to be trusted. "How long have you known he's a potential rat?"

She cocks her head. "Since he left you to rot in that place."

"Him getting me out now isn't a coincidence. My father said he's got someone lined up to take out Duke."

"Honey. I told you once. Dante is a disease. That man is a stone-cold killer. He's going to either drag you down with him, or he's going to be the death of you."

"I need two untraceable IDs before then," I nod at the wedding invite on the desk.

After a minute, she sighs. "I'll see what I can do. I might know someone, but you'll need a lot of cash."

TWELVE

VIOLA

MY ROOM IS the same as when I left it, but someone took the time to clean up the blood—Dino's blood. I shower and change, putting on some of Quinn's pajamas. She has so many pairs and loungewear sets I'm beginning to think the girl lives in nothing but them.

Dante is waiting for me when I come out of my room. The sneaky fuck. I didn't even know he was there.

His arms are folded, and he's looking at me strangely.

"What?"

"They're a bit revealing, aren't they?"

I look down at the cute t-shirt and shorts I'm wearing with the words 'Pillow Fight Queen' on them in big fluffy letters and a tiara hanging over the Q. "They're Quinn's. And you've all seen me in less."

And that's true. Even Quinn has seen me naked.

He blinks at me and then exhales. "Tell me what you need."

"You want a job?"

"I can't sit here and do nothing."

"I thought you had work?"

"That's done. I told you I had to straighten it out. From now on, I'm all yours."

I narrow my eyes at that. Dante only cares about work. He wouldn't give that up for me.

"My father said he'd hired someone to kill Duke. Is that you?"

He cocks his head. "I would have done it a thousand times over if it was me."

He's right. I can't dispute that. Dante wouldn't let something like that slide.

"Then there's nothing I need you to do for me," I say, shaking my head. "You've done enough. Unless you can get me a car."

The muscle in his jaw clenches. "You're being a brat."

"Am I?"

"Yes, you are." He tilts his head, trying to figure me out. "And I think I know why. Is it the redhead? You're still blaming yourself?"

I open my mouth to make a scathing remark back, but I suddenly don't have the energy. I walk off, leaving him standing there. He can psychoanalyze me all he likes because he's wrong. I don't think anything about Dino, nothing at all.

Because if I do, I'll fall apart.

When I head down to the apartment's open-plan sitting and kitchen area, Jude and Lorcan are waiting. Lorcan is the first to notice me. He's on his phone, standing in the kitchen, scowling at something he's reading on there when he looks up.

"Fuck, V," is all he says, and then I'm in his arms.

He kisses me like there's no tomorrow. When I break away from him, his woodsy cologne is still in my senses. Hand on my waist, he frowns, drawing me back to him.

"Where the fuck do you think you're going?" Lor asks.

My eyes dart over to Jude, leaning back on the sofa, beer in hand, a soft smile edging onto his lips.

"Oh, right," Lor says, taking his hand away. He runs it through his hair. "You'll want to see Jude too."

"I want to see both of you," I say practically.

Jude snorts. "Where's Sinner when you need him to make everyone feel super awkward."

At the mention of Dino's nickname, all I see is blood and feel the darkness slide over me. Finding my release with Dante held it at bay for most of the day, but it's back, slithering under my skin. I suck in a breath, shove it away, and stalk over to Jude. He puts his beer down and pats his knee.

"Sit that fucking delightful ass right here, baby."

I roll my eyes but straddle him anyway, grabbing his head to kiss the life out of him.

"You fucking lied," he says in a shitty tone after I've sucked every last drop of beer from his lips. "You told me we were leaving together."

"Just shut the fuck up," I scold him lightly. "I've had a crappy day at work." I'm done with men whining. Someone starts to massage my shoulders, and I don't look to see who it is. It's Lorcan, making up for the lost time, easing the pain.

"Is this what you need?" he asks, voice soft and seductive.

"Fuck, yes," I say, looking deep into Jude's hazel orbs, which are practically glowing now. For a split second, I wonder if he's sober. Probably not, if the beer on his breath is anything to go by. But better beer than benzos.

I need Jude alert and firing on all cylinders if I'm to pull off my plan.

Lorcan starts kissing my neck, so I close my eyes. I don't open them when Jude starts lifting my pajama top to massage one breast and suck the nipple of the other, causing waves of pleasure to erupt from my core.

"Please tell me I haven't just walked into an orgy starring my brother and my ex," says a bitchy voice.

"Okay, who let the Pirahana in?" drawls Jude.

I open my eyes to see Saskia standing in the middle of the

kitchen with her hands over her eyes. "Fuck off, Jude. Have you quite finished whatever disgusting thing you were doing to Viola?"

"Sorry, Sassy. I forgot you were home early," Lorcan says to his sister.

Jude snorts a laugh as I tug my pajama top down. Lorcan just exhales, stepping away from me, and goes to welcome his sister. I don't know how to greet Lorcan's sister, so I give her a look. It's not a hateful look, so that's an improvement.

I also get off Jude's crotch.

As much as I enjoyed being on top of it, I doubt Saskia would approve.

I shoot Jude a look. "Saskia lives here?" I say in a low voice while Saskia talks to her brother.

"Apparently," he shrugs.

"Lor was worried about my safety," Saskia says, cutting in. She comes right up to me and throws her arms around me. "V, so good to see you." I stiffen in her embrace. What is it with all these people who want to hug?

"Sorry, I forgot you hate being touched," she coos, stepping back with a smile. "Oh, my goodness. You've lost weight. You look amazing."

I blink at her.

"The food was like shit, and some days we didn't eat, Sas," says Jude, not bothering to get up, taking another sip of his beer.

She rounds on Jude. "I wasn't talking to you." Her eyes run over him from top to bottom. "Although you've lost weight too, you look fucking awful for it."

Lorcan rolls his gaze upward, and Jude looks thunderous, but Saskia doesn't seem bothered. I haven't seen her in so long, but it's coming back to me why I decided to like her. She takes no shit from anyone. I can respect that.

While Saskia goes off to put her shopping bags in her room, I take Lorcan aside.

"Saskia is staying here? With Dante? Is that wise?" The last time they were under the same roof, Dante tried to kill her.

Lore shrugs. "She moved in when Dante fucked off. We didn't think he was coming back. It's fine. Me, Jude, and Dan have taken up one of the other apartments. This is now the girls' apartment."

I give him a strange look. "Dan? He lets you call him Dan?"

Lorcan's brow creases. "It's his name. What the fuck do I call him then?"

I shake my head, suddenly wanting to sleep for a thousand fucking years. I close my eyes, breathing in and out, and then drag my lids back open. Lorcan is looking at me with a weird look on his face. I have to tell him there's a hit out on him, but I'm too tired to form more words right now.

"Fuck, you must be shattered. I didn't even think about what your father—" Lorcan stops talking and rubs his chin. "Come on, let's just get you to bed."

I shake my head. "I need to talk to you," I say. Byron is still in the facility, and there's what he said about Lorcan's parents that I need to tell him.

"It can all wait until tomorrow," he says.

He's right. I need sleep. But the last thing I want is to close my eyes and see fucking Dino covered in blood. "Come with me?" I say, unable to believe I'm asking him to come to bed.

"You know it's only six?"

I look out the window, and it's already dark. "Pretend it's eleven."

Lorcan shrugs. "Want me to get Jude?"

So they're openly sharing me now.

"Get Jude," I say. "I'll be in my room."

I note that Lorcan doesn't ask if I want Dante. He goes off looking for Jude while I climb the stairs to the top floor.

I'm tucked into bed when the boys walk in. I let my eyes run over their broad shoulders, sculpted abs, and the v just before their hips as they strip quickly and efficiently down to their boxers and climb into bed. Lorcan takes the far side, and Jude takes the side close to the door, leaving me trapped in the middle.

"I can't do this," I suddenly say, sitting up. They're too close. There are too many of them. I've had a solo bed or Jude only for the last few months. How can I go from that to two of them, or even three if Dino comes back?

If he comes back.

I don't even want to think about Dante.

"We've got you," Lorcan says. He pulls me back down in the bed, so I'm facing him. I look into his shattered green orbs. He smoothes the hair out of my face and then brings his lips to mine. Kissing Lorcan has always been like finding myself. He gets me. He knows what I need without me having to ask. I devour him back, and once I'm lost in the feel of him, Jude tentatively places his hands on my waist, massaging and kissing the back of my neck. When I don't freak out, he moves closer, spooning and nuzzling me from behind.

It's not bad. It's not too much.

It's nice and safe.

My monster settles like a stray cat under a firm hand.

When I come up for air, Lorcan runs a thumb over my brow and then shifts so that I'm the big spoon, taking my arm under his so I'm holding him from behind. It's the only way he can sleep.

"Pretty soon, this ass is mine," Jude whispers.

The smile is on my lips before I can stop it.

Trust Jude to ruin the fucking moment.

THIRTEEN

JUDE

VIOLA IS BACK, and it shows in the dynamic of the place. Before, there was no cohesion whatsoever. Everyone had an agenda. Especially that fucker Dante, who looked like he'd gut you with his toothbrush if you looked at him funny.

"Oat skinny latte and a macchiato," says Lore, handing Viola a steaming cup. I shoot him a look as if to say where's mine? But he flips me a finger and stalks off back to the kitchen. We're sitting in the main lounge room, waiting for Quinn to get her shit together and Saskia to finally emerge from her cocoon.

Dante—fuck knows where he is. I don't trust him, despite what Lorcan has told me about him helping them find Rebecca. There's just something off about him. The fact that he's a murderer probably doesn't help.

When Lor comes back with more coffees, the fucker hands me one. As I take it, my hand decides to shake like a bitch. It doesn't go unnoticed. Viola and Lorcan stare at me as I clench and unclench my fist to get it to work.

"Maybe you should lay off the beer, mate?" fucking Lor has the balls to throw at me with Viola in the damn room.

"How about you lay off being an absolute cunt?" I say back to him.

Viola rolls her eyes, and Lor frowns, creasing up his holier-than-thou brow like a goddamn prick as he takes his coffee and sits on the other side of our girl. Fucking tosser.

Saskia walks in, looking like she raided a fashion house. She takes a mug of coffee from the tray her brother put on the table and then sits on one of the armchairs,

"What did I miss?" she asks, taking out a goddamn notebook, ready to take fucking notes.

"Nothing yet. We're waiting for Quinn," Viola says, sipping her drink. She looks better today. No one got up early, so we all had a long lie-in. After her mini-freak out in the bed, I got a text from Lorcan saying not to fucking try anything and let her sleep. Do you know how difficult it is to sleep with your dick pressed against Viola's luscious fucking ass? I spent most of the night aware of her every movement until exhaustion kicked in.

Not that I've been able to sleep much since St Michael's. Withdrawal has been a bitch. I really want a beer, but after Lorcan's remark, I can't just head over to the goddamn fridge, so I reach for Viola's hand instead. When she lets me take it, the need for a drink subsides. Lorcan sees us and places his hand on her thigh, his fucking FOMO going off the charts.

And that's how we are when Psycho Charlie walks in. His eyes take in me and Lor, either side of Viola, claiming her for the world to see.

We're like a bunch of fucking wolves, marking our territory.

I'm expecting him to react, but all he does is walk over, grab a coffee, and then head to a spot by the kitchen island to stand against it. He doesn't bat a fucking eyelid at Viola sitting with us. Before I entered St Michael's, Dante tried to kill us all. And now he's fucking drinking coffee with us, and we're sleeping in his damn school.

Call me paranoid, but I don't like it.

When Quinn arrives with her laptop and a bunch of notes, no

one is talking. "Well, tell me who died because it's like a funeral home in here."

"More like a pissing contest," Saskia sighs. "Let me get you up to speed. They all want to fuck Viola, but no one is willing to make the first move now she's back for fear of hurting her or not being allowed to share."

Viola snorts into her coffee.

Dante frowns.

Lorcan grimaces.

"Nailed it." I raise my mug to Sas, who rolls her eyes, but there's a faint smirk on her lips.

"Can we just get on with the briefing?" Dante asks. "I've got things to do today."

Viola's brow furrows at that, but no one says anything else as Quinn sets up and hands out paper copies of what she wants to go over. It's like being at fucking school. I don't remember signing up for this. I care about Viola just as much as anyone else here, but this. *What is this shit?* I flip through it, toss it onto the table, and take a sip of my coffee. But it's like drinking soil now it's no longer hot.

Fuck, I need a proper drink.

The briefing was short, thank fuck. Quinn wanted to go over the security measures she'd put in place around the campus to protect the girls and keep everyone safe. Viola gave everyone her update on Byron and her father. There was some discussion on getting Bryon out, and Lor said he would handle it.

Lorcan and I gave everyone the shitty news—no one knows where Adrien is keeping Dino. After that, Dante fucked off as soon as it was over. Saskia announced she was going shopping to cope with the stress. And Lorcan took the hint and went with her since it was on the way to his lawyer's office anyway.

Getting Viola alone is a luxury I don't have anymore, so I

volunteer to go with her to check over all the entrances and their locks.

"You don't trust Dante?" she asks me outright when we get to the far entrance gate.

"I get it that he saved you and that he's always been there for you. But he tried to kill Saskia and you, and now he's strolling around acting like a right cunt."

"Is that a no?"

I sigh. "It's not a yes."

She seems to contemplate this. "I don't trust him either."

I stop walking and look at her. "Then what the fuck are we doing here? Let's just leave this place."

She turns to me. "No, I need to see this through to the end."

"The end of fucking what?" I stare at her.

"Adrien. I have to kill him. I need to get Dino back."

I understand that. I get that. "You don't need Dante for that. You've got Lor and me. And that hot Asian who knows fucking everything…."

She cocks her head, giving me an annoyed look. "That's not your call to make. I decide if we need to keep him close or not."

I glare at her, not getting her at all until I do. "You don't want to give him up, do you? Even if he's going to fuck us over one day, and he will. I know his type."

"You know nothing about him."

"Neither do you," I scoff.

Our voices are raised at each other now as we stand in the woodland beside the long rear entrance driveway that leads to the school. There's no one here, but anyone could be listening. Viola seems to check herself as she looks around.

After a pause, she speaks again, in a more level tone. "Then help me, Jude. Get close to him."

I scrub my hand over my face. "How do you expect me to do that?"

"Dante knows about addictions. How to manage them."

I snort a laugh, shaking my head at her. "I was waiting for this talk."

"No talk, just pretend you need help. Get him to open up. You're the only one I trust to do this. And you owe me for your uncle."

She's got me there. I lift my hands. "Fine, fine." I don't have my inheritance yet and probably will never get it.

When we get back to the boarding house, Viola drags me upstairs. I sit and wait on her bed while she digs around in her things.

"You'll need these," she says, handing me something heavy wrapped in cloth. I know before unraveling it that it's my brass knuckles.

"Fuck, look at that, " I say, holding one up. They've been cleaned. I glance at Viola. I could kiss her right now for this one thing alone. "You found them?"

She shrugs. "They were in your car. Filthy, I might add."

I slip one on. The weight I've lost means it doesn't fit as well as it used to, but I don't fucking care. "You know, there was a time I lived in these."

She raises a brow. "I can imagine that."

"You fucking beaut," I say, kissing the cold metal.

"Shall I give you two some time alone?"

I grin at her. "Come here." I pull her toward me, tangling my hand with the knuckle duster in her hair. She lets out a small moan as her lips find mine. "I'd rather have a threesome," I tease in her ear.

She frowns. "There's no way that's fitting inside me," she says, making me chuckle. "And we can't. I have something to tell Lorcan. I told him to meet us up here when he's back."

"Fine, I can wait," I smirk at her.

Viola gets her blades out instead and cleans the fuck out of them until Lorcan walks through the door.

"I don't give a fuck. Just do what I tell you," he says down his phone. He puts his cell away and returns to where we're sitting on the bed. "Fuck Joseph's company," he mutters, eyeing the impressive array of knives and switchblades Viola has already worked through.

"Did you speak to the lawyer?" she asks, glancing up at him.

He sighs and runs his hand through his hair. "Yes. They're going through his papers as we speak. We might have to get him transferred to the place Quinn moved Rebecca to until we can get him signed off as not mentally unstable."

"Can't we just get rid of the file as we did with Viola?"

Lorcan shakes his head, sitting on the chair next to the bed. "No, Viola was never in under her own name."

"I was," I say to him. "You got me out."

"No, Jude Marques is still inside St Michael's or whoever you switched with. We're still working on officially getting you out too." He glares at me. "Another reason you can't just fuck off. You do anything to alert the authorities that you're not where you're supposed to be, and you go right back in, got it?" He sighs, putting his head in his hands. "How the fuck did I become the babysitter in all this?"

Fuck this.

I start getting up off Viola's bed.

"Where are you going?" he snaps.

"I'm going to get a beer. That alright with you, mate?"

Viola gives me a look like I'm not helping, making me want to run my fist through a wall. I stalk out and head downstairs. The kitchen is empty for once, so I take longer than usual to grab a beer. I sit on the sofa and flick through social media on my phone while I drink it. Lor can be a right prick when he gets it in his head that he's running the show.

I'm still scrolling through my phone when Dante walks in.

"Where is she?" he demands.

"Fucking Lorcan," I say just to irritate him. He narrows his eyes but doesn't fuck off, so I put my phone down. "They're talking about Byron," I say, taking a swig of my beer.

"Tell her I found the redhead." And with that, he walks off.

With a sigh, I get to my feet and chase after him. He's getting into his car when I walk down the boarding house steps. The engine is one. He must have left it idling.

"Hey, Dante." He looks up at me as he slides behind the wheel, one hand on the driver's door, ready to close. "Viola said you could help me with something," I add lamely.

He stares at me with unreadable eyes and then nods. "Get in. Not the beer. Chuck that."

With a long-overdue sigh, I place the beer on the side, stroll to the passenger side of the Mustang, and get in.

Fucking hell, what am I doing?

What Viola needs me to do, and I'll do it every fucking time. No questions asked.

FOURTEEN

VIOLA

THE NEXT FEW days go by too slowly. As soon as Dante told me where Dino was, I wanted to go to him or at least stalk him. But Lorcan tackled me to the floor while Quinn talked some sense into me.

They only let me up once I agreed to wait a few days. Lorcan likes to plan, and so does Quinn. The two of them together are annoying as hell. But as they explained, not rushing in gives me time to heal and everyone else time to formulate a strategy. I get the latter part. I'm a paid killer. I usually don't rush into things. But if a job lands on my desk, I like to scope things out immediately. I have to see how the land lies for myself. Trusting intel only can get you killed.

For the healing part, I beg to differ.

All I've done is recuperate. I'm done with waiting.

Jude, at least, seems to be on board. If he's not spending most of his time between doing the perimeter checks with me, he's with Dante. I don't know what they do all day, but it's given me a little bit of breathing space that Jude is keeping an eye on my mentor and that my mentor is helping Jude deal with his demons.

Dante is good at that, at least.

Now all I have to worry about is Lorcan. He didn't seem interested when I told him about the hit on him and what Byron said. He told me to forget about it.

"It's not important." Those are the words he uses as he looks at me with those intense green eyes.

"My father is trying to kill you."

He gives me a shuttered look. "Someone is always trying to kill me."

"And you really don't want to know your real parents?" I ask to be sure.

He shrugs. "If what you said is true, they gave me away. Why the fuck would I want to know them?"

All my life, I've thought about what it would be like to have different parents. Being the daughter of a monster means one day I will turn out just like him. That's probably happened already. I can't escape it.

Adrien made me who I am through both nature and nurture.

Lorcan is upset with them, so I understand he doesn't want to know because of what they did.

But I would be curious.

That's the difference between him and me.

I don't hold grudges.

Well, not easily.

"Fine," is all I say with a shrug. He sighs and draws me closer, inhaling as he wraps his arms around me.

"I still can't believe you're fucking here. Don't you ever leave me again, or I'll hunt you down and tattoo my name on your goddamn ass cheek."

To pass the time quicker, I train with Dante, and we settle into a routine of early morning boot camp and sparring sessions after breakfast. Sometimes Lorcan joins us, sometimes Quinn, but not Jude. Never Jude. The boy likes to have a lie-in way too much.

Dante makes it his mission to get me to yield in as little time as possible. I make it mine to cause him as much pain as I can. Usually, he wins, but occasionally I get a sly dig in.

"You're favoring your right side because of your wrist. It makes you predictable," he says one morning. It's been about three days since we found out where Adrien is keeping Dino, and we're still here, pissing about. The raw frustration at being unable to do a damn thing, a prickling heat under my skin, has been eating away at me. I want to really hurt someone.

Especially Dante.

"Knives," I say, huffing. "Let's go with knives next."

Dante's mouth twitches at the corners. "That bad?" We're alone today, so I won't scare anyone if I go supernova at my ex-mentor. I know he can take it.

I. Just. Need. Release.

Fucking hasn't been enough lately.

Not that I'm not complaining about that. But since St Michael's, Dante hasn't touched me, and Jude and Lorcan together seem to think they're going to break me.

Well, they're not.

Dante heads over to his training gear and selects two very blunt-looking blades. He tosses me one. I catch it easily, frowning when I run a finger over the edge. Dull as dishwater. I give him a look.

"Do you have any real knives?"

He snorts and heads over to his killing tools. He takes out a material wrap and selects two of the meanest, fuck-off strike knives. This time he doesn't throw one at me. He walks over and hands it to me, hilt first.

"Please don't accidentally kill me during edged-weapons training," he says.

"What about deliberately?"

He stares at me for a few seconds until I flash him a grin.

131

"Just be careful," he says with a shake of his head.

I'm not careful, far from it. Every time he gets too close, I funnel my rage into slicing parts of him off. He dodges quickly and efficiently every time. Pretty soon, we're both sweating, bruised, and covered in small bloody gashes, mostly me. Our clothes haven't fared too well either. Where I haven't sliced him, I've managed to cut ribbons into his clothes.

"This was my favorite shirt," Dante chides, eyeing me with what looks to be newfound respect. I should hope so. I've not let up once.

"It's black, just like every shirt you own," I say.

He gives me a look, an evil-looking one, and lunges. I block, barely.

"Stay outside of kicking range," Dante says in a smooth voice. He lunges again, and I move quicker this time, giving him a wider berth. "Come on, V, defang the snake. Why am I still holding this weapon?"

I snarl at that. "You have better timing," I say, and he does. For every strike I get, he gets five more. If this were a real fight, I'd be dead.

"Feel for that split second when you can connect to your target and then strike. Don't hesitate."

I lunge for him, missing by a centimeter. He uses my mistake to give me a warning cut on my hand.

"That would have disarmed you." He pivots and slashes again at my throat. "And that would have killed you."

I'm so fucked off with him that I do what I've wanted to do this entire time; I throw the knife at him. It narrowly misses, plunging into the gym wall behind him.

"If you're trying to kill me, that was a piss poor attempt," he snaps, whipping his attention back to me after seeing where it landed.

Now, I've upset the beast.

He seizes my knife from where it's stuck. I tilt my head, jutting out my chin as he marches up to me and hands it back.

"Here's my fucking heart, Viola," he says in a clipped voice, stepping in dangerously close, ice blue eyes tearing into me where I stand. "You want me dead, then do it."

Viola. He called me Viola.

I glare at him, and he stares back. He's so close; I could take him out. I could end Dante Black for good.

My heart thuds in my chest, my mouth runs dry, and I do nothing. Absolutely nothing.

He takes my hand, gripping the hilt, and places the blade's tip over his chest. The piercing slice of his eyes is almost demonic as he looks down on me.

"Here is my heart." He puts pressure on the knife. "Now cut the damn thing out."

My eyes become slits as he carves the edge over his skin. I glance down, seeing the well of blood under his shirt.

"You think I won't?" I grit out.

"No…I think you will. I just can't be bothered dancing around your games any longer." He stops slicing and starts forcing the blade into his flesh, his jaw clenched, eyes burning with ice-cold rage.

I try to yank my hand away, but he has it locked around the knife. I can't let go.

"Stop it," I snarl at him, my breath coming in shorter and sharper as I try to pull back.

He advances, making me step back faster. Every time I pull the knife away from him and increase the space between us, he pivots around and yanks me closer, pushing it in deeper.

"No, this isn't—" I choke on the last few words.

"This isn't what? Fun? Nice? What isn't it, Viola?" he seethes, digging the knife into his flesh. The tip of it scrapes against bone every single time.

"This isn't what I want!" I rage at him.

He drops the knife, and I snatch my hand away, my whole body practically vibrating as it clatters to the floor. I've already skittered back, but Dante grabs the base of my skull, fingers curled in my hair, and hauls me to him, crushing his lips onto mine.

His lips are cold, and his tongue warm. But the blood is hot. My hands, pressed against his chest, are becoming slick with it. There's so much blood pouring from the slashes and cuts on his chest, but he doesn't seem to care.

He forces himself inside my mouth, branding me from the inside with his tongue and teeth. Every suck and bite takes me close to the edge of a desperate pain where pleasure is just beyond reach.

The bitter tang of blood is everywhere. He even tastes of it, making me wild, bringing my monster to the surface. I dig my hands in his blood chest, making him hiss. I moan as he tongues me, running his hands all over me. And then, somehow, he picks me up, and I wrap my legs around his waist as he moves to pin me to the wall.

"You're going to be the death of me," he says in my ear as he pushes me up against the plaster.

"Shut up and just fuck me," I pant, biting his ear.

His hands drag across my body, tearing down my leggings as I yank down his shorts.

"Tell me, V, what you want," he groans, his cock hard between my legs, his chest slick with blood as I claw at him.

"Fuck, Dante. I want you." Our need for each other has spiraled out of control as we writhe against each other mindlessly.

There's no right or wrong anymore. No distrust. It's just our raw need, this moment, and so much fucking blood. As Dante grabs my hips, I angle myself to meet him. And then he thrusts himself inside me before I can catch my breath.

The punch of his cock, coated with his hot blood, has me riding him to the hilt, biting down on his neck from the shock of pleasure rising from my core. He doesn't take it slow this time. He fucks me like he's a man possessed, slamming into me, filling me deeply over and over.

"Is. This. What. You. Want?" he asks, thrusting deeper with every word as I grind down on him. I moan in answer to that, eyes tightly closed, pulling at the hair on his head, gnawing my own damn lip.

He licks my neck and then tells me to look at him. When I do, his gaze penetrates—darkening with every snap of his hips.

"You want me to come inside you, V? Is that what you want?" he grits out.

I stare back, meeting his thrusts with mine. "Leave your mark," I say.

He grimaces. "Because I trust you."

He kisses me then, brutally, his tongue sliding over mine. He tastes of sweat and coppery death as he fucks me without mercy, taking everything I am in that one moment and destroying it. Blood is everywhere—messy, mixing with the slickness between my thighs, coating us both as he pounds me against the wall. His dick swells inside me as pleasure erupts, and every stroke is absolute control gone out the fucking window.

This is what I need.

And I feel it as I see it…his eyes glazing over, shuttering as the blaze of light within him falters. His arms, holding me upright with immense power behind them, quake enough for him to slam a palm at the wall as he leans against it, keeping us upright.

Keeping me close.

This is what I need.

To be the one taking as life slips away.

I clench around him, seething, screaming, holding him to me as he bleeds for me.

That's when I come, falling into the abyss of sweet release, clinging to him as he falls to one knee. His breath quickens as his cock tightens inside of me, and he comes with a violent shove of his hips. I'm still wrapped around him when he drops one knee to the floor and then the other, emptying deep inside me until there's nothing left.

And he's got nothing left to give.

"Fuck, you're heavy," he says, panting as he rests my back on the lower half of the wall, pale blue eyes, glassy almost, as he takes me in.

"Asshole," I say softly, in retaliation. His cock is still sheathed inside me and twitches as he stares deep into my eyes.

We slide further as he falls, slipping.

Blood everywhere.

"Dante?" He doesn't respond, so I wriggle to get free. "You need to get off me. Fuck, D.

He doesn't move, only his eyes as they flutter closed, breathing less and less as he puts all his weight on me.

"You're the fucking heavy one," I glare at him as I try to push him off. I manage to roll him off onto his back. There's blood and cum everywhere. All over him and all over me.

It looks like a massacre.

"Dante? What the fuck?" I slap his cheek, hot sex all but fucking forgotten.

"I'm going to need you to stop the bleeding," he murmurs, passing the fuck out. "I think you nicked a vein."

FIFTEEN

VIOLA

FUCKING DANTE.

I've no idea why he would nearly kill himself to prove a point. But I move quickly, getting him to the medical bay as soon as he's out for the count.

With Dante out of commission, detained by Quinn, I shower, washing the dried blood off my body and cleaning it out of my hair, before changing and then go snooping around in his things. He might trust me, but I don't trust him. I'm no closer to my goal, and just sitting around has done nothing, so I take it upon myself to move things forward. That's always been my specialty —stab first, deal with the consequences later.

I'm done with waiting.

His room is neat and bordering on empty. There's his laptop which is locked, a few piles of clothes neatly folded in the wardrobe, and his backpack. I open the last one up to find three files inside, jobs from the agency and one containing his birth certificate and newspaper clippings of his parents' death. I go for the jobs. It's been a long time since I did one. I'm curious about what kind of things they've been sending him.

Lorcan's head on a plate, perhaps?

They're not. I rifle through them, noting his shorthand in the margins where he's written down some additional information. He's even highlighted the fee being offered. My eyes widen at that. These jobs are high-end. Trust Dante to get the good ones. I could retire on the amount just one of these jobs would give me.

When I check the dates, it dawns on me that these jobs should have already been completed. That's what he was doing when I was inside. He was earning fucking more money.

I shove the files inside Dante's bag and head back to my room. If I want those IDs Quinn promised me, I need to figure out how to earn that kind of money myself. But I'm pretty untouchable now that Polina has put the word out that I renege on my contracts. The bitch has cut me off. I need to get one last job somehow.

Maybe I can pretend to be Dante?

After dinner, I head down to the medical rooms where Dante is. I know he's okay because Quinn told me he was. He's sitting up, bandages all over his chest, hooked up to an IV to replace the lost fluids, reading a goddamn book like he's on holiday. He's not. I got Quinn to handcuff him to the bed while he was out of it.

"Cuffs, really?" he says, holding up his wrist.

"I want an explanation," I say to him.

Dante puts the book down, exhaling. "Is there anything you don't want? That might be easier."

"Don't blame me for nearly bleeding to death. I didn't stab you in the chest."

Quinn walks in with freshly squeezed orange juice on a tray. She hands it to him by extending the tray. "Here. One fresh orange juice. That's the last time I wait on you," she says in a pissed-off voice.

"Then I appreciate it even more," he says, taking a huge gulp.

"Those jobs in your room. What are they? When did the agency give them to you."

He gives me a look. "They're not important." He doesn't even bother to ask why I was in there. He finishes the juice and waves the empty glass to Quinn. She makes an annoyed face and comes over with the tray.

"Because you've already done them?"

"Yes, I did both when you were in St Michael's," he sighs, putting the glass on the tray Quinn is holding for him just out of reach. Suddenly, he seizes it, jerking her toward him as she yelps with surprise. I'm ready for him when he does. I jab him with a concoction of drugs enough to put a grown man down in seconds. He grimaces, letting go of Quinn. Red blooms on his chest where the clean bandage is. Good to know he's not fucking superman.

"That is why you shouldn't be moving," Quinn says, scuttling back, even more pissed off than when she came in.

"Why the fuck am I in cuffs?" he huffs, straining against them and the drugs.

"Just tell me if you've met Polina yet to collect the money. They were cash-only deals," I say.

Jaw clenched, he shakes his head.

"Then I'll collect it." It's only polite to offer.

Quinn makes her fucked-off, mother hen face. "You will not."

Dante frowns, eyes muddy and dark as the drugs start to work. "Out of the question. She still has a hit on you," he pants, agreeing with her.

"Then send Jude. I'll go with him but stay out of sight. She'll never see me," I say.

He actually glares at me. "Why do you want to meet Polina?"

"I want a collector's fee," I lie. Okay, it's not a lie. It's a half-truth.

He stares at me for a few minutes and then relents. "I'm not having you go there with just Blond fucking Fight Club for backup. He has no idea how to shoot a gun, never mind drive a car."

I was going to keep Lorcan out of this because he's got a

target on his back, but this is my idea, so I know it's not a trap. "Fine, I'll take everyone."

Outside the medical center, Quinn draws me aside, her voice low. "This is for the IDs, right?" When I nod, she adds, "I don't get why you can't just ask Lorcan for the money you need."

I just look at her. "Quinn, when have I ever liked to beg money from a man?"

She rolls her eyes. "This is hardly begging, and he's loaded. He can afford it."

I shake my head. "I can't ask for more. Not for this." *Not when I'm planning on using it to leave him.*

She sighs. "Fine, I get it. Just don't get yourself killed."

She walks back to a spaced-out Dante and starts fussing with the bandage.

I don't tell Lorcan what we're doing straight away. I ask him to drive me to the address Dante sent me to pick up a courier drop-off, which seems harmless enough. Jude comes too when I ask him, mainly because he's bored. I don't blame him. We're both going out of our minds having to stay on the school grounds all the fucking time.

Saskia coming along was not my idea, but she gets in the car with us anyway when Lorcan drives Dante's Mustang around to the boarding house to collect everyone.

Lorcan glares at his sister in the rearview mirror. "Sas, what are you doing?"

"If you're all going, I'm not staying here alone with that killer," she says, clipping her seatbelt.

"He's drugged and cuffed," I say to her.

"And what if he escapes? No, I'm coming with you."

Lorcan grits his teeth but doesn't argue. I'm sitting shotgun, so I glance in the mirror at Jude, who is tapping his fingers anxiously on the door car, staring out of the window. He looks much better than when we first got out of St Michael's. The haunted look has gone. And he's not drinking, thanks to Dante's influence. As much as I hate Dante right now, he does have a positive effect on the boys.

The abandoned warehouse arranged for the meet is halfway between London and Whitechapel, in Hayes. It's getting dark by the time we get there, which works out for the best because it's easier to park closer and still stay hidden in the shadows.

Lorcan pulls up and switches off the engine. "So, what am I looking for?" he asks as he opens the car door.

"There will be a black duffel bag inside the main area. Just get it and come back out." I produce two of Dante's guns. "Take this." Lorcan hesitates but then takes it, checks it, and tucks it into his jacket.

I hand one to Jude through the seat headrest. "Jude, go with him. He'll need back up." I don't know if Jude knows how to take the safety off, but there's only one way to learn.

"I wouldn't say no," says Jude.

Lorcan frowns as Jude gets out too. "What the fuck for? You said this was simple equipment pick-up?" he spits at me through the open car door.

"I lied. Polina is dropping off payment for Dante. He told her you'd be collecting it for him."

"You fucking what?" Lor says, seething at me. "Fucking hell, V—" he runs his hands through his hair. "We're not doing this. Jude, get back in the car."

Jude gives him a skeptical look as another car's headlights beam into the warehouse's parking lot. "We'll look like right dicks if we left now, mate." He sighs.

"If you don't do it, Saskia and I will do it," I hiss at him, leaning over the middle partition so I can look at him.

"I'm ready to. Just hand me the gun," Saskia adds, backing me up, scooting forward to join the fray.

I took Saskia to the shooting range the weekend before her supposed wedding. She asked me to, and I was trying to fill my day with things to distract me from Dante stalking and hunting me. I was also gathering as much information about Joseph as I could. It turns out that Saskia, like her brother, isn't a bad shot.

That clearly sends the fear of God into Lorcan because he gives me a crazy look, slams the door in my face, and storms off toward the warehouse doors. Jude strolls after him, looking back only once to give me a wink.

"Jude knows how to shoot a gun, doesn't he?" asks Saskia, her voice filled with worry.

"I have no fucking clue," I say, letting all the air out of my lungs in one go.

She glances at me. "Did you bring any more guns?"

I nod at her. "Of course I did." I take another couple out of the bag and hand her one.

"There's a plan, right?" she says, checking the barrel and the safety like I taught her.

"Yep." I check my own gun. When the people from the other car have gone inside. I nod at Saskia. She's giving me one of those Cheshire cat smiles as I tell her the plan: "We're going to kidnap Polina while the boys create a diversion."

SIXTEEN

LORCAN

THERE'S nothing on the floor when we walk into the main area of the warehouse, but at the far end, a few heavy-set-looking guys appear.

"Which one of you is Duke?"

I indicate that's me, and they come over and hand me a fuckoff heavy bag. "Dante must trust you a hell of a lot," he says. Both men wait, watching us count it. Once I've confirmed it's all there, they walk off the way they came.

Jude shakes his head. "Why do I feel like we just got off too easy?"

"Because this is Viola we're talking about," I say to him. "When is anything ever easy when it comes to her? Come on."

When we get outside, the Mustang is running, and Viola is behind the wheel. "Get in," she says, revving the engine as she pulls the car up in front of us, so close she almost runs over my goddamn foot.

"What the fuck? You almost ran me over."

"Just get in, hurry," Viola snaps.

Jude takes the bag, and I jump in the front seat. We're just belting up when there's a shout from men from the warehouse that something is wrong. Viola peels away from the warehouse as fast as the deathtrap that is Dante's car will let her. Behind us, the two guys are running after us, shouting. They can't catch us, not on foot, but they look extremely fucked off.

"Viola, what did you do?" I ask her, holding on to the inside door card handle.

She says nothing, glancing in her mirror and then back to the road.

"Why were they chasing after us?" I ask, rephrasing just in case she didn't understand my first fucking question.

I look over my shoulder at my sister. "What did you both do?"

"What makes you think we did something?" Sas hisses at me.

There's muffled thumping from the trunk.

Jude starts chuckling. "I fucking knew it," he says, shaking his head.

"Is there someone in the fucking trunk?" I look at Viola, who's still pretending not to hear me. The banging continues, telling me that they do indeed have someone in the fucking trunk. "Is that why those men are chasing us?"

She finally deems me worthy of a glance. "Relax, I slashed their tires. No one is chasing us, and no one is coming after us."

"Who is in the trunk?" I repeat.

"My old boss."

"Why the fuck—" I shake my head.

"Because she's trying to kill me, is that good enough reason?"

I stare at her for a good full minute. "Jesus fucking Christ, Viola," I finally exclaim, turning back to the front, unable to say anything else. I have no words. No fucking words.

Viola doesn't drive us back to Sacred Heart. Instead, she takes us to the middle of nowhere and parks up. There's nothing but dark wood all around and not a patch of light in sight, apart from the moon.

'Where are we?" I say, completely done in.

"The cabin used to be here," is all she says. As she gets out of the car, I sigh. I tell Sas and Jude to stay put and get out too. I walk to the trunk. Viola is already there, waiting. I place my hand on the trunk before she opens it. "Before you do this, what's your plan?"

I know what she's going to say. I've seen that look in her eyes before. I don't know that I want to hear it, but I have to. What kind of pussy would I be if I didn't.

This is what I signed up for. I knew she was fucking psycho.

"I'm going to interrogate her. She knows if Dante is a rat or not."

"Here?" I gesture around. "In the middle of the damn woods?"

She shrugs. "The cabin basement is still intact."

"Is she tied up in there?"

Viola nods.

I run my hair through my hands and nod. I may not like it, but she's fucking right. We have to know if that bastard can be trusted. "Fine. I just need to take my sister home. I don't want her around this fucked-up shit."

Her brown eyes peer into mine. "Take the car, and then come back for me."

Despite everything, I've never wanted her so badly than in this moment. I grab her and kiss her hard, shoving my tongue into her mouth, bruising those sweet, luscious lips. When I pull away, she's panting, looking at me like she wants to devour me.

"I'm so angry at you right now for lying to me," I say. "But I get why you did."

"So am I forgiven?"

"Far from it, sweetheart, when I get back, I'm going to punish you by fucking you so hard and deep that you won't be able to walk for a week."

She smirks. "I look forward to it."

I give her lips one last teasing suck and then let her go so she can open the trunk.

Inside is a small woman with dark hair and dark brown eyes. From the angle Viola seems to have wedged her into the trunk, she doesn't look comfortable. Her clothes are in disarray, but enough that I can see the edge of a familiar-looking tattoo. There's also one on her hand, a small star. She rages at Viola from behind her gag, only stopping short when she sees me.

She mumbles something into her gag that's incomprehensible unless you know the language.

I give a shake of my head. "You've got to be fucking kidding me. She's Camorra mafia," I say, closing my eyes for a minute to massage the bridge of my nose. "But you know that, don't you?"

Viola gives me a sideways look. "It changes nothing."

I glare at her. "It changes everything. You can't kill her."

"If she gives me what I need, then I won't have to," she says calmly.

The woman is still trying to say something to me. If only I'd paid more attention to the lessons Joseph used to make me attend. I catch only a few words like 'traitor' and 'son of whore'.

Fucking charming.

I make Jude take Sasia back to the school, then I stand and force myself to watch while Viola uses her knife skills to extract information from her old boss. Viola doesn't hesitate to do what a grown man would.

She's our Angel of fucking Death, alright.

Only once do I avert my eyes—when Viola is cutting her eyelids off. That's not something I want haunting my nightmares. Her screams, though….

They will never leave me.

But all the things she has done for the firm, all the things Polina has already admitted to, tell me she deserves it.

When Viola finally puts Polina out of her misery, her eyes are burning with an intensity I've only seen once—when she had me tied up on her bed in the farmhouse. *Viola was supposed to kill me then, and she didn't.* I don't know how I feel about that, so I take the stone steps to the outside world to get some fresh air. Viola casts her eyes over me as she works, but she doesn't stop me. There's relief behind her eyes, as though she would rather be alone with her prey.

That suits me just fine.

Outside, there's a fresh breeze and only the sound of the wind in the trees. I check for messages from Jude, sitting on a bit of burnt-out cabin wall to wait for him. I told him to bring back some accelerant so that we could burn the body. The Italians are already going to be after us. I'd rather they didn't find what is left of their dead boss.

Viola emerges a short while later. There's blood on her face and clothes, but otherwise, she looks peaceful.

"How did you know she was mafia?"

"Her hand, there's a small star tattoo. An ex-girlfriend of mine had one. Joseph used to make me date the daughters of the mob bosses so he could gain intel on them."

"Makes sense. Polina could withstand everything I did to her, even until the end."

"So does that mean you don't believe her?" I ask her as she comes and sits next to me.

"About you or Dante?" she asks.

I turn to her, putting my arms around her shoulders, drawing her close. "All of it," I say, taking a long breath. Polina said some fucked up shit about my father—my biological father. I don't know whether to throw up or fuck something up.

"She was lying about Dante. She was just trying to confuse me," she says, leaning back, resting her head on my chest.

"So do you think she was lying about me?" I say quietly.

"Who the fuck knows."

"But it makes sense if what Byron said was true about my parents."

She looks up at me. "Byron said your parents had to give you up to cover a scandal. That doesn't sound like something a head of the Italian mob would do. And that doesn't explain your sister."

I nod at her. She's right. The bitch had to be lying.

"I think there were girls who had babies from Joseph's prostitution ring. And that agency used them to solidify ties with highly influential people desperate for children, or at least blackmail them."

According to Polina, my father's illegal prostitution ring fuelled an even darker secret—a black market adoption agency. Just the thought of it makes me uneasy. I should have burned his business to the ground the moment I inherited it.

"Do you think your mother was one of the girls in the prostitution ring?" Viola asks, breaking me out of my dark thoughts. "I could ask Quinn to look," she says after a pause when I don't say anything.

I'm saved from answering by the dip of headlights as a car turns into the clearing. It's the Mustang.

I stand up, offering my hand to her. "Come on. Let's burn this shithole to the ground a second time. I still have nightmares about this place."

"Nightmares?" she lifts a brow.

I roll my eyes at her with a smirk. "And fucking wet dreams, alright."

"I was never going to kill you, you know," she snorts, taking my hand.

"Good," I say, hauling her to her feet, groping her ass as I devour those sweet lips. "Because I was always going to fuck you."

SEVENTEEN

VIOLA

I DON'T KNOW how to tell Dante that I killed Polina, so I just send a picture of her tattoo using Quinn's secure drive and message Quinn to deliver it to D.

When we get back to Sacred Heart, he's waiting for me in a makeshift prison cell Quinn has seen fit to fashion out of the equipment storage room. It's the only place in the school with a huge cage door and a massive lock. Gym equipment is expensive, apparently. Although, everything that was in the store room is now dotted around what was an empty gym hall. All that's in there with him now is a mattress and bucket in the corner of the store area.

When I enter the gym, Dante looks at me with an unreadable expression on his face. The only way I know he's annoyed is because his arms are folded.

"V, can I talk to you in private?" his eyes flick to Jude leaning against the wall. I can only imagine Jude was the one who dragged Dante in there when he was unconscious. I give Jude a look.

"I'm not leaving you alone with him," he says.

I roll my eyes. "He's behind a locked cage door."

"Fine, I'll be out in the hall."

The floating feeling I got from killing the bitch from the agency is all but gone. But that's fine. It never lasts long. I know that. After Polina told me many secrets, I felt the urge to sleep for a long time. But I need to speak to Dante. The things she told me are too confusing without his input.

Blood drips down Polina's face from a cut on her forehead. She grins at me, unbothered by the pain of my knife cuts. She's been taught to with-stand more.

"Having fun, Viola dear?"

I blink at her, unmoved and uncharmed. "Who is Dante working for?"

She snorts a laugh. "Apart from himself. No one. Why are you asking such idiotic questions?" She closes her eyes, body swaying. She's dealing with the pain the way I was taught, taking it inside her, consuming it, and drifting away as if it's happening to someone else.

I exhale, trying a different approach. "Does the agency belong to my father?"

Her eyes open. There's a sneer on her lips. "No and yes," she says, talking in riddles again.

I take my knife and slice another sliver of her flesh away. Polina doesn't react, but she does look me in the eye, grinning. If she passes out, I won't get to ask any more questions, so I need to take this slow.

"I'll ask again. Does my father own the agency?" Dante once told me he did.

"You should be asking who it does belong to."

"You could just tell me."

"And you could go to hell." She spits blood in my face and then laughs with red-stained teeth. She must have bitten her mouth trying to deal with the pain.

My shoulders are tense, and my neck is stiff from hunching over my prey. I roll them back, cricking my neck as I walk around Polina, who is tied to a chair that survived the fire, looking for the next piece to remove. Lorcan is watching me. I don't know how I feel about that, so I ignore it or try to. Every so often, he'll wince or frown when I'm working. It's fucking off-putting.

"Who have you got working the Duke job?" I say.

She smiles—a twisted one as I dig the knife in. "No one you know." She grimaces. "Your replacement."

More blood. More pain. "Do you have a name?"

"All I can tell you is that she is very sad, a bit like you were when you joined us." The agency thrives on recruiting young men and women into its ranks. New blood is the only way they can keep up with the demand for work and keep the more significant share of the fee. If they have a recruit on Lorcan, I'm less worried.

"Let's go back to the adoptions," I say, playing my knife along the skin at the back of her neck.

Polina hasn't been entirely closed-mouthed. She's given me some tidbits about my father, depending on what she thinks I already know. And she admitted the agency was selling the babies from Joseph's prostitution ring, using them to blackmail their high-profile fathers and the couples they sold them to.

"Tell me, who maintains the list of all the sales?"

I didn't know about the adoptions, but it makes sense Adrien would use whatever he could to gain leverage with certain groups of people.

When I get to the front of her chair, Polina's eyes are fixed on Lorcan. "Why, are you looking to see if a certain boy toy is on it?"

Lorcan stiffens.

Polina laughs. "I can see why you didn't kill him. He's handsome, exactly like his real father."

I stab my blade into the softness of her side, making her hiss. She hasn't yet started screaming. She will. I haven't even started yet.

I crouch in front of her, so she has to look at me. "Who is Lorcan's father?"

She shakes her head slowly back and forth. "Now that would be telling." She says something suggestive in Italian, making the muscle in Lorcan's jaw tense.

Bitch.

I take my knife and start removing another piece. When I'm halfway done, and she's no longer smiling, I try again. "Who is Lorcan's father?"

She shakes her head. "I will tell you something about your precious Dante, though," she pants, gritting her teeth with a grin. "You should look for him on that list."

"I don't need to. I found his birth certificate in Adrien's office."

"Did you look closely? Birth certificates can be faked or altered."

I narrow my eyes at her. "What do you mean?"

She laughs, which turns to her coughing. "We're an agency that specializes in fake identities. Why do you think your father wanted our help? He needed to hide one child in particular."

I stare at her, slowly taking in what she's saying. "What child? From who?"

But Polina just smiles, and that fucks me off even more.

"You kidnapped Polina?" Dante asks as soon as Jude is gone.

"Correction—I killed her."

He looks at me blankly, so I start telling him everything she told me, from the black market adoptions to the fake birth certificates. The whole time Dante stands there, face unreadable, blue eyes boring into my soul through the cage door.

"You need to get it together," he says finally. "You know what happened last time."

"Have you heard anything that I've been saying?"

"Yes, I have, and none of it matters."

"You're always telling family is the most important thing in this fucked up world."

"Because it is, V," he says, cocking his head at me. "*You're* my family. No one else."

"What about money?"

"I'm wealthy. What do I care about money." He glances at the duffel bag at my feet. "Keep that, all of it. You've earned it."

"What do you mean, I've earned it."

"I told you I needed to do those jobs. When you got arrested,

I went out of my mind. I almost gunned down the police station trying to get you back. Lorcan was the one who told me you had a plan. Doing those jobs was the only thing keeping me from killing every fucker standing in my way. I took those jobs for you to give you the time you needed."

When I don't say anything, he sighs.

"Polina also said that my father didn't own the agency. You lied to me," I say.

He shakes his head. "I didn't say your father owned it. I said Iskar works for your father."

I frown at him. "Why is everyone speaking in fucking riddles?"

"I told you once—there are things you don't know about and I can't tell you."

"That was before."

He sighs. "Just for once, trust me."

I walk out of the gym with the duffel bag, waiting until I'm alone to exhale loudly.

I don't know that I can.

I take Dante's money, all of it, to Quinn. She's not in her office since it's late, so I guess she's in her room. I guess right. She's on the floor in some kind of yoga pose, eyes closed, when I enter.

"Saskia is good at yoga," I say, for want of anything to fill the silence.

She opens one eye. "I thought it was you. No one else can sneak around like a cat in here. Most people knock."

"Here, it's all there." I dump the bag of money on her floor.

Quinn frowns and gets to her feet to inspect the bag's contents. "How much is there?"

"Enough and some left over to pay you for everything you've done for me lately."

"I don't need paying," she says, brow furrowed. "I'm here because I care. People do that, you know."

I sit on the end of her bed while she stuffs the bag with the money into her wardrobe. I know enough about Quinn to know that money will be squirreled away somewhere safer tomorrow. I never have to worry about Quinn.

"I'll use what's left over to pay Rebecca's residential fees."

I nod at her. "Just let me know if you need more."

"Is it true? Is Polina gone?"

Word travels fast. "I wanted to know if Dante could be trusted."

"And?"

"I have no fucking clue. She started talking about some list of babies."

"Oh, that."

"You know what she's talking about?"

"My contact, who is getting you your untraceable IDs. They provided everything your father needed…national insurance numbers, birth certificates, even fake doctor's reports."

"So you know where this list is?"

She nods. "I can get it for you. But it's encrypted. Not even I can hack the original names."

"Who has access?" I know who does as soon as I ask it and that I've fucked up.

"In the agency? Only Polina. And her boss, I would imagine."

Iskar. Who works for my father.

I find Lorcan and Jude in the gym the next morning in tank tops and shorts, flashing abs and corded muscles on their arms as they work out. Both are dripping with sweat as they mop their faces, taking sips of water. I walk over, wearing an animal print dress with boots, and my hair is up. They have no idea why I decided to dress up, but they seem to approve.

"I'm going to see Dino," I say. I contemplated not telling them, but every time I hide what I'm doing, it gets me in trouble. So this is me, trying something new.

Lorcan frowns, and Jude raises a brow, but neither says no.

"We're coming with you," Lor says.

"Fine," I say. I knew they would be. I expected nothing less.

A phone rings. Lorcan grabs his device from the side bench and looks at the screen. "Shit, I have to take this." Then he walks off, answering with a gruff hello.

Jude looks at me. "How are you doing, babe?"

I give him a blank look. "Why are you asking me that? I'm fine." Now that I'm looking at him, I can see he looks better than he has in weeks.

He shrugs and then grins. "Are you checking me out, Hawkes?"

I shrug back.

He saunters over, still grinning, looping his sweaty towel over the back of my neck, hauling me closer to his lips. He tastes of sweat, sports drinks, and himself. There's no hint of alcohol on his breath at all.

I pull away, slightly breathless.

"Fuck, I've missed you," he breathes.

"I haven't gone anywhere," I say.

"No, but I had you all to myself in St Michael's. Now I have to share you with Lore and Psycho Charlie."

"You sleep in my bed every night," I say to him.

"I want more," he teases. "I'm going to claim that ass very soon."

I roll my eyes.

He chuckles, dropping the towel around my neck, but not before running a thumb over my lip. I dart my tongue out to lick it. He's salty from the workout.

"That was Grandfather," Lorcan says, walking back over to where Jude and I are standing.

"What did he want?" Jude asks.

"He wants to talk about the inheritance. I sent him a message that Byron is alive."

I tilt my head. "Are you going to see him?"

161

"Not yet. I need to know who my real father is first." That's different. A few days ago, Lorcan wasn't even interested. He must see my face because he adds, "Saskia wants to know too."

"I spoke to Quinn. She can get us the list. Then we need to talk to the head of the agency, Iskar."

"I can speak to him," says Dante from his holding pen. We all look up at him, and then the boys look at me. They're waiting to see if I've decided what to do with him. I still don't know the answer, but there's only one way to find out.

"I'll have Quinn set up a meeting," I say. "If anyone is speaking to him, it's me."

EIGHTEEN

VIOLA

"ARE YOU OKAY?" Lorcan asks me for the hundredth time. We're in the car driving to the east coast. The address where Dino is supposed to be is forty-miles east of London, a stud farm. Since one of Dino's mother's passions is breeding and racing horses, it makes sense. The farm is not in the Vice's or my father's name, for that matter. It's a Donovan-owned enterprise. Lola was a Donovan before she married Liam Vice, Dino's father.

"I'm fine," I say to him. It's just the two of us in his Mclaren. Jude is following in his Aston Martin. The deal is that I ride there with Lorcan and back with Jude. The boys are still squabbling over me, no matter how much of myself I give them.

"Are you sure you're okay? You're scratching the hell out of the leather with your nails," he chides, glancing at me between keeping his eyes on the road.

I glance down. My nails are shorter now, but my fingers clutching the leather still leave a mark. I relax my hand and place it on my lap, fighting the urge to fiddle with the radio.

"Are you worried about Dante?"

"No."

"Is it that we're going to see Dino? Because it's okay to be nervous."

"I'm not nervous."

"He will want to see you. This is Sinner we're talking about. He's worshipped you since the moment he met you."

"That's not—" Fuck. I shake my head. "Just turn around." *This is a mistake.*

"We're not turning around. We're going to get him back. I'm more worried that we will have to fight our way out of this. Sinner wouldn't have stayed away this long unless they made him."

For once, the darkness is quiet and withdrawn. I don't feel like I'm losing. I feel like I've lost and am trying to salvage something out of the mess that's left. This wasn't how it was supposed to go. Dino promised me he would never leave me, and yet he fucking did.

Because I turned on him.

I didn't mean to hurt him, but I couldn't control it. And what if it happens again? The blood at the edge of my vision is back, staining the car's insides a dark red. With every mile closer to the coast, I feel like screaming.

But I can't lose it again.

"Viola, the fucking leather."

"Fuck the leather," I snap at him.

Lorcan sighs. "Here, take my hand." He offers his palm, unturned, and I take it. I grip hard, shoving all my pain and grief into that hand. Lorcan says nothing, but when I look at him, he's occasionally wincing as he cruises us down the freeway. When we pull off, he takes his hand back to handle the car better around the corners.

"Are you ready?" he says, pulling off the main road and into a long driveway lined with horses in fields.

"Yes," I say, sucking in a breath. "Yes, I fucking am."

The Donovan farm is vast, with several brick buildings, yards, stable blocks, and outhouses. The main house is newly built with cream-painted walls and huge arching windows. The central courtyard is packed with cars that have spilled out into one of the fields. The only thing that stands out as 'Dino' is the line of racing bikes near the house. I recognize one of his Ducatis in the middle.

Lorcan takes my hand as we walk up to the front door.

"We're just going to knock?" Jude asks, catching up to us. "Looks like they're having some sort of party."

Lorcan gives him a look. "You got a better idea?"

"Fuck, no," says Jude. He leans over and presses the doorbell. Inside, you can hear a load of dogs going crazy.

After a few minutes, Jude knocks, hammering on the door as loud as he can.

The door swings open.

A woman in a floral dress with light brown hair and dark brown eyes opens the door. "More guests. Please come in. Everyone is in the back."

We pass through the house—a mix of old brickwork, beams and cream-painted plaster, and new leather and metal furniture dotted around marble units.

The garden is filled with people, all dressed up for a summer party, and there's staff moving through the groups serving drinks and canapes. There's even a violinist playing in the middle of it all.

Dino is there too.

In a dark blue jacket and a light blue shirt and chinos, his red hair brushed back, his blue eyes the same color as his shirt. His jaw clenches as soon as he sees us, making his dimple pop out. Then a dark look settles on his face, and the dimple fades away.

Flashbacks of him covered in blood cloud my vision.

I focus on his now bluer-than-blue shirt.

Dino excuses himself from the group he was talking to and comes over.

"Dino, you're fucking alive, *mate*," Lorcan says. He squeezes my hand, anchoring me to reality in another way.

"Fancy us having to drive all the way out here to see if you were," Jude says, looking around, taking a mini slider from a passing tray and eating it.

"Duke, Marques, what do I owe the pleasure?" he asks, all smiles until his blue orbs, filled with black hate, fix on me, searing my damned soul to shreds. I can do nothing but stand there, gripping Lorcan's hand.

And then….

He blinks, and just as quickly as it was there, the darkness in him is gone. The ends of his mouth curl up into an empty smile. Though, the smile falters slightly when Lorcan gives him a man hug.

"Come inside," Dino says, his voice smooth, smile plastered on his face. "Let me get you a proper drink." He walks through to the next room, and we follow him. I can't help but notice that he walks with a limp, though he makes every effort to hide it.

"Bourbon, if you have one," Jude drawls.

"Ignore him. He's driving. We'll all have a soda." Lorcan says, taking a seat at the breakfast bar. I sit next to Lor because he has my hand in an iron grip.

Dino pours our drinks, serves them, and then pours himself a large whiskey. There's a slight tremor in his fingers as he grips the glass, leaning against the kitchen counter.

"So," he says, taking us all in. "You're all here? Why?" His gaze settles on me, and it's not warm. It's cold and almost calculating.

That makes everything turn fucking red across my vision. I blink several times, forcing it away.

"Why are we here? Have you heard yourself?" Jude exclaims. "I went to fucking juvie for you."

"We're just here to see how you are. Lola wouldn't let us see you after…." Lorcan tails off.

"I'm fine. Still recovering, but I'm fine," Dino says, running his hand through his hair. The look doesn't suit him. The whole charade, his hair, his clothes—looks like Kristian. "I'll get over it," he says acidly. "So will you," he says to Jude, knocking back his drink.

Lorcan frowns. "Who are all these people? Why are they here?"

"Mostly family, friends of Kristian," Dino snorts, not looking at Lor but directly at me.

Jude's eyes narrow. "Are you taking the family business on now?"

"Someone has to," Dino sneers. "Now I need to go. It was good to see you all." He turns his attention to me. "Viola, try not to kill anyone."

And then he leaves, grabbing the bottle of whisky on his way out.

I narrow my eyes at him as he goes.

Fuck all this pretending, playing nice.

"Let's go. This is fucking pointless," I mutter, getting off the stool, but Lorcan won't let go of my hand.

"Well, he's evolved into a right cunt," Jude proclaims.

"We came here to get him, and we're not leaving until he's in the car," Lorcan says. He looks at me. "You need to speak to him alone."

I raise both brows at him. "He hates me."

Lorcan sighs. "Look, hate is better than no emotion at all. You can work with hate. I hated you when I first met you."

I glare at him. "That doesn't help."

"If we're sharing, I hated you too," Jude says, holding up his hand.

"Then, you're both assholes," I throw back.

Lorcan cocks his head, still gripping my hand tight. "Maybe this is Dino's time to hate you. Don't let this one little mistake fuck over the best thing that ever happened to you because that guy out there was there for you, even when you told him he meant nothing. Prove to him that you fucking care."

I stare at Lorcan, trying to take it all in. "Fine," I finally say. "Just let me go."

He does, and I stalk out in a huff.

Dino is on his own, drinking at the far side of the garden when I enter it. He doesn't see me at first and scowls when he does. He watches me walk over, and the hatred is so intense that I can almost feel the heat from the burning pits of hell in his eyes.

"You hate me, I get that," I say as I stand before him. I'm no fucking good at saying I'm sorry, so that's the best it's going to get.

His jaw tightens, his hand white knuckles around his glass for the longest time, and then he shakes his head. The rage I could see and understand is gone, and in its place is just an emptiness. He smiles, not a nice one.

"Why are you fucking here, Viola?"

"We came to bring you back home."

He smirks. "I am home." He takes a sip of his drink and looks over my head as though I'm not there.

I nod at him, letting out a breath. Oh, how the tables have turned. There was a time when he begged me to come home, and I think I said the same thing. I walk over to where he is and stand next to him, seeing what he sees.

There are a lot of people here. Most of them look like bad news, flashing guns under their jackets and mob affiliation tattoos on parts of exposed skin. The Vices are reputed to be the nastiest of London's crime families. This party is just here for decoration. Something else is going on.

"Something is going down tonight, isn't it?"

"How very astute. Is that the trained assassin in you, or are you just a nosy bitch?"

I shoot him a look. "I may deserve everything you say to me after what I did to you, but I am sorry for what I did."

He doesn't say anything after that. He just stands there drinking, dimple going wild on his cheek. When it looks like one of his family members is coming over, one of his uncles, he shoots me a look. "You should go."

I don't listen to him, because when have I ever listened to any of the boys? I stand my ground.

"Kards, my boy. How is my favorite nephew?" the guy walking toward us says. He's got the same piercing blue eyes as Dino, but he's wider, if not just as tall as his nephew. He grabs Dino and kisses him on both cheeks, then jovially, he looks at me.

I tense. I have no idea what Dino or Lola told them about me.

Did he tell them I nearly sliced his heart out?

"And who is this?" he asks Dino.

"Oh, just some whore, forget about her," Dino says. "Come on, let's go inside where we can talk."

The insult washes over me, and I let it. I know why Dino said it, but I also know it's the wrong thing to say because the older man suddenly grins. "Some tasty fucking whore." He turns back and throws an arm around my waist, pulling me along with them. "Come with us, beautiful. Come sit on my lap and keep me company while we talk business."

Dino's face is a picture, but I can't worry about that now. I know this type of man. He thinks anything that's not tied down is his. Dino should have introduced me as someone important to him.

His mistake.

But it's not mine.

I force everything inside me not to react and shoot Dino a look.

Fix this, or I will.

If I'm expecting Dino to hesitate or be his old morally conflicted self, I'm dead wrong. Dino looks down and smirks. When he looks up, he turns to his uncle, in the middle of the garden, surrounded by all his friends and family.

"I told you to fucking forget about her," he says, taking out his gun, shooting his uncle, calmly and cleanly, in the head. No warning. Nothing. The pistol has a silencer, so the only sound is a quick zip, and the big guy drops to the floor like old trash.

No one moves.

Dino looks at everyone staring. "What the fuck are you looking at? Go back to what you were doing, drinking my fucking expensive champagne and getting wasted."

The effect is immediate; everyone, and I mean everyone, resumes what they were talking about, going back to their drinks as if nothing happened. Two men hurry over and start dragging Dino's uncle's body away.

And then the music starts up and the party carries on.

I should be scared, but I'm not.

I'm intrigued.

Lorcan and Jude are entering the garden, brows furrowed. They're probably wondering what the fuck just happened. I don't have much time. I stalk over to Dino, link his arm in mine, and lean in enough to breathe in the citrus and cinnamon of his cologne. "Take me upstairs, now."

Dino's eyes tighten at the corners, but he nods.

I give the other boys a 'stay here' look as Dino escorts me out of the party.

Upstairs is just as grand as the ground floor. Dino's room is at the far end, a huge master with a connected bathroom and walk-in wardrobe. The furniture and decor are straight out of Country, Home & Living magazine—dark wood, rustic beams, and a four-poster bed with vintage covers and rugs. There's even a goddamn fireplace.

"Lola's taste," he says as I look around. He walks over to the bed, takes off his jacket, and places his gun on the side table and something from his pocket—a pair of red dice.

He comes to me, eyes roving over every part of me as he takes the collar of my dress and rips at it. Buttons go every fucking where. Then, his lips find the curve of my neck. He unhooks my bra and carries on kissing me, moving his lips over my shoulders, and then traveling down to bite my breasts. I'm shaking as his hands snake under what's left of my dress to pinch and knead without mercy.

Mostly, he looks the same. He even sounds the same. But that's not my Dino. I've seen all types of monsters, but I never expected to see one behind Dino's eyes.

"I'm going to tie you to this bed and fuck you until you bleed," he promises.

I see the monster now.

NINETEEN

DINO

SEEING Viola turn up at my fucking house with nothing but that look has me reeling.

Lola's not here today, thank fucking God. I don't know what Todd was thinking, letting them in the main gate. A bright, yellow Mclaren and a silver Aston Martin. I watched them through the kitchen window as they all got out, taking in my mother's yard.

They really shouldn't fucking be here.

Even if we're supposed to be married in a month, I'm not ready to see her.

Because I fucking hate her….

And madly in love with her at the same time.

But I can't see her. Not yet. I lose myself when I'm around her. And I'm not that person anymore. I never wanted to see her again, yet somehow, I see her every fucking night in my dreams. Over and over, she's killing me. It took me a long time after the hospital just to get through one night without me waking the entire damn house with my fucking screams.

Kristian dying, Viola getting arrested. Me, almost fucking

dying. I gave her everything, and then I lost it all in a split second.

But all of that is in the past.

Was in the past.

Until now.

They knock on the door a second time, making the dogs go fucking nuts.

"Cuz?" Sorrow asks, brushing her dark hair out of her face, and taking off her riding boots. She's just come in from a ride. We have guests, and she's just fucking strolled in smelling like the fucking yard. "Aren't you going to get that?"

I clench my jaw and nod at her. "Bridget will get it. You need to fucking go and showered and get changed. One of these pricks is going to fuck you tonight, so look fucking nice for once, will you."

She glares at me, eyes like slits. "I thought you were different, but you're just the same as Kristian."

That hits me in the gut like Viola's fucking knife.

"Just do as I fucking say," I grit out, locking the dogs in the back kitchen. I hobble through the open plan area to the garden, grabbing a drink off a passing tray before they can ring the doorbell again.

I don't want to see them. I can't. Not yet.

"Kardinal, there you are," one of my uncles calls me over. Gregor, Pieter, and fucking Angelo are all waiting for me to say that I'll do it. As part of my initiation, I have to kill one of my family in cold blood. It could be anyone.

For no fucking reason.

I killed my brother and have done worse since I got back, but none of it is enough. These pricks want more. They won't ever follow me or trust me if I'm not someone to fear, and with the engagement hanging over my head—they need to fucking know I'm not going to let Adrien control me.

I know the moment she steps foot in the garden. I can practically feel her presence like a black hole sucking my life away into it. Wherever she is, it's like I'm a fucking asteroid being pulled into her orbit. Any minute, we're going to collide, and I will explode.

They start walking toward me, so I excuse myself from the group and cut them off before they can fully enter the party.

"Dino, you're fucking alive, *mate*," Lorcan says as our eyes meet.

"Fancy us having to drive all the way out here to see if you were," Jude adds, like the prick he is.

"Duke, Marques, what do I owe the pleasure?" I say, looking between the guys, leaving *her* till last.

When our eyes finally connect, my heart fucking jumps like I've been electrocuted. I want to grab her and kiss her, and at the same time, I want to take the gun strapped under my jacket and blow her fucking brains out.

I close my eyes and count to three. When I open them, she's still looking at me. My heart is thudding like crazy. I have no idea what to fucking do. Lorcan saves me from having to do anything because he embraces me like I'm his long-lost brother.

I was once.

Before I lost my real brother.

"Come inside," I say, forcing a smile onto my face. "Let me get you a proper drink," I say, taking them through to the kitchen part of the open plan area. Sorrow is nowhere to be seen, so I offer my old friends a seat, and then it's awkward as fuck.

"Bourbon, if you have one," Jude says.

"Ignore him. He's driving. We'll all have a soda," Lorcan adds. I take my time making their drinks and then pour myself a large whisky. The nerves of my right hand were damaged when she stabbed me. I wasn't trying to stop her; my hand just got in the way. But the result is that I can't fucking use my hand much anymore. Riding a bike is a bitch. It's a good job that I'm left-handed, or I wouldn't be able to hold a gun either.

"So," I say, turning around, bracing myself for the internal destruction that comes with her eyes on me. "You're all here? Why?"

Why the fuck are you here? Now? I waited for weeks in that hospital bed for one of these fuckers to come and visit me. And no one came. I only found out later she got arrested. But I fell into the darkest fucking pit of despair during that time.

Only in my dreams did she come, Viola and my goddam brother, fucking haunting me.

I never wanted to end it more than those weeks after.

I even tried.

But they stopped me—my family. They reminded me that this life is all I have.

I am my family.

"Why are we here? Have you heard yourself?" Jude seethes. "I went to fucking juvie for you." I just stare at him. What a cunt. I never fucking asked him to.

"We're just here to see how you are. Lola wouldn't let us see you after...." Lorcan tries, but I don't hear it. I only have eyes for the bitch that tried to kill me *after* I told her I loved her. I never loved anyone as much as I loved her. I take a swig of my drink and let her see how much I fucking hate her. She still looks the same, maybe a bit skinnier. Her brown eyes are shuttered, closed off. I tried to get her to open up, thinking she had emotions.

Now I know....

She's dead inside, just like me. *Maybe we deserve each other?*

"I'm fine. Still recovering, but I'm fine," I say, staring at Viola as she stares back like no one else exists. "I'll get over it," I say in a shitty tone to Jude. "So will you,"

How am supposed to fucking marry her?

I can't even be in the same room as her.

"Who are all these people? Why are they here?" Lorcan asks.

"Mostly family, friends of Kristian," I say absently, still watching her intently. The darkness inside me is crawling under my skin. Every time I look at her, I want to hurt her.

Jude's eyes narrow. "Are you taking the family business on now?"

"Someone has to," I sneer. "Now I need to go. It was good to see you all." I give one last look at the bitch who ruined my fucking life. "Viola, try not to kill anyone."

I can't bring myself to speak to anyone else, so I stand off to the side, drinking like a damn fish, getting drunk because it's better than being fucking sober right now. Somehow, she finds me. At first, I'm sure if she's real or not. Most of the time, she's not. Until she speaks….

"You hate me, I get that," she says. Ghost Viola usually just tries to kill me, which you get used to after a while.

I grip my glass and think of the shitty fucking things I've wanted to say to her after she chose Jude over me. I can get over the stabbing eighteen times; that was a walk in the park.

No.

It was her leaving me again.

"Why are you fucking here, Viola?" I shake my head. I can't even be fucked to tell her.

"We came to bring you back home."

A bit late, isn't it? You left me to the sharks.

I give her a dark smile. "I am home," I say, drinking, looking anywhere but at her because a part of me wants to tear her clothes off, hold her face down in the long grass, and fuck her until she runs out of fucking air.

"Something is going down tonight, isn't it?" Her words rip me out of my little dark fantasy.

This is what she does to me.

I've become my fucking brother.

She's standing to my side, watching everyone like I am. I can guarantee she's noting the fuckers here, the ones to watch out for, mentally taking down their weaknesses. She'd make an excellent wife in this life. As long as she didn't accidentally (or purposely) fucking kill me.

"How very astute. Is that the trained assassin in you, or are you just a nosy bitch?" I say acidly, not looking at her.

I feel her eyes on me, burning me to the ground with her contempt. "I may deserve everything you say to me after what I did to you, but I am sorry for what I did," she says, sounding not sorry at all.

She doesn't have a fucking clue.

At that moment, Marco spots me. Out of all of my uncles, he's the fucking worst. I caught him yesterday trying to rape Sorrow in her room. I very nearly killed him. I should have done. His eyes are on Viola immediately. If he, in any way, thinks she's mine, he'll try and take her from me.

She's not yours anymore.

"You should go," I say to Viola.

Marco comes up to me and kisses me on both cheeks. He's playing for the audience. I know the bastard hates me. He was a firm fan of my brother and his methods. I know Marco thinks I'm a pussy and will try something soon. I can tell by the way he looks at me and talks to me.

It's disrespectful.

His greedy eyes are still latched on to Viola. "And who is this?"

"Oh, just some whore, forget about her," I say dismissively. "Come on, let's go inside where we can talk." I need to get the bastard away from her. He doesn't move, though. He stops, devouring her with his fucking pissholes for eyes. "Some tasty fucking whore," he says as he puts his arm around her.

Viola's eyes connect with mine. Her goddamn accusing look is all it takes.

I see fucking red.

Red like the dice in my pocket. I roll them in my fists as I take them out, feeling the hard edges, and then look down.

Six and a three.

I win.

All the hurt, anger, and despair shuts off. "I told you to fucking forget about her," I say, feeling void of emotion as I calmly place my empty glass on a passing tray and reach inside my jacket to take out my gun. I aim at Marco's head and pull the trigger. Funny that only when I'm killing does the shaking and pain subside.

There's silence while I put my gun away. Everyone is fucking looking at me. Even Viola. "What the fuck are you looking at? Go back to what you were doing, drinking my fucking expensive champagne and getting wasted," I snap.

They do, quickly.

I've begun to earn a reputation for being a cunt, and a little crazy after my brother died. It's not a rumor I try to discourage. I can't be weak, not with my family.

And certainly not with fucking Viola in my bed.

Viola is the only one looking at me now. Her big brown eyes have a wicked glint to them that I used to be afraid of.

Now they get me fucking hard.

She comes over and takes my arm. "Take me upstairs, now."

It's like she read my mind.

When I get her to my room, she's hesitant. I've no idea why. I remove my jacket and gun to place them on the side table with the dice.

"Lola's taste," I say as she glances around, taking in the over-the-top decor.

Her eyes are glittering with a mix of lust and devious hate. She doesn't try to stop me as I take the collar of her button-down dress and yank it hard. The buttons snap off in unison. I kiss her exposed neck, unhooking her bra as I run my lips over her shoulders, and then bite her breasts, massaging under her ruined dress until she's quivering in my arms.

"I'm going to tie you to this bed and fuck you until you

bleed," I say softly in the shell of her ear, my grip vice-like as I draw her roughly to the bed, barely keeping the anger from sweeping in.

My silk tie is still in my pocket. I pull it out and use it to tightly bind her arms and hands around one of the posts at the foot.

"You weren't joking about the tying up part," she says as I pull the silk tighter. There's a flash of anger in her eyes, but she can get fucked. I don't care. I want her hands taken care of, unable to claw or stab.

When I'm done, I move around, holding her waist to stand behind her, tracing my fingers under the remaining skirt of her dress to find her soaking wet.

"Dino," she hisses as I stroke and thrust my fingers into her, making her body shudder against me. Her knife is strapped to her thigh. I unsheathe it and slice off the rest of her dress, leaving her in just a strip of lace. That comes off, too, with a rip of the blade before I chuck it onto the side table on top of the red dice. They clatter off the side and fall between the bed and the table.

Her head whips up when they fall, and then she looks at me with sinful eyes, begging me to do fucked up things to her. *Fuck I want to.* She fucking deserves it…to be used by me. But…I need to see where they landed—two and a five.

I fucking win again.

I grab a fistful of her hair, turning her to look away. I don't want to look in her eyes anymore.

I don't want to fucking look at her.

"I've wanted to do this to you since I woke up in the hospital, and you weren't there," I say, running my other hand between her legs. She's soaking wet between them.

"Do it," she breathes. "Fuck me, Dino."

"Gladly," I say, undoing my belt and trousers. "I'm going to fucking use you, just like you used me." Pulling her head back, I force her legs apart and push my cock into her tight hole, making her gasp. With every thrust, she clenches around me.

Her eyes flutter as I ram into her, pull out, and then fuck her again. She's clinging to the post as I take what's mine.

No one else touches her.

Not my uncles, not my family. Not ever again.

She's fucking mine.

TWENTY

VIOLA

HE FUCKS me rough and hard like he has everything to live for and die for. He tells me everything he wants to do to me, how much he hates me, and what he's going to put me through. He uses me because…it's what he needs.

I saw it in his eyes. He needs control back. He craves it. He needs to let go. He needs to hurt me.

And I can give that to him.

It's easier now that I can't move or leave. But I don't care. *I need this too.*

"Do you know what I want to do to you most?" he asks, dark and desperate, in my ear, as the fire of pleasure, from dragging his cock into me has me panting and gasping against the wooden post. When his hand slides around my throat, taking my breath away, I know what he will say.

"I dream about killing you," he grits out, squeezing his fingers until I see stars. I feel the release burn, chasing through my pussy as it clenches around his cock.

But I need more.

"Hurt me. Do it," I seethe at him, grinding back, searching for the sweet pulse building with every stroke.

"Fucking gladly," he hisses.

He pulls all the way out and then slams into me. Again and again. I'm shoved so far forward that my hips are rammed against the wooden post, now wet with my juices as it slides over my clit. I can't help but shake and twist against the restraints, against his hand wrapped around my throat like a loving vice.

I'm using him just as much as he's using me, even if he doesn't like it. Even if he wanted to hurt me. *But Dino, my sweet, I can't be broken.* His brother tried and failed. He tried and failed....*it just makes me want him more.*

He finishes with a vicious thrust, emptying deep inside me. And I come hard, too, shaking against him as my orgasm shatters through to my core.

After he's breathing hard, leaning on me, his total weight pinning me to the bedpost, I say, "Get that out of your system, did you?"

He stiffens and then moves off me, leaving me tied to retrieve my knife and what's left of my dress. Cool air from the open window plucks at my sensitive nipples as he cuts the silk holding me to the post.

"Get the fuck out," he says coldly, handing me my things.

I can feel his cum dripping down my leg, but I pay it no attention and tug my dress on, fastening what's left of the buttons. There's a huge rip up the side where he cut it away, but there's enough material to tie it in a knot around my waist. When that is done, I take my knife and shove it inside my boot.

"I dream about killing you too," I say softly. "Your blood is on my hands every fucking night."

And then I leave. Not once, looking back.

· · ·

"Viola, you're going to want to see this," Quinn says, walking into the cafeteria where I'm drinking my coffee alone. It's been a few days since I saw Dino, and ever since, I've wanted to be alone. I know I'm moping, but I can't help it.

He's alive. That's what matters, Lorcan said to me on the way home. And he's right. But there's a missing piece inside of me that I can't quite let go of.

Jude was less impressed. He gave me a dark look that said, *You're missing that?* It was after he discovered that Dino shot his uncle in the head for touching me.

That turned me on, but apparently, that means he's falling apart, just like when he tried to kill himself. My father wants me to marry Dino. Dino hates me. I want to kill my father. Dante wants...who the fuck knows. There must be an easy solution, but everything is a mess in my head.

For once, I don't know what to do.

"Earth to Viola, are you with me?" Quinn says, taking a seat at the table I've taken to sitting at every morning. It's the one the teachers used to sit at during lunch as it has the best view of the lake.

"Did you get the list?" I ask, seeing her laptop in her arms. She nods and turns it on the table to face me. On the screen is a spreadsheet of names and addresses.

"These are all the families that have adopted children illegally through the agency. And these,"—she clicks on another window—"are the girls, first names only, who bore the children for the agency after being brainwashed into Joseph's prostitution ring. We think these in bold are those who just happened to get pregnant by someone Joseph wanted to blackmail."

She scrolls a very long list of names. Some are bolded. Each name has a sum of money next to it and several codes.

"What do the codes mean?"

"Each code contains a date of birth and three letters. Possibly, the letters are the gender and the father's initials, but I'm still cross-checking that assumption."

"So separately, we have all the data we need. Is there any way to link the two?"

She shakes her head. "Iskar wasn't helpful. He doesn't want to talk to you after Polina. I managed to get what we have with Saskia's help."

I raise a brow. "Saskia is helping you?"

"She's good at yoga like you said," Quinn says. "We got talking during Shavasana."

I just look at her.

"Corpse Pose," Quinn offers. I have no idea what she's talking about. "Anyway, it seems she knows her way around a computer and where most of her adoptive father's company files are kept. Or actually, who to threaten to get those files," she carries on.

I nod. That makes sense.

"It's in Saskia's interest to find out the truth," I say."

Quinn shrugs. "She thinks she and Lorcan could be part of this black market adoption ring."

"For that to happen, they would have to have been adopted together, wouldn't they?" I ask her.

She nods at me. "So, I thought that and highlighted the names of girls with more than one child adopted. This one had two—a boy and a girl over eighteen years ago. The dates and initials of the father are the same. Could they be twins?"

I take a sip of my coffee, noting the mother's name. And then the letters of the supposed father's name...*ES*. I don't recognize it, but *Tatiana*...where have I heard that name before?

Suddenly, it comes to me. "Jude's aunt, Byron's mother, is called Tatiana."

"There's also a girl who got pregnant by this mysterious ES seven years earlier." She highlights a second entry on the list.

This name I don't recognize—*Ophelia*. I say as much to Quinn.

She flattens her lips in response. "Do you think Polina was

telling the truth? Lorcan's and Saskia's biological father is someone important? This ES person?"

I shake my head. "We still don't know enough. We need to find out who ES is." It might not mean anything, even if he is Lor's birth father. I have to tread carefully.

"And Dante?"

I shake my head. "I don't know how he fits into all of this."

"Didn't you say that you found his birth certificate? I could check if it's real or doctored in any way. If there's a name on it, it might match the list?"

"Dante has it in his room somewhere. He doesn't want me digging into any of this." I also don't want to look for the files since they'll be covered in Dino's blood.

The last time I had them in my hands was after the church....

"That's what people say when they're hiding something," Quinn says, interrupting my dark thoughts.

"Which is why I don't trust him," I sigh, rubbing my temple, tired all of a sudden. The itching under my skin has been back since we visited Dino. It's been keeping me awake at night.

"I don't disagree with you locking him up, but wouldn't it be easier just to kill him?"

I shoot her a look. "It would, wouldn't it?" But my current plan is to deal with my father while Dante is indisposed and then leave without a trace. Once Rebecca and I are far away from here, I'll let him out. I'm not sure how possible that is, but it's what I've got.

"Just be careful, V," Quinn sighs, getting to her feet.

"Does Saskia know about her aunt's name being on the list?" I ask her before she leaves.

She shakes her head. "No, I didn't speak to her about that yet."

"Let's keep it that way for now. We don't know for sure that it is Tatiana Duke." It could be another girl who just happened to have the same first name.

After Quinn returns to her office, I stay and drink the rest of my coffee, letting the silence and the lake view soothe my thoughts, trying to make sense of what Quinn just told me and Polina's words. It all feels like an agency red herring to distract me from the real mission—killing my father. *More rich prick distractions. As if I don't have enough of them.*

But....

Something doesn't sit right. If Tatiana is Lorcan's birth mother, it'll mean he's the rightful Duke heir. So why would Joseph hide that fact? Unless he didn't, Lorcan's family already know who his mother is. *And also know that ES is his father.*

I take out the new phone Lorcan got me and call him. There's only one way to find the truth—go straight to the source.

"Where are you?" I say to Lorcan as soon as he answers.

"We're just leaving St Michael's. We've got Byron. They released him today. Now, we're on our way to see grandfather."

"Do the initials ES mean anything to you? Someone important to your family, someone Joseph might want to blackmail?" I ask him.

He pauses. "My ex-girlfriend, Kat, has an uncle called Ed Savino. Joseph did business with him often."

"The Camorra Don?" It fits, now I know who Polina was working for, but I need more evidence.

"That's him. Why?"

"I'll tell you later." Lorcan doesn't need to know about my suspicions just yet. If I'm wrong, I'll have given him concerns over nothing. At least now I have a starting point. "Is Jude with you?"

"Right here, baby," he drawls, obviously listening in.

"Tell me," I say once he picks up the handset. "When you spent time with Dante. Where did he take you? What did you talk about?"

Jude lets out a breath. "Addiction mainly. And how much he cares about you and Rebecca."

I let Jude waffle on for a bit, listening to how he bonded with Psycho Charlie. He sounds pleased with himself. I'm almost tempted to tell him 'good boy' down the line to see what reaction I get. "I need you to show Byron a picture of Adrien."

"Why?"

"Show him. Ask him if that's the man his uncle was talking to."

There's some talking in the background as Jude switches to speakerphone and does what I ask. Down the line, I hear Byron say, "Yes, that's him."

"Did you get that?" Lorcan cuts in. "Now, are you going to tell me what's going on?"

But I don't bother to reply. I'm already hanging up and walking toward Dante's cell in the gym. I need to get the rest of my answers from him, and then I can explain everything to both Lorcan and Jude later. I have to, or they won't be happy. *How on earth did I get to this—needing to explain my actions to the men in my life?*

My gut is churning when I get to the gym, and rightly so because the store room that Dante was locked in is wide open and empty when I get there. The fucker has gone again.

He left me.

I call Quinn to let her know so she can increase security. Then I sit there staring at the empty cell, thinking about what Polina said about Dante being on the list, and the other baby boy, born seven years before both Lorcan and Saskia, making their half-brother twenty-five years old….

Conveniently, the exact age as Dante.

TWENTY-ONE

VIOLA

I WAS wrong about the hit.

A new recruit can be just effective…if you give them a bomb.

Lorcan calls me from Windsor General Hospital just before midnight, finally answering my messages. There was an explosion on the news just outside of Ascot Hills.

My first thought was that Dante had gone after Lorcan for my father. But Dante doesn't do bombs. He sees them as messy, and he much prefers the cleanliness of a gun with a silencer attached. It was also Gordon Duke's vehicle rigged with an exploding device that went off just before the boys got to the family home.

If Adrien doesn't have a hit out on Lorcan, and it's his grandfather, Gordon Duke, that he wants dead, this whole charade is a play for the Duke empire.

With my father at the helm of it all, pulling at the fucking strings.

I say this to Lorcan, who takes it in his stride. "My grandfather's alive; that's what matters," he says. Apparently, Gordon heard the trigger just before the key turned and managed to jump out. "I've got to talk to the police, and then we'll be coming back to the school. Just tell me *you* are okay? Quinn said Dante fucking escaped?" he adds, the edge of fear in his voice crystal clear on the phone.

I give him my usual answer—*yes*, and then wait for him to keep probing me for more information to make himself feel better, but he doesn't. He just sighs with relief. "Look, I have to go. There's fucking police everywhere...I'll be home soon." There's a pause. "Where are you? You sound like you're in a car?"

I am in a car. I'm driving Jude's Aston to visit Rebecca. Quinn gave me the address the day after I got back, but there was no time to see her until now. I give him some bullshit about popping out for a coffee and then hang up.

When I get to the assisted living residence Quinn moved her to, I park up and walk straight to the reception of the refurbished stately home, through the tranquil gardens full of squat trees shaped into animals of all things.

My phone lights up with a message from Lorcan just as I walk through the doors to the place.

> *This isn't a time for secrets. Where the fuck*
> *are you?*

Oh, but it is. I haven't told the boys where my mother is. I'm not telling anyone. The last thing I need is for Adrien to find her again and use her to control me. She's the only one who can tell me the truth. I'm just hoping my mother is having one of her good days so I can get to the bottom of all the lies.

Lies I keep on adding to.

I click my phone off and then sign my name on the register using the fake one I sometimes use just for this purpose.

"Oh, you must be her daughter?" asks the pretty brunette nurse, reading the name I've given her from the registration form. It's the same surname as Rebecca's name while she's here. A temporary measure until I take her away for good. I nod at her, forcing out a plastic smile, and the nurse beams. "You've come on a good day. She's going to be over the moon to see you."

She leads me into the main room where most residents are watching TV and points to Rebecca in her chair next to the window.

"I can go over there myself," I say to the nurse.

The brunette nods. "Okay, call me if you need anything."

I won't but tell her I will, and then I make my way across the room to where Rebecca's chair is parked. My mother is reading, which is a good sign.

"Rebecca," I say as soon as I'm within hearing distance.

She looks up, a frown creasing her brow as soon as she sees me, but it immediately turns into a wide smile. "Viola, oh, my baby girl. Come here." She drops the book on her lap and opens her arms.

I hesitate for a second but then make myself physically available to the woman who birthed me, bending slightly to allow her to put her arms around my shoulders. She smells of linen and lavender and feels fragile, even with the weight of her body bearing me down in a hug, which is not a lot. I'm stiff in her arms, but she doesn't seem to notice. Rebecca never seems to mind anything, and that's always been her downfall.

I count to ten in my head. *Ten seconds is long enough to be affectionate with family, surely?* While counting, I check that what I came for is still around her neck. It is—golden and warm against her skin, the pendant I found in my father's office long ago and have been wearing ever since. It's also the necklace that Quinn installed a listening device in for me when Dante was stalking us the first time, and I needed something to make him bite.

I asked Quinn to leave it with Rebecca for safekeeping while I was at St Michael's.

And now I need it back.

I wait until the embrace starts to feel clunky to pull back. Rebecca's grin broadens as soon as she gets a good look at me, brushing the hair out of my eyes. "I've missed you so so much," she says, voice cracking, her eyes moist.

I look at her in the same way, minus the tears. "Do you have everything you need?"

Rebecca nods, smiling and crying simultaneously like she can't quite decide what to do. "Yes, it's great. There's an amazing library which I'm sure you know about," she says, touching her thumb to my chin as she used to when I was a kid.

That was my one stipulation to Quinn. My mother likes to read, and it's all she has, so she needs lots of books.

"I'm glad," I say, and it's not a lie. I want my mother to be happy and content. She was the only one who tried to protect me when I was younger, and now I can do the same for her. I perch on the chair next to her and try to act like the sweet, attentive daughter the staff here think I am. It's tedious but necessary.

After my mother has finished telling me about the other residents, her walks in the garden, and her books, she cocks her head and looks at me in a way that reminds me of myself when I look in the mirror.

"You're miles away," she says. "Is it one of those boys you've met?"

"All of them," I say honestly.

My mother's brows raise, a smug smile easing onto her face as if to say, 'that's my girl'. "And you came here to ask me something?"

Rebecca could always read me like a book in her more lucid moments. "The necklace around your neck. Have you seen it before?"

"The necklace?" Rebecca frowns, hand closing for the closed pendant dangling from her neck as she looks at it. "I…" Her frown deepens as she looks down and opens it to see the photographs inside. She glances back up at me. "I honestly don't remember, but it's got you and Dante in there, so I'm assuming it must be your father's. Did he give it to me?"

Adrien would never give her anything, but I don't correct

her. It would just confuse her. Rebecca likes to forget what a bastard he is. "Do you know the girl in the photograph on the other side?"

I always assumed it was Adrien's sister who died long ago, but now I'm not so sure.

Rebecca looks at it again, twisting it toward her to get a better look. "No," she says, shaking her head. She looks up again, eyes level with mine, but not at me, instead through me, her brow creased like it hurts to think. "Should I?"

Her smile has gone now, and that's how I know I'm losing her.

I pushed too hard.

I give her a pleased look a dutiful daughter should. "No, don't worry." Then I lean in to kiss her on the forehead, removing the necklace as I do, slipping it into my pocket before walking out.

When I get back, Lorcan and Jude are waiting for me. I ignore their annoying looks to take a shower and then dry off, changing into my pajamas. My hair is still wet, but I don't give a fuck. It's the clothes that cling to me, making me feel suffocated and restricted, so I take the pajamas off again. The boys watch with dark eyes as I strip completely and crawl into the sheets between them.

The ugly buzzing is back under my skin, driving me fucking crazy. Short of peeling it off, I don't know how to stop it. Well, I do, but slicing someone up right now is off the table.

I *need* the boys.

But I don't want to fuck.

I might kill someone, lost in the moment if I do.

Lorcan is the first to get it, sigh, and wrap himself around me. And then Jude, who wriggles out of his boxer shorts.

"If we're getting naked, then we're fucking getting naked," he drawls.

Then I'm stuck between the two of them while they update me on their grandfather. I'm shattered by the time they finish but feeling less erratic, so I stifle a yawn and tell them about my meeting with Quinn and my visit to Rebecca, leaving out anything to do with Dante. I still don't know if it is him on the list. It's a hunch I have triggered only by Polina's goadings. Until I know for sure, the boys don't need to.

Finally, Lorcan spoons me from behind, maybe sensing I need him more than he needs me. I lie there with my head on Jude's chest, his arm around me, hand lazily stroking circles over my skin, and my ass nestled in Lorcan's groin while he hugs me to the length of his body like he won't ever let me go.

And then I sleep.

And dream of killing Dino.

Like I always do.

In the morning, the darkness inside me is somewhat sated by sleep and skin-on-skin contact so that I can get up reasonably early. I run and then have breakfast in the boarding house kitchen. Just a slice of toast until Lorcan gets up and makes me a full English fry-up.

Jude wakes up late and steals some bacon off my plate before pouring himself a coffee from the pot, joining us at the table.

It's a weekday, so Saskia has had to go to school, much to her annoyance. After I told Lorcan that there's a good chance the infamous Ed Savino is his biological father and that he and Saskia might be twins, he begrudgingly told his sister. I heard her shouting at him in the early hours while I got ready for my run and stayed far enough away that I didn't have to get involved.

"She already knew some of it from helping Quinn, but she wasn't thrilled to find out we might be the same age." Lorcan snorts.

"It's only a year older," I say, brow creasing, taking a sip of my scalding coffee with a shrug.

Jude grins at me. "See. This is why I fucking love you."

I don't see, but I'm not in the mood to try to understand. "Did you speak to your aunt, Tatiana?" I ask Lorcan, rolling my eyes at Jude.

"Not yet. We're treading lightly. Tatiana is summering in Turin with the family. We're going to fly out there after all this is over and speak to her," Lorcan says, moving his food around his plate, not looking at me. He hasn't all morning and has been in a mood since returning from the hospital.

"And Ophelia?" I asked them to look into the name of the other woman who possibly had a child with Ed Savino, too, seven years before their Aunt, but I didn't tell them why.

Lorcan frowns as he answers me. "Quinn found one Ophelia Valle in the southeast who used to attend Sacred Heart. According to the obits, she died in a house fire over twenty years ago." Finally, he looks at me, his frown deepening. "Who is she again? And why do we care?"

I clutch at the necklace in my pocket. "No reason yet. Just see if she can locate a photograph." If the woman in the pendant is Ophelia, then I'm going to hazard a guess she's Dante's mother.

"It must get so tiring, keeping fucking secrets all the time," Lorcan snipes at me. But I don't have time for his tantrums, so I'll just have to ride this one out.

"What the fuck are we doing about Dino?" Jude asks, reading the room and changing the topic.

Good boy.

"I'm going to go through with the wedding," I say, taking a sip of my coffee.

Jude's brows raise.

Even Lorcan looks surprised until he shutters his gaze. "Are you now?" he counters, sitting back in his chair.

"Oh, don't be jealous," I scowl.

"Sweetheart, if you're marrying anyone, it's not fucking Sinner," he drawls.

I cock a brow at him. Jude seems to want to say something too, so I talk quickly. "I said...I'm going through with the wedding, but I'm not marrying him. It's the only way to make certain you're all with me at my father's estate when I take him out."

When they say nothing and just look at me, I add, "I'll do a deal with Adrien to call off the hit on Gordan Duke in return for my compliance. He'll think he's won, and that's when we'll do it."

Fucking silence.

I slit my eyes at both of them. This is why I don't tell them things. They just get annoyed. "I'm telling you instead of leaving you in the dark like I usually do because I need both of you to help me," I say, trying to convince them one last time. I shoot a look at Lor. "I'm trusting you not to throw a tantrum." I switch my gaze to Jude. "And I'm meaner than you and older, so for fucking once, just do as I ask."

There's the sound of the coffee machine finishing its daily rinse, and then nothing but the birds outside after that. Jude and Lor are just staring at me.

For fuck's sake.

Why is this so damn hard?

I shake my head, totally fucking done. "Or I can do it myself, and you can both get fucked." I'm *really* not in the mood today.

"Fine," says Lorcan after burning me to the ground with his shitty glare. "We'll help. Just give the fucking order," he says, getting to his feet. "Now, if you'll excuse me, I have a ton of work to get through."

As he walks out of the open-plan kitchen and dining room, I close my eyes. There's an annoying pulsing just behind my left eye. All this boy drama is giving me a headache.

"He's just going through some things," I hear Jude say.

I snap my eyes open and look directly at the blond jock whose twinkling, hazel eyes seem to mock me. "Tell me what things because I can't take his moody shit anymore."

Jude shrugs. "His grandfather nearly died. He just found out his ex-girlfriend, Kat, is also his cousin. And his dad, Ed Savino, is one sick, nasty motherfucker. They call him the Barbaric Don, for christ's sake. Saskia is having a paddy about her age. And *you* are keeping secrets again."

Right. "He doesn't like not knowing everything."

Jude snorts a laugh. "You're clueless, and that's what I love about you, but Lor doesn't give a shit about that. He's more worried about being in the dark because you think you don't need us, but you do. Every fucking night, you *need* us. And now, you're talking about selling yourself so that you can get close enough to your father to kill him?" His brows raise, as does his voice. "He has a hard time getting his head around putting you in danger without ever getting a say in the matter. We both do."

I slit my eyes at him. "He shouldn't be worried about me."

"He worries. We both do. It's all we fucking worry about."

"I don't need—"

"Shut the fuck up, Viola," Jude sighs, sliding his hand through the back of my hair, pulling me to him. His lips are warm and taste of toothpaste with a hint of coffee. He's not touched a drop of alcohol since I asked him not to, which makes the tightness in my shoulders lessen slightly—one *thing less to worry about.*

As he pulls back, teasing me with his mouth on mine one last time, he cocks his head. "There. Made you less fucking spikey. Now listen. We will always fucking worry, and that's our burden to bear, but the dictatorship has to fucking stop."

"Have you finished?" I ask, thoroughly conflicted, looking at him with feral eyes.

"Yes, now go after him."

"I don't even know where he went," I huff, getting to my feet.

"Yes, you do," Jude muses, slapping me on the ass as I squeeze past him between the tables.

I leave Jude and walk toward the boathouse. Jude's right. I know where Lorcan will be because it's where he always goes when he's fraught with all kinds of internal conflict that I don't truly understand.

"Funny work," I say as I walk along the pier toward Lorcan at the end of it.

The dark-haired Adonis, who caught the eye of my monster a long time ago, glances over his shoulder. As soon as he sees me, he squints and shakes his head, returning his gaze to the lake.

"I needed some air," he says as I sit down beside him on the wooden end of the dock. He already has his bare feet in the water, so I strip off my shoes and socks and do the same. It's become our ritual. Or it was before I got arrested.

The water is ice cold and restful. It helps to clear my head. And soften the serrated edges of my internal mood that seems sharper, nastier these days.

"I know why you keep things to yourself, but it fucks me off every time you do it."

"You want to know everything?" I say to him.

"Yes, I fucking do."

I drink down the fresh air around me, filling my lungs until all I can do is exhale. And then I tell him everything I know and suspect. All the maunderings trapped in my head, all the dark musings that could get me locked away for a very long time—I say it all to Lorcan.

Only the crisp, cold water strung around my ankles and feet like icy barbs of truth, spearing through me, stopping me from running away.

A few seconds after I finish, he blows out his cheeks. "Viola, this plan—it could all go fucking wrong. I don't see why we can't just fuck off to Australia or wherever you want to go."

"It could," I say, for want of anything better. "And Australia is too damn hot."

"Fuck—" he says, letting out a breath, scrubbing a hand over his face. "I preferred it when the only thing I had to worry about was you trying to kill me." A smile ghosts his lips as he says it, glancing my way.

I'm not sure why that's amusing, but he seems to find it so. *Is it? Me trying to kill him instead of someone else...is that funny?* Sometimes, I just don't know what frequency he's on.

I give him a strange look and then change the subject. "I'm doing this so that Adrien will think he's won. I can only kill him if he's caught off guard." I tried to do it last time, and I failed. I need every advantage I can get.

Lorcan's expression sobers. "The ceremony will be packed with his men."

I did already have a plan. I would have one if Dante weren't such a fucking asshole. "We need back-up. I have a plan to get us that."

He shoots me a look. "Does this have something to do with a certain assassin?"

"No," I say, looking over the lake, watching how the ripples rip through the water from the movement of my feet. "Not this time. I'm counting on Dino to help us,"

"Dino is fucked. He's not even answering my fucking messages," Lorcan sighs, taking out his phone to check.

I let out a breath, leaning back. "He'll come around," I say, keeping my feet moving in the water. Every kick in the cold, dark water sends a shiver down my spine, reminding me—I'm alive.

Not dead. *Alive*

Lorcan casts a glance at me, frowning. "How do you know?"

"Because..." I close my eyes, shutting out everything but the cold. "I'm going to tell him what he wants to hear."

TWENTY-TWO

LORCAN

VIOLA IS TRYING NOT to keep secrets, but she's been doing it her entire life. I have no idea what she's decided to do to get Dino back on board. Quite fucking honestly, I don't want to know. But I agree with her that we need him with us for her plan to work. However, to get to him, she needs to be in the same room as him.

And since the fucker isn't seeing us...

Once Viola tells her father that she's on for the wedding, it's like everything snowballs toward the big event. Three of Adrien's men turn up the next day to escort Viola to her father's estate. The last time she went home, she nearly didn't come back. I'm not fucking happy with how things are going, but I have no choice but to grit my teeth and watch while my girl leaves.

"It's only for a couple of weeks," she says, leaning in to kiss me the following day. "And then you'll be there for the rehearsal dinner."

She tastes of peaches and smells of spring walks by the lake. I groan into her mouth as she grabs my cock in her hand and gives me a hard tug. *How can I let her just walk out of here?*

Jude is waiting for her outside, so I reluctantly let her go. When she proposed going alone at first, until the week of the wedding, I was dead against it. But she's right. I have to learn to trust her too.

And Dino. He'd better make sure nothing fucking happens to her.

Or I will personally…

Fuck. Him. Up.

The only reason I'm letting her go is that I still believe in him. As much as Sinner is acting like a prick right now, I know my best friend is still fucking in there and that he won't let Adrien hurt her. He will come through. I just have to have faith.

And I have to let Viola go, *even if it kills me.*

Viola's always saving us, but it should be the other way around. We're the ones who should be guiding her back when she's lost or losing it and be there for her every single time, no matter what. I *will* be. Even if I have to endure her torturing someone every fucking day for the rest of my life.

God, so help me; I'm in love with a girl who likes to cut eyelids off people.

After she's gone, I send a message to Sin on his old number to make sure he heeds my fucking demand to see that she's kept safe. He's not been reading or picking up any of the messages I sent him, but as I said, he'll come around.

Or I'll fucking kill him if he doesn't.

> **If anything happens to her,**
> **I'm holding you fucking personally responsible.**

I get one back straight away.

> **Still a controlling cunt, I see. Don't you worry,**
> **mate.**
> **I'll see that she's well looked after.**

I'm livid at his attitude, but I let it slide. He has a stick up his ass for some fucking unknown reason, but knowing Viola, she'll sort him out.

"This is going to come back and bugger us up the ass this is," Jude grimaces as we drive to see Grandfather.

We've piled into Jude's Aston so we can take Byron and his wheelchair with us. Gordon and his troupe of lawyers want to see him in person before they put the kid back on the will. The poor sod hasn't had any fucking rest since he got out, but at least he's out.

"Fucking Joseph," Saskia snarls from the back seat. "This is all his fault." I don't correct her. He really did a number on this fucking family.

"What I don't get," she carries on as we get out of the car, drawing me behind the others once I've helped Jude with Byron's chair. "Is why he adopted us in the first place?"

"We're Edrei Savino's kids," I say with a shrug. "Joseph was using us to ally with the Camorra mob, maintaining his control over The Five and promising Savino a slice of the Duke empire if I inherited."

"And why fake Byron's death?" she asked.

Jude is wheeling Byron up front, and the teenager is talking the fucking leg off him about football. He has no idea that Jude lost his place on the team after the school started clamping down on drugs, but Jude hasn't said a word to the kid about that. I wait until they're out of earshot to reply to my sister.

"It is the only way Joseph could protect his nephew from Savino. And ensure I inherited everything."

"That's fucking stupid. As if you would give everything to them."

"I would if it meant keeping you safe," I say to her. The 'friend' Joseph was marrying her off to was a supposed Italian diplomat, old enough to be her grandfather. I know I would have done anything to get her back if she had married him.

It should have been me killing Joseph.

Not Viola.

Once again, I'm reminded that our Angel of Death has done nothing but rescue us over and over. It's high time we repaid the fucking favor.

"If we are Tatiana's kids, then we are Dukes too, right?" The hope in her voice slices through me.

"Dukes and Savinos," I say, making her grimace. I get why she's asking, but the potential answer is giving me a sick churning in my fucking stomach.

The Dukes and the Savinos have been at each other's fucking throats ever since Edrei tried to take over back in Italy. When I spoke to Grandfather, he admitted that Savino's men took his daughter, Tatiana, to send him a message. When she became pregnant by Savino himself, with us, we were given to his son, Joseph, and his wife, who couldn't have kids, to keep what happened a secret.

Only when Carl found out Joseph was working with Savino to siphon off the Duke fortune, he tried to have us killed.

Grandfather didn't mention rape. But it's so fucking obvious. No one tells the truth. We all keep secrets and tell lies.

I'm not sure I even want to know.

Saskia's hand reaches for mine, and I let her squeeze it until her nails dig in. I grit my teeth and let her. She's fucking petrified, as I should be. Edrei Savino is no joke. When I was dating Kat, she would often throw it in my face that her uncle would crack my nuts open like eggs and eat them for breakfast if I looked at another girl while I was with her.

Kat; who is now my fucking cousin.

"Fuck. I still haven't called Kat. I won't be long. You should catch up to the others, or Jude will claim the title of the favorite cousin from under you," I say.

Cece and Saskia have been visiting Byron every day since he

got out. Saskia has made it her personal mission to make up for all the shit Joseph has ever done.

"Jude can kiss my ass," she scowls. "Just tell me you're okay." She looks into my eyes.

I roll my eyes. "I'm fine, Sas."

I watch her stalk off in her high heels toward the other two, and then I take out my phone. I dial Kat's number and wait, hoping she won't slam the phone down on me after I failed to call her back months ago.

"Hello," purrs a feline voice. "Lore, you fucker, is that you?"

I suck in a breath, steeling myself for a world of pain. "Kat, long time. Sorry for calling out of the blue. I need to speak to your uncle, Edrei Savino."

"Interesting request. Can I ask why?"

"Because I fucking know...." I close my eyes, unable to believe I'm about to say it.

"Know what?" the bitch taunts.

"That he's my father," I grit out. "Now arrange for me to fucking speak to him."

There's a pause and then a sigh. "And why would I do that, dear cousin?" Her voice is like silk.

"Because I have a deal for him that he won't want to miss out on."

She sighs. "I'll speak to him, but I can't guarantee he'll agree."

"Just do what you can," I say and hang up, the tightness in my shoulders making my entire upper body ache like I've done a fucking workout.

TWENTY-THREE

DINO

"WHERE IS THE BLUSHING BRIDE?" Sal, my cousin, and current keeper, asks me as Adrien's assistant greets us in the foyer of the main house.

"Miss Hawkes is…indisposed. She will hopefully be along later for dinner. She sends her apologies," says Adrien's EA. Jules, I think she said her name was.

Sal gives me a look. "The bitch fucking hates you, alright."

It's a week before our wedding, and my family is arriving in droves at Adrien's estate, and Viola was meant to be here to act as hostess, but she's nowhere to be seen. *Why am I not surprised?*

I clench my jaw and force a smile for Jules. Viola not being here, acting like we're not ex-lovers or ex-friends, reinforces my story that Viola stabbed me in a rage after seeing me kill Kris in cold blood. But it still fucking hurts. Just when I thought my heart couldn't be ripped from my chest because there's nothing there to rip out, she does a number on me.

I grip the dice inside my pocket as I consider going to fucking find her. But then the darkness passes, and I'm able to release them.

It's funny how life fucks you up the ass. I would have given anything to marry Viola before, and I still would. But now there's a vast fucking canyon of death and destruction between us. Part of the agreement between Vice and Harper-Black is sanctioning this damn union. My family is superstitious, as well as religious as hell. Viola was my brother's fiancée, meaning I either agree to marry her or suffer the damn consequences.

"Let's just get this over with," I say gruffly as Jules leads into the depths of the house.

They give us one of the wings in the main building on the estate, enough rooms to house my mother and her current husband, most of our immediate family, and my men. There was no way we would set foot in this fucking death trap without everyone and his dog. The Vices are notorious for having trust issues, regardless.

I'm on the balcony in my room having a smoke when there's a knock at the door.

"Come in," I say to whoever it is. It's probably Sal. The bastard hasn't left my side since I took over the family business. No doubt, my uncles aren't yet convinced I can fill my father's or my brother's shoes.

"Nice fucking place this," Sal says as he strolls in.

I give a shrug. The plush carpets, gilded walls, and luxurious furnishings don't do anything for me. The last time I was here, Viola was treated so fucking poorly…

No, stop thinking about her.

I'm just as bad. I tied her to the bedpost and fucked her like she was nothing to me. I deserve to have her hate me.

Sal comes out onto the balcony where I am and takes in the view of the estate. I have a clear view of the river and the woods from here. And just below is the garden where the house staff is busy erecting marquees for the big event.

"Lola's room is clean, and the boys are checking the rest. I've come to make sure there's no funny business going on in yours,"

Sal announces, taking out a handheld scanner and showing it to me.

I give him the nod and let him do what he needs to to make himself feel better. I wouldn't put it past him to plant a few of his own devices while he's at it.

"Lola wants us all to have dinner tonight," he says to me from inside as he finishes. "With the Harper-Blacks."

He comes out onto the balcony when I don't bother to respond. "Kards, you shouldn't piss your mother off or your father—"

"He's not my fucking father," I say abruptly.

"Riccardo has been like a father to you all these years," Sal corrects, his blue eyes entirely focused on me.

Ric has, and I had called him dad in the past when it suited me, like when Lola was fucking out of it, and the schools needed to speak to a parent, but the reality is Lola married Liam's brother the second his dead body hit the ground. Kris and Lola planned it from the start knowing too well the tradition of marrying your dead brother's wife would get them both what they wanted—someone they could manipulate.

"He wants you there. He hasn't met Adrien's daughter yet, and we're all fucking intrigued. Kristian kept her locked up good and tight when he announced it to the family. We are all dying to meet her," Sal carries on.

No one knows that Viola killed Kristian. No one was there apart from me. I took the blame because I'm the only one who could have killed my brother and not had any backlash. My family also bought the story that Viola turned on me because of what I did to Kris. Again, it's the only way they would accept what she did—a crime of passion, an act of revenge. Either fucking works.

Adrien knows precisely what happened and that I lied to save her. He reminded me as I was lying in the hospital bed, in no uncertain terms, that he didn't give a fuck about her. All he cares about is getting his hands on our business. And so, I have no choice but to go along with what he wants because if my family ever finds out what she did to Kris, they'll hunt her down, brutalize her, and bury her with the fishes.

And me along with her for covering it up.

So here we fucking are.

About to get fucking married.

If only I didn't hate the bitch now.

I give him a dark look. Internally, I want to tell them all to go fuck themselves, but I manage to pull a smile out of my ass and plaster it on my fucking face.

"Dinner sounds good. Arrange it." Sal's eye twitches as he looks at me. Giving Sal orders is like poking a fucking shark, but I do it anyway. He's been up my ass crack day in, day out. I'm meant to be running the business, not him, and certainly not fucking Ric.

I give him a look that says, 'piss me off, go on, I fucking dare you'. All he does is grind his teeth and nod. I go back to smoking my cigarette, enjoying how the hot smoke burns my damn lungs, making me feel for a second that I'm not dead.

I didn't die when she gutted me, but some days...I fucking feel like it.

When I finally leave my room to head down to dinner, wearing a dark shirt, silver tie, with a gray suit, the jacket swung over my shoulder; everyone is already seated and waiting. I can see them through the hallway door as the staff bustle in and out with drinks on trays.

Except for Viola.

She's standing at the top of the stairs like I am, on the other side of the staircase, wearing a black satin dress with a slit up one side—the side that has the branded H. Her blonde hair is braided down the back of her head.

She looks fucking divine. And the part of my chest that usually feels fucking empty aches.

My hand tremors on the stairwell railing, making me grip it

so fucking tight I'm sure she's noticed. It's what she does…read body language like she's reading fucking minds.

That alone makes me hesitate.

I'm supposed to pretend to everyone here that I feel nothing for this girl when the exact opposite is true—I feel everything.

I can't fucking do this.

But I need to.

If I don't, and my family finds out what she did, she's as good as dead. My family is fucking monstrous.

I indicate for Viola to go down first. She lets out a sigh and walks down ahead of me, not once looking back. When we enter the dining room, everyone around the long, rectangular table looks up. Lola is seated at the far end next to Ric. She frowns at me, a question on her lips about why we're together. Lola is probably the only one here who knows Viola and I were an item in the past. So she's reading into things, looking for connections that aren't there anymore.

She's worried about this deal, and so am I.

Ric cocks his head at my arrival. "Ah, here's my stepson." He glances at Viola. "And his pretty soon-to-be wife. Already getting acquainted, I see."

"I'm sorry I couldn't be here when you arrived. I trust Jules saw to it that you have everything you need?" Viola asks smoothly like she's been living under this roof her whole life and didn't just move in a week ago.

When my family confirms they have, she gives a polished smile and takes her seat, the one opposite Lola and Ric. Next to Viola on her right, Sal immediately starts engaging in conversation about the history of the main house, which is apparently a listed building. His primary business is burying bodies in real estate, so he'll always start there if you let him.

Sorrow is next to Ric. She looks up at me with a hateful glare. I ignore her, greeting my uncles seated at the far end, and then take my seat at the top of the table on Viola's other side.

Adrien hasn't yet arrived.

I'm aware of Viola's every fucking move during the first course. She's the perfect hostess, asking questions about menial stuff, and making my family laugh. Sal seems to love her already. I know her enough to see that this is all a facade—her agency training coming to the fore. She's playing a role. Immediately, it makes me fucking miss the real Viola. The one who's salty and direct, who busts my balls if I fuck her off.

But I also despise that Viola too.

Every time I glance her way, I have to grip the cutlery I'm holding in my hands and make myself stay in my damn seat. I need more time to get over this, whatever it is. Life is fucking ass raping me right now and laughing about it.

I close my eyes and then drag them open, hearing Sal laugh at something she said. I'm staring at whatever plate has been put in front of me when Viola's hand suddenly rests on my thigh. I jerk like I've been burned and then glare at her. She's still talking to Sal, making no indication that she's touching me outwardly.

Fucking bitch, what's she playing at?

When she starts moving her hand, rubbing it over my trousers, I have to sit there and try to eat the pheasant or whatever the fuck it is. Until I can't eat because her hand is stroking over my cock that's now rigid in my fucking pants.

"Kardinal?"

"What?" I say quickly, glancing up into the disapproving eyes of Lola opposite as Viola unzips my trousers and slides her hand into the opening.

Jesus *fucking* wept.

"Riccardo was talking to you. He was asking you if you'd chosen a best man yet."

I blink at my mother, understanding only half of her words. All I can think about is dragging Viola upstairs to my room and fucking her brains out.

"I'd be interested to know that too," Viola says as she teases the tip with her nails. It's the first thing she's said all night to me.

I can feel her eyes boring into me as she plays with me, hidden from the view of everyone else.

I have no clue what her game is, only that everything else has gone out the window.

"Who will you pick? Jude or Lorcan?" Her voice is dark velvet, taking me back to the night I fucked her tied to the bedpost.

"Lorcan," I grit out after a pause.

"Interesting," Viola says.

"The Duke boy?" Riccardo asks, his brow furrowed. Sal shifts in his seat and the rest of the table quiets.

Fuck, I wasn't thinking. I was supposed to say, Sal. I can't back out now. I'll look like a right knob.

"He's been my best friend for years," I say dismissively.

I actually don't care who my best man is. I just want to punish Viola six ways from Sunday for the agony she's putting me through right now.

Dessert comes not a moment too soon. She's awoken some kind of beast inside of me, and all I can do is grunt whenever someone asks me a question. I'm not even eating.

I've never wanted someone so badly. As soon as this shit dinner is over, she's mine.

All fucking mine.

Our plates are cleared, and everyone talks among themselves, paying us no attention. I lean in and discreetly whisper a promise in Viola's ear.

"You fucking brat. I'm going to annihilate you when I get you upstairs."

"You'd better," she snipes back, under her breath, pausing in the attention she's given me all night.

That's it. How can I bear another fucking second in this room with my family? I seize her upper thigh, squeezing as I slide up the split. Her breath catches until my palms cross over the H branded into her skin, and she stiffens. My grip tightens. Viola shoots me an unfathomable look and draws her hand away, leaving me reeling.

Leaving me empty and desperate.

How can she still have her claws in me after what she did?

I glance at her, talking now to my mother about horses, making that smooth transition from my private whore to the pretty hostess in seconds. I'm half listening, half sulking. I didn't know she could ride horses. It dawns on me that I know nothing about Viola at all. After all this time, she still doesn't talk about herself.

Well, if we're going to be married, that's going to fucking change.

Dinner is finally over. My mother, stepfather, and two uncles take their drinks into the parlor to talk about the wedding and the business deal. Sal fucks off to wherever he goes at night—the casino, probably. Sorrow, my cousin on my mother's side, shoots me a burning look, which I ignore. I don't want to talk business or family shit tonight. I want to fuck my fiancée and then sleep until morning.

Sorrow gives up when I don't immediately come over and stalks out of the room. We're the only two left in the dining room. I still can't look at her, so I don't. But Viola leans in any way as we walk to the door, her sweet perfume taking me back months to when she was in my arms most nights, and she was all mine.

"I'm heading upstairs. I suggest you do the same in a few minutes," she purrs.

I nod at her, running a hand through my hair.

With my family in the house, it's dangerous ground, but I don't give a fuck. It's expected of me to fuck my would-be wife. What kind of Vice would I be if I didn't?

Viola disappears up the stairs. I don't follow her. Not yet. I know where her bedroom is. The parlor has an outside terrace attached. I take my drink and head out. Lola and Ric are deep in conversation by the fireplace. Lola's on her meds, thank fuck. Ric is good at keeping her on them, so I don't have to worry about her going off the rails when he's around.

It's bitter and wet on the terrace, but I let the cold seep through my shirt, enjoying how it feels against my skin as I take out a smoke and light it.

"What a miserable fucking evening," says a gravelly voice.

I turn back to see Sorrow stepping on the terrace, hugging her arms around her, trying to keep the cold out. She gives me a shitty look as she shuts the door behind her.

"What do you want, Sorrow?" I say, taking in a lungful of smoke.

Her eyes narrow, and her lips become a grim line as she steps up next to me, looking into the dark surrounding the house. "I wanted to apologize for being a bitch lately."

I shrug. "You're a Vice." All Vice women are absolute bitches, my mother being the main one.

"I also wanted to thank you. You stopped those bastards from...whatever they had planned the other night. I know my father wants me off his hands, married to some pig, but appreciate you looking out for me."

I take another drag of my cigarette, leaving it balancing on my lips, and then reach into my pocket to take out my pack, offering her one. Sorrow doesn't smoke, but she takes one anyway and holds it to her lips while I light it.

"There's more than one way to be useful," I say. "If you can stomach it."

She cocks a brow at me. "Oh really, even you are pimping yourself out for the greater good."

She's got me there. This deal with Adrien all ties into this sham of a marriage. Viola hates me. I can't look at her without wanting to hurt her. It's all fucking screwed. "Do what Sal does. No one will make you marry anyone you don't want to if you're an asset already."

We smoke in silence for a few more minutes.

"It's not that easy, and you know it," she grimaces.

"Want me to speak to Lola for you?"

She shakes her head. "Fuck no." After a pause, she adds. "Sal has asked me to do something for him."

Sounds fucked up. "Do I want to know?"

"Ew, not like that." She rolls her eyes. "He wants me to get information from someone and then get rid of them for the good of the family. I haven't decided if I'm going to do it yet."

"Who?" I keep my voice light.

She side-eyes me. "I can't tell you."

I shrug and finish my smoke, stubbing it on the low wall. I'll just have to ask Sal directly. Fucking bastard, roping Sorrow in to do his dirty work.

"What do you think I should do?" she asks.

"My advice…do what needs to be done." She seems to consider that. "No one else is going to save you," I add before going inside.

Lola gives me a concerned look as I walk through the parlor. "Dino," she says, calling me over.

I know what she's going to say; she's going to tell me to stay away from Viola because she knows that I'll be strung up if my uncles suspect that Viola and I killed my brother together. Killing family is tolerated for ambition but not fucking love.

Never for love.

Not that I'm in love with Viola anymore.

That emotion died the day she left and didn't fucking come back.

TWENTY-FOUR

VIOLA

I DON'T KNOW how to get through to Dino. Trying to navigate his rollercoaster of emotions isn't a skill set I'm trained for. I'm a killer. I know how to charm, seduce, target, and take out. I don't know how to bring someone back from despair or beg for their forgiveness. The apology I gave him last time was the only one he'll get from me; that's all I know.

Other than that, I'm winging it.

I try seduction first because that's what I excel at.

To get him alone.

So I tease the hell out of him, taking him to the edge, stopping only before we both fall into the dark crevice of no return. When he promises to hurt me, a shiver runs down my spine tearing me in half between wanting the innocent boy who wormed his way into my dead heart and the guy next to me who doesn't seem to give a shit.

I get a text from Lorcan asking how project 'Win Dino Back' is going because everything rests on him being on our side. I can't kill my father if he's going to just fuck everything up because if he gets in my way, I may hurt him, and that's the last thing I want to do.

But I will...*if needs must.*

I don't reply to Lorcan because Dino comes barging into my room. He doesn't knock, acting like he owns this room and everything in it, including me. And he will if the deal with my father goes through. The deep blue depths of his eyes suck me in as he stalks over. I once said Dino would stand there with a hard-on and do nothing. Not this version, and not right now. His hands are all over me, running under the satin dress, searing my skin with his touch. His mouth is on mine, bruising my lips with the harshness of his kiss. I could get lost in his kiss so easily.

For several seconds, I let him eat me up, enjoying the sensation of him in my mouth, on my skin, under my defenses. His kiss wraps around the ragged edges within me. His hands, rough from working on his bikes, piece me together bit by bit.

When we come up for air, an emotion I'm not equipped to figure out flits across his cold, hard gaze.

"I hate you," he hisses, his hands tangling in my hair as he looks down on me. "So why can't I fucking walk away?"

I glare back at him, not letting him see the need in my eyes. I don't show anyone that side of me, not even Lorcan. "I'm not stopping you," is all I say. "You don't have to be in here. This is my room."

"Fuck, Viola, what is wrong with you?" He lets go of me and shakes his head, striding over to the other side of the bed, as far away from me as he can. He stares out the window that looks over the courtyard for a minute, breathing hard, jaw clenched, anger dimple begging to be bitten.

He needs to look at me.

"I don't know what you mean," I say as I smooth my hair where he savaged it and then walk over to the vast wardrobe on the far side. I strip down to my underwear to hang up the satin dress. Baring skin has always worked in the past, so I shamelessly flaunt my body, scars and all. When I glance back, Dino is watching me with molten eyes filled with desire as well as disgust; fists clenched at his sides. He can't avoid looking at me now, even if he is upset that I'm practically naked. Using my flesh to get through to him is a low blow, but I don't know any other way, and I don't actually care.

"You do know, but you don't care," he says, drinking me in with his baby blues. "But you need to care because this isn't a game anymore, Viola."

"I don't think it was ever a game," I snort, bending over to rifle through my loungewear drawer.

Dino groans loudly. I steal a look at him as he scrubs his face with his hand. "Will you stop fucking turning me on for a minute so that I can talk to you?"

I blink at him, moistening my lips as I stand up straight. "You said you would annihilate me. I'm waiting."

He stares at me and then shakes his head before beckoning me over. "Then come over here and put your money where your fucking mouth is," he says. He places a pair of red dice on the sideboard and then undoes his trousers.

"Don't you mean your cock?" I ask as he eye fucks me for what it's worth, pumping his dick in his hand.

I take my time to get to him. When I finally do, he forces me to my knees, one hand on my shoulder, the other fisting my hair. I look up at him from under my lashes as I take his velvet-hard cock between my lips. The taste of him is everything I've been missing and more.

"Fuck," he breathes, eyes closed, tearing my hair at the roots. "You know exactly how to destroy me, but that's not how this will go."

He holds my head on either side and trusts into my mouth. He's big enough to make me choke, but I focus on opening up for him, swallowing him down completely as he slams into the back of my throat. Dino makes a low sound, halfway between a sigh and a moan, and then continues to fuck me between the lips, his scent making me wet just as much as the feel of his shaft sliding over my tongue.

I'm being generous, giving him control over me for a second time. I don't know why I'm offering him this side of me. I fight in the bedroom, or I take. There's no situation ever where I give myself up like this. I'm making a sacrifice this one time.

For Dino.

I let him pump into me, using my mouth as he needs it. His cock swells over my tongue, becoming thicker and harder with every thrust.

"Fuck," he keeps saying, over and over again. "Fuck, fuck, fuck, Viola."

Between my legs, I'm soaked, desperate for my own release. It sweeps through me in sharp waves that I dig my fingers into his hips. He cradles me then, hand around my head, holding me to him while he shoves his hips forward. And then he comes with a groan, a bittersweet tasting moment. I swallow everything he gives me while looking into his guarded eyes as he breathes in and out, taking every last detail of me in.

After, I climb my way up to him, pulling myself to my feet, to kiss him deeply. Fiercely. That wakes him up. With his lips on mine, tongue inside my mouth, the remnants of his bitter release swirling between us. He pushes me back until I'm on the bed, and he's on top. I'm tearing at his shirt as he's ripping off my bra and knickers. His trousers are shrugged off, and I can see he's instantly hard again in no time at all.

"No," he says, grabbing my wrists and pinning them above my head. "I need those claws away," he grits out, his knees knocking my thigh apart, easing his cock between my dipping, aching folds. And then he's inside me, filling me completely. He slowly rocks his hips as he holds me down, making me squirm with frustration. The pace is not my ideal, but I have no choice, and that annoys me.

"I just let you use my mouth," I snipe at him. "You don't get to dictate how you fuck me too."

"I'll do what the fuck I like," he scoffs, thrusting slowly again but this time deeper. "You keep taunting me, pushing me to the fucking edge. What did you think was going to happen?"

I'm so wet; my body doesn't protest when he bottoms out inside of me. I lie there and take it for a few punching strokes, enjoying the feeling of being used this way too. And then I lose it. I'm done playing nice.

"Fuck me properly," I snap. When he doesn't speed up, I scowl and bridge my hips, trying to buck him off, and I almost do. But he wraps his arms and legs around me and latches his mouth on mine. His mouth consumes me as we tumble in the bed, wrestling to get one up on each other until I manage to get away, bruising his lips with my teeth, biting his ear, and scratching his back until he pins me beneath him.

"I said no claws," he snaps, pinning my hands back onto the bed.

"Go fuck yourself," I say with a vicious smile.

He snarls and flips me over, pushing my face down into the soft pillows, managing to angle his hips behind me so he can thrust into me again, drilling me into the bed. I push back, moving to meet his as he fucks into me. His thick length, filling me completely, is enough to send me over the edge.

As Dino holds me down, one hand threaded through the hair on my scalp and the other dug into my waist, I come, gripping the sheets, panting, the air ripped out of my lungs, while he jerks his hips harder and harder, driving deeper and deeper. He gives one last thrust. Then he finally comes too, his warmth spreading into me, dragging the heat and pleasure deep into my body.

We lie there later with him draped over me, keeping me close. He hasn't said a word since we both came, and neither have I. I'm not ready to talk or do whatever energy-sucking thing is required of me next. I just want to be here and stare at nothing, letting the heat of his body shield me from the buzz beneath my skin and the darkness lurking where there should be a soul.

I must have fallen asleep because it's dark when I open my eyes, and I'm suffocating under the heat of the covers...and Dino. He's wrapped around me; his face barely inches from mine. The sound of his breathing, deep and even, is what tells me he's fast asleep. My phone is on the side table, lit up from a recent message. Shifting slightly, I reach for it, but Dino's arm tightens around me as if to keep me from vanishing. I wait in the darkness, filling my lungs as he does, waiting until he relaxes.

I don't want to wake him up.

Another message flashes on the screen. It's probably Lorcan demanding to know what the hell is going on. I wait, counting the seconds that turn into minutes as Dino's breathing evens out. And only then do I ease out of Dino's embrace and the bed.

I'm too hot anyway.

I slip out of the covers, snatching a dressing gown from the end of it, and walk over to open a window. The cool air instantly soothes me as it caresses up my robe, playing over any exposed skin. But it's a soft kind of stroke that isn't jarring. Usually, I need to freeze my ass off on nights like this to remind me that I'm still alive. Killing isn't enough, and it hasn't been for a very long time, so the cold keeps the need that crawls over my skin under control.

Dante understands. He needs to feel alive just as much as I do. When you're dead inside, it's a damn requirement.

But....

Lately....

Other things have sated the hunger.

I glance at Dino, letting the unexpected tug in the pit of my stomach stir and then steel down my spine. Like a monster creeping through the shadows, I watch him sleep, enjoying how he looks when he's not pissed at me. *Like I could eat him alive.*

My phone lights up, screaming silently at me. With a sigh, I move away from the window to pick it up. It's Lorcan, only about fifteen times. I read every message and then send him one back to say that it's all under control. I slip the handset into my gown pocket, where there's also a syringe I prepared earlier.

As I stand over Dino, I let my gaze run over his sleeping form, holding the needle between my fingers, still hidden in the pocket. I could easily slip a needle into his vein and keep him out of harm's way until all this is over. But if I do that, it's over. He will never trust me again.

Never.

I'm not an idiot.

I know enough about human relationships to know that he would not take that kind of treatment very well. Especially after I stabbed him. Dino needs to trust me.

And I have to trust him.

I let go of the needle.

His eyes fly open, even though there's no sound in the bedroom but our breaths and the wind as it whispers in from the open window.

"What the—" His gaze narrows as he sits up slowly and deliberately. "Why the fuck are you watching me sleep like a stalker?" His eyes burn into mine, and then a quick flick of his gaze left—to the gun on the dresser.

I have a split second to decide.

Prick him with my syringe, or talk to him?

I'd much rather shove a needle into him than try to form words that mean nothing and make no sense, but I force the air out of my lungs and take a seat on the divan opposite, drawing my legs up onto it, tucking them beneath me.

It's a pose that says I'm not a threat.

I'm not here to kill you, love.

"Let's talk," I say, soft and easy. I told Lorcan that I knew what Dino wanted to hear. I just don't know if I can say it.

Dino just stares at me like I've grown a second head…

And then, slowly, like he's coming back to me from a deep sleep, he nods. The tension leaves my body as he slides back onto the pillows, moving away from the weapon on the bedside table. His pose is also non-threatening, but his dimple is puckered, and his jaw is set. He's ready to listen but also ready to hurt me if he needs to...

Yes.

It's going to be a long night.

TWENTY-FIVE

VIOLA

"THIS PLACE LOOKS like Adams Family owns it," Saskia exclaims as she walks through the door. Quinn walks in behind, surveying my childhood home with the same intensity. I've never brought Quinn here before. I've no idea what she makes of it as she takes in the deep dark wood, almost black furniture, the gold-accented wall art, and the rich flocked wallpaper. It's all Adrien's taste, and it's horrendous, suffocating.

The security men at the door search the girls and their many suitcases. And then they're free to follow me to the Western wing. The bride's guests will stay until after the wedding.

No one said I couldn't have bridesmaids, so I took it upon myself to invite Quinn and Saskia.

"So who is planning this shotgun wedding, and where is your dress?" Saskia asks the moment we get behind closed doors.

I blink at her. "How the fuck should I know?"

Saskia's eyes almost pop out of her head. "Please tell me you're joking?"

I look at Quinn, silently asking for help. But Quinn raises a brow as she walks over to where her suitcase is and heaves it onto the bed. "I'm not getting involved. I'm just here as tech support."

"She's not, is she?" Saskia asks, looking at me in horror. "You need two bridesmaids. Three would be ideal, but two will do. You can't have one. It'll ruin the symmetry."

I open my mouth to reply, but nothing comes out.

Thankfully, I'm saved by someone knocking at the door. It's Sorrow Vice, Dino's cousin, with a stormy expression on her face —brows furrowed, eyes narrowed, lips thin and taut.

"I'm supposed to try on a dress?"

I let out a breath and then step back to let her in.

"Saskia, Quinn, this is Sorrow. She's the third bridesmaid." Lola came and found me earlier in the day to inform me of that fact. I don't care either way, but Saskia's face brightens, so I suppose that means it's good for the damn symmetry.

"The dresses are in here," I say, leading the three girls into a second adjoining room that used to be a study. Someone brought the dresses around earlier. Saskia immediately screeches and runs up to the boxes and begins opening them.

"You didn't even hang them up?" she snarls, looking back at me.

Quinn purses her lips at me and then mouths 'run'.

I roll my eyes and walk out of the room. I can't right now. I just can't. I'd rather torture someone for information than do whatever is happening in that room.

Any day of the fucking week.

An entire morning of girl talk has my head exploding and my left eye twitching. After Saskia finds out that Lola is the wedding planner for the event, she makes her join us for breakfast cocktails and dress fitting. Lola is happy enough to get trashed at 10 a.m. She's also delighted to stick a few pins into me while helping Saskia take in the dress.

It needs to fit me like a second skin, apparently. Having lost a lot of weight from my stint in Juvie, Saskia hasn't stopped complaining about how awful it looks. I don't see what her problem is. It's a dress. All wedding dresses are meant to be hideous, aren't they?

The sharp needles are a welcome distraction from Saskia's cutting remarks and the celebrity gossip around the band booked for the wedding—a romantic scandal that I'm not the least interested in involving the sister of the famous singer, Lana Langfield. I've no idea who that is, and I don't care. But Lola and Saskia seem to revel in revealing what they know and what they don't.

I've never understood idle speculation. Why discuss an unknown fact that could or could not have happened? What a waste of time. When Quinn joins in the debate of which guy the sister is fucking, I know I've had enough. Especially when Lola refuses to adjust the dress to fit my dagger underneath.

"There won't be any weapons at the ceremony," she sniffs at me.

I would stab her had Saskia not been there. Quinn doesn't care. And Sorrow looks like she wants to stab Lola too when she deems the conversation riveting enough to tear her eyes away from her phone.

But…Lorcan would not be happy if I lost it in front of his not-so-delicate sister. Throughout the day yesterday, he sent me several messages warning me not to lose my temper in front of his sweet Sassy. The guy is delusional. Saskia is vicious as she is fashionable. I've already taught her how to shoot, and she's bugging me to teach her self-defense. I'm waiting for the day she asks me how best to part someone's jugular and not get blood on her dress.

Something of which I'd love to know myself.

I extract myself from the room when Lola and the girls switch their attention to the bridesmaid's dresses. Not that there's anywhere else to go. Dino and his family have taken over the entire house, making me on edge, as well as Gigi. Whenever one of Dino's uncles passes by, I feel for my knife, just as her hand hovers over the gun tucked under her suit jacket.

On the bright side, Gigi seems to have forgotten I exist with the Vice family in residence. I have enough on my plate to deal without her beady eyes following my every move until Adrien returns—Adrien, who still hasn't bothered to return from his business trip to Turin. A good thing, too, because if he *were* here, I might have already tried to kill him out of sheer frustration.

Dante would say that it's essential to plan this right.

There's no room for fuckups.

Lorcan and Jude know what I need from them. Quinn is doing her magic around the estate without anyone noticing. And Saskia is providing the necessary distraction. The only potential fuck up was Dino, but I've got that under control—I hope. *Can he be trusted? Or will his distrust of me get in the way?*

With the wedding happening so fast, I've not had time to reflect on the fact that I have no idea where Dante is. He's the wildcard in all of this. He won't reply to my messages and hasn't given any indication of where he is.

Fucking Dante.

When the boys, Jude and Lorcan, arrive later in the day, heralded by the dogs barking their heads off at the roar of high-performance car engines, the tension in my shoulders eases a touch. As they step through the doors, Jude strides over and possesses my mouth, hands all over my body, in a move of pure ownership. He smells of vanilla and bergamot and all things Jude. I close my eyes briefly, allowing my mouth and senses to be invaded by him and only him. I've let myself forget during the two weeks at home how much they ground me.

"Tell me you're fucking okay?" Jude demands, breaking the spell and the kiss to raze his eyes over me from the bottom up.

"I'm fine," I say without fanfare. We have an audience. Gigi and her men escorted them in, unhappily, I might add, but they are part of the wedding party, so she has no fucking say. As well,

I outrank her. Adrien at least made good on his word to announce me his second for a short time before my eventual union to Vice.

Having walked in with the cases, Lorcan comes to stand behind me, claiming the space so no one else can. He slides a hand around my waist. The second Jude shifts his own to my ass, sandwiching me between them.

"You're a fucking sight for sore eyes," Lor drawls in my ear, nuzzling and nipping my neck with his lips and teeth. His scent penetrates through my shitty mood and teases a sigh from my lips. "Edrei has agreed to meet here," he says in a low voice.

"Did you speak to him?"

"No, Kat's arranged it with him. He'll be here the day before the wedding."

I give a soft nod, sorting through my head the deal I need to make with Dante's father, the agency's owner. I don't need D. I can go above him. Since Dante told me Iskar worked for my father, I assumed that meant Adrien owned the agency. But Polina and Iskar are both Camorra mafia. Dante has never stopped working for them, even when going against Adrien. It was easy enough to put two and two together.

I show the boys to their rooms, not trusting anyone else to see that they get there without issue, and then leave them to settle. There are a thousand things to be done when planning a fucking wedding. *Who knew?*

But now they're here, all three of them, under my roof, it's evident…

One alone is not enough.

I need them all.

Jude is my rock. Lorcan is my faith. And Dino *was* the light to my darkness.

I just need to get through to him.

Just as I'm leaving, walking down the hallway that connects the East Wing with the rest of the house, I spot Sorrow Vice hovering at the end, gaze sweeping past me toward the room where the boys are located. She hasn't seen me and almost jumps out of her skin when I say her name.

"Fuck, you scared me," she says, color draining from her face when she sees it's me.

I raise a brow at her. "That wasn't my intention."

"Sorry, jumping at shadows today," she mumbles.

I narrow my eyes at her. "I see. Are you lost? This wing is for guests of the bride only."

"Saskia sent me to pick up a bag from her brother."

"Lorcan and Jude are at the far end."

She nods at me and then shuffles off in that direction. Something about her seems off, but Dino turns up with some men flanking him at that moment. I give him a look as he gives me one. His dimple pops out, begging me to bite it out. I suppress the urge and carry on walking, letting my attention run elsewhere, even as it wanders back to our 'talk' the night before.

If you could call it that.

"Some talk," Dino says after a few minutes of us both staring at each other, listening to the rain patter outside the window. He cocks his head at me, brow furrowed, waiting.

Talking has never been my strong point. I'm a stab first, ask questions later kind of girl.

Where to begin? What to say.

Dino has always been the one who knows what I'm thinking before I think it, but lately, he's too consumed with his hurt over what I did. I may not understand human emotion, but I know anger when I see it... and fear.

Dino is afraid of me.

As usual, that gives me goosebumps, tiny electrical pulses trembling through every cell in my body, telling me it's time to hunt. But there's also another reaction—my heart feels heavy, my breathing strained, and my gut twists harshly, all when I see the uncertain way he looks at me. I'm used to all kinds of rawness in his blue orbs because out of all the boys, Dino is an open book. But fear has never been there....

And I like it too much.

"You're afraid of me," I say, just coming out with it.

His frown deepens. "I'm..." He stops to run a hand through his hair, breaking eye contact. His eyes are flintier, harder when he looks back at me. "I'm not afraid. I just don't know if I still love you."

I tilt my head, waiting, mainly because I don't know what to say next. I don't even know what love is anyway.

"After...what happened," he carries on. "The first thing I wanted when I woke up was to see you. I know you didn't mean it. It was the rage in you, reacting. You were in your zone, and I fucked it up. I took your outlet away from you." His eyes burn into me as he says the next part. "That's why I held you. Didn't try and stop you." He almost chokes on the last part. "I let you use me to let out the rage."

Something dark and feral tugs in my chest. I swallow it down, stifling it before it can rise and become me. "I could have killed you," I say on the surface, matter-of-factly.

His dimple puckers. "And I would have let you," he counters.

"But why?" I'm glaring at him now, unable to keep the anger from rising. Why the fuck am I pissed at him?

"Because..." He stares into my eyes, unflinching. "I would have done anything for you."

"And now?"

He shakes his head, drawing in a breath. "Now, I can't stand the sight of you." I don't say anything to that. I wait, watching him search for the words. "I waited in that damn hospital. Everyone I hated was there; my mother, my stepfather, my uncles, even your fucking father, but not you."

"I was arrested," I say, blinking at him.

"I know that now, but I didn't back then. And when I found out, I was so fucking pissed off at you for not even bothering to come to see me before...." He drops his eyes, unable to look at me anymore, hands becoming fists. "You decided to save Jude instead."

"I came to see you," I say slowly.

His snort turns into a sneer. "When? You didn't try that hard, obviously."

"Lorcan and Dante tried to keep me away," I say, thinking back to what happened. "But I ditched them, stole Dante's car, and drove to St Guy's Hospital." Dino's gaze, still shuttered, shifts upward, resting on me as I speak. "I walked in through the emergency entrance because I was covered in your blood and didn't want to draw attention to myself. I got as far as the corridor to your room," I say, letting Dino see the truth in my eyes. "But my father saw me, and then I couldn't go any further. I turned around and walked out. I'd already called the police and turned myself in before I arrived, so they were waiting when I left the hospital. And then it was too late. I couldn't go back."

Dino doesn't say anything. He just looks at me, eyes searching my face.

He wants more. He needs more than that. I drag in a lungful of air and then shift in my seat. My legs are falling asleep. Dino is still watching, waiting. But I don't know what the hell to say next.

"Why did you want to see me?" he asks after a few beats."

"I wanted to see you because everything inside me was…falling apart." I give a slight shrug. "It still is."

"You need me," he says. It's more of a statement than a question.

"No, I don't."

He frowns.

"I don't need anyone, but I want you. There's the difference."

"Why?" he practically growls out the word.

"Because…" I search my newly created relationship arsenal for something to say he'll accept. "You're the light to my darkness."

He closes his eyes, letting out a long sigh. When his baby blue eyes refix themselves on me, the furrow in his brow is gone, and the weight behind his eyes is less.

"Come here," he says, opening his arm and gesturing me to come to him. I gladly untuck my legs from where I'm sitting and go over to him. He pulls me onto his lap, holding me, kissing me on the brow. He smells of his usual scent, cinnamon and citrus, but he also smells of me. My perfume is all over him, marking him as mine.

"Thank you for telling me that."

"I thought it was obvious," I say with a shrug.

He gives a strained chuckle. "No, you're a fucking enigma, Viola. I have absolutely no idea how you feel."

I frown but say nothing. I have no idea how I feel either, but it's probably not the right time to admit that.

"You were right. I was afraid," he says in a low voice after a few minutes of holding me. "I was afraid that I was too soft for you. You kept asking me to be darker, harsher. I wanted to, but...fuck. I was afraid if I didn't change, I would lose you. And that you would never love me the way I love you." His body tenses in my arms as if waiting for a confession too. But I say nothing because, truthfully, love is something I have no measure for.

And have no need for.

I didn't mention that I would leave after this all goes down. Telling Dino that I'm not tying the knot with him, but leaving, is not a discussion I wanted to have in the dead of night. Not after his eyes changed, and my heart stopped fluttering about in my chest like a dying fucking bird.

Not after I felt peace for the first time. And the buzzing under my skin for the first time ever....

Just stopped.

TWENTY-SIX

JUDE

WHEN WE ENTER the reception room where the evening drinks are being held the night before the wedding, Viola is there talking to Dino's family while he stands next to her with a dark look on his face, his arm around her like he can't quite bring himself to touch her. I know he's putting on an act because V messaged us the night before to say Dino was on our side again.

I didn't even know the fucker wasn't.

There's so much I missed while I was in juvie that it hurts my head just to bloody think about it. It's like I've come back to absolute carnage—Dino hating us, Kristian dead, and Dante killing people for us. That was a joke. Either that, or he has some fucking balls playing both fucking sides.

If I ever see that smug bastard again, I will smash his fucking face in. In my pocket, my good hand closes on the cold metal of one of my brass knuckles. I brought my party trick because you never know when you might need to break someone's jaw, and ever since I stopped drinking and Dante decided to switch sides again, I've been itching for a fight. Broken fingers or not.

I've no idea what she saw in Dante.

No fucking idea at all.

I have to be there to hold her together, catch her when she fucking falls. Lorcan might be the one she turns to when she's losing it, but I'm the one who finds her before she gets to that state and keeps her from going off the edge.

She wouldn't have hurt Dino if I'd been out and there for her.

That, I can guarantee.

"What's the plan?" I ask Lorcan as we head to the makeshift bar in the corner where proper drinks are being made instead of the weak-as-shit champagne in glasses being offered. Fucking gangsters are everywhere you look. The Vice crew. Adrien's men. The place is crawling. The amount of testosterone in the room makes me so desperate for a damn drink that I slip the metal of the brass knuckle over my fingers instead.

Not a great move.

I'm so fucking wound up tight. Who knows what will set me off.

"The plan is to be here for Viola in case she needs us," Lor says, getting the bartender's attention as he casts his eyes around the room.

Our girl glances briefly around the room too. I haven't taken my eyes off her since we walked in. Lor is doing his best, but even he can't stop staring. She's looking stunning, as per usual. Blonde hair poker straight, red lips, smokey eyes. She's wearing an off-the-shoulder red dress with a heart-shaped cut-out on the back exposing her creamy skin, which is very fucking apt if I pay attention to the fucking feelings clogging up in my chest whenever I think about losing her.

I only just got her back.

I kept my expression blank when she told us her idea to leave because what the fuck else could I do? Lorcan seemed to take that bit of news in his stride. I almost choked on my coffee when she found me in Quinn's office to tell us he'd escaped. Lorcan already knew it would happen. I could tell by his face. Quinn raised a brow but said nothing. I wanted to punch the fucking door in, but with Viola's brown eyes daring me to question her insanity at not going after him, I just gave her a shrug.

She can do what the fuck she likes.

Her reasoning makes sense, but that doesn't mean I like it. I actually fucking hate it. I still don't understand why she has to change her name and disappear. She's giving Dante everything. He fucking wins. But I get that she's always been running. As much as she's a ruthless killer, she's also a survivor. To do what she's had to do, over and over, she's come up with a pattern of throwing everything to fucking dogs and running for the hills.

That's going to have to change. Even if I have to throw her over my shoulder and drag her back home cave-man style. Even if I must follow her to the ends of the fucking earth....

She's not running away. Not from me. I'll hunt her down and chase her to the end. *Viola belongs to me.* I look at Lorcan and Dino, and I know they think the same.

She belongs to us.

"Whiskey for me. Coke for him," Lorcan says to the bartender.

I shoot him a pissy look. "Fuck, no. A whiskey for me too."

"You've been sober for weeks. You're not breaking your sobriety tonight," he says, brows furrowed.

"I'm fucking dying of thirst here," I exclaim.

"I doubt you're dying," he says, like a fucking bellend, drinking a mouthful of his whiskey when the barkeep hands it to him, rubbing that shit in my face.

"Just give me the fucking coke," I grit out, taking the soda and swigging it back. I would give anything to add a dash of Blue Label to it, *anything*, but I keep that thought to myself. Lorcan can be a judgmental cunt when he wants to be. I don't need him looking at me like I'm a fucking liability.

We stand there like dickheads, scanning the crowd. Saskia and Quinn join the party with one of Dino's cousins. I forget her name, but I've seen her around.

"This is Sorrow," Saskia says by way of introduction. The dark-haired girl with bright blue eyes gives us both a sullen look.

"So you're the dickheads who got my cousin in so much trouble?" she asks, tossing her hair, unable to tear her pretty orbs away from Lorcan.

Saskia notices her staring at her brother immediately. "He's taken."

Lorcan hasn't even noticed. His eyes are still fixed on V. I don't think they ever left.

I snort a laugh, and the girls shoot dark looks my way. Sorrow practically glares but follows Lorcan's gaze, her frown deepening when she sees who's got his undivided attention.

They always go for the tall, dark, tortured one. It used to fucking piss me off when we were kids. I can't look at an orchard the same way after he deflowered my first-ever girlfriend against the biggest fucking apple tree in the field behind his house. That was when I decided it was easier to share them with him, and then later, with Sinner. I also decided to date his sister then to piss him off.

Look at us now, sharing the girl of our dreams.

"She can't be dating both of them?" Sorrow says, brow furrowed.

"Three of us," I say, taking a drink of my flat fucking coke. "She's with me too."

Sorrow looks me up and down. "Three guys. How? What the hell does she have that we all don't? I don't get it."

"Speak for yourself," Saskia says acidly.

Quinn turns back to join us, having ordered the drinks from the bar. She hands Saskia a glass of wine and Sorrow what looks to be a Redbull and vodka. "Are we talking about Viola? Because I would say, she's got me too."

When everyone looks at her, including Lorcan too, she shrugs. "I would if she would have me. She's amazing in bed," she says simply. "Her pussy practically sucks you into it."

Now we all look at Quinn...wondering what Viola's pussy has sucked up and when.

Lorcan grimaces, brow full of fucking deep ass furrows. "Can we not talk about this with my sister standing there?"

"I'm not a fucking prude, Lor," Saskia glares at him. "If I went that way, I'd do her too."

Lorcan chokes on his drink, and Quinn laughs softly into hers. Only Sorrow looks confused. I can't help but snort again. It's the wrong reaction because Saskia gives me a death stare, taking a long sip of her wine before adding, "Well, Jude isn't that great. He's lucky to be included. That's all I have to say."

I almost do a fucking Lor and choke on my pisspoor drink, but I'm saved by the fucking Angel of Death looking over and catching my eye. Then she walks out of the room, leaving Dino, as per the plan, to distract his family.

Time to get this show on the fucking road.

I shoot a look at Lor and Quinn before sauntering out after the only girl ever to suck me up, spit me out, and leave me begging for fucking more.

Viola is waiting for me in the bathroom at the end of the hall. It's not locked because, apparently, there are no doors with locks in this damn house. So I just barge in to find Viola standing there, waiting for me with a faint smile on her lips.

I'm on her in a fucking heartbeat.

All that talk of pussy sucking has me shoving her back against the bathroom mirror, running my hands over her tight body under that dangerous dress. The bathroom and the bedrooms are the only places where there aren't any cameras, so they are the only places we can talk without some fucker listening in. It's the only place I can do what I've wanted to do since the second we got here.

I delve a couple of fingers inside her, stroking her clit with the ball of my thumb. It has the effect of making her mewl like a goddamn kitten.

"I heard some very interesting things from Quinn," I say, getting down between her legs, hitching her skirt so I can get better access, tearing her silk panties aside with my fucking teeth.

"Quinn likes to exaggerate," she breathes as I plunge a tongue inside her, teasing her slick, wet folds.

"No, I don't think she does," I mutter between licks. She tastes like the most delicate fucking liquor. Her hands, nails now they've grown back, are digging in my scalp, making my dick rigid in my pants. That can wait. I want to eat her up first.

Viola clenches her thighs against me as I push her legs apart so I can devour her deeper. She's greedy for me, panting and shaking, her moans driving me fucking crazy. I'm hard as anything as I bring her to a quick climax. Out of all the ways I get to claim her glorious body, I absolutely love making her come. If I can't get my kicks elsewhere, then I'll fucking need to do this more often. I'll probably turn into a sex addict.

When she finally gives one last shudder, her pussy flooding my mouth with the sweet taste of her, I almost blow my load. She's so fucking tight and wet. I just want to sink myself inside her. Giving her one orgasm isn't enough. I want to fuck her so damn hard, giving her as many as she can handle, taking away all the fucking goddamn anger out of her.

I told her once my gift was fucking…

I meant it.

"He's arriving soon," Viola says, interrupting my devious thoughts. "Lola informed me just now." She means Adrien. Great. "And Edrei?"

Like fucking always, we don't have time.

"Lorcan hasn't got an update from Kat yet." I grab her ass in the palms of my hands, thumb softly stroking her slick hole as I get to my feet. "When are you going to do it?" I'm not sure if I mean anal or killing Adrien. Maybe I mean both.

Viola's eyes are glowing. She's practically boneless in my arms. "If Edrei gets here soon and agrees to my deal with the agency. I want Adrien gone and dealt with tonight."

"Sounds good to me," I say, still teasing her rear. I enjoy making her squirm. "Just tell us what you need us to do."

"I just need your brute strength. I can't move him on my own," she says, eyes fluttering half-closed as I slip right into her ass.

I take the opportunity to seal her mouth with mine, tasting strawberries and fucking champagne as I lap up everything I can. When I pull back, she's looking at me like a cat who got the cream.

"You're making this harder," she sighs, clenching around the knuckle of my thumb inside her, looking up at me with languid eyes.

"No," I say, using my other hand to place her palm over my trousers so that she can feel how solid my cock is. "You are. This is how much I fucking want you right now."

She grabs me through the material with a smirk. "Good to know. Although I already got the gist. You're taking liberties."

"Oh, this?" I pump her asshole a few times. "Just a little pre-wedding present so you don't forget what you love about me."

She gives me an amused look. "That would never happen."

"Good, because I'm going to fuck this first chance I get," I remind her, thrusting my thumb deeper. "And I don't want to have to wear you down all over a fucking again."

"Is that what this is…wearing me down?"

I lean in close, inhaling her vanilla scent, briefly closing my eyes as she sticks her hand down the waistband and runs her nails over my raging cock. "This is all just foreplay, baby. I'll rip you a new one when I'm finished with you." I pump into her a few more times as she rakes her nails over me.

"Promises, promises, Jude. When are you going to deliver? When Adrien gets here, I won't be able to talk to any of you."

I grin at her. "That fucking bastard can't keep me away." I kiss her one last time. "Now, stick your hand in my pocket?"

She frowns but does as I say, pulling out a black box with a bow. "What the fuck?" She looks up in askance.

I take my hand from between her legs because I draw the line at that, I think, and take the box from her and open it to reveal the family fucking heirloom—a perfect yellow diamond ring. Then I get down on one knee, which is annoying because I just came from there. Her eyes glitter like dark fucking stars in the low light of the bathroom as it dawns on her what I'm about to do.

"What the fuck are you doing?" she asks in that emotionless way of hers.

Fuck it. You only live once. "Miss Viola Hawkes, will you do me the fucking honor of being my wife?"

She stares at me like I've lost my mind.

I probably fucking have.

TWENTY-SEVEN

VIOLA

JUDE, of all fucking people, is one knee in front of me, proposing like it's the answer to everything. It's not. It's so far from what I need right now that I almost want to laugh. Instead, I just stare at him, speechless.

And with a goddamn diamond ring.

First Dino, and now Jude. I can't marry him. I can't marry anyone. Why the fuck can't any of them understand that. Instead, I just stare at him, open-mouthed. I hate being lost for words. It's like losing. I'm usually quick-witted enough to fill boring gaps in dialogue, but this is more than chit-chat or deep conversation. This is Hell incarnate, and Jude is the damned Devil. The ass play was fine. I let him have that.

But this—I do not fucking need this right now.

My gut reaction is to punch him, but that would be extreme even for me.

"Viola, you're fucking killing me here," he says, a dark look crossing his face.

I shake my head. "I can't be anyone's wife."

His brow creases up. "You've agreed to fucking marry Dino."

"For a deal with Adrien," I exclaim. "It's not a real union. I'm not even going to marry him. I told you. It's all fake."

"I get that, but after this is all over…." He frowns, not getting it. "You're really just going to walk away?"

I need air, but Jude is trapping me in the bathroom by kneeling in front of me. I'd have to squeeze around or climb over him to get away from him. *Is that possible?* No, I wouldn't get very far. He'd have to grab me or stand in front of the door. I'm not going anywhere. I drag in a breath as my eyes scan the room once more and then settle on the ring still in Jude's outstretched hands. Punching him in the guts is looking more and more appealing.

"I get it," he says, breaking my train of how-to-escape thoughts, eyes becoming shuttered and dark. "You want it to be Lorcan." He takes the box, closes it, and shoves the offending thing in his inner jacket pocket.

You've got to be fucking joking me.

I glare at him. "I do not want it to be Lorcan."

"Yes, you do. All the fucking bitches love him more." He gets to his feet, glaring back like I've skinned his pet cat to make a fur coat.

"You're an idiot," I say for want of a better insult. Any minute Adrien is going to arrive, and Jude is acting like the love-sick jealous boyfriend I never knew him to be. Suddenly my head pounds. I really don't get men. Minor things seem to trigger them.

"And I thought you cared, but maybe I was fucking wrong about that," he sneers at me. When I don't say anything back, he scowls. "Fuck this. I'm going to get a drink." He leaves me in the bathroom, not looking back as he storms out.

I don't chase after him.

I don't have the energy.

After he's gone, I splash cold water on my face and re-apply my makeup. I can't focus on anything but Adrien—not the boys acting like jealous assholes, not Dante still not answering my messages, and definitely not the decision I've made to leave after this is all over.

Like she said she would, Quinn came good with the IDs I asked her for. She slipped them into my hand when we were trying on the dresses in the morning. It's everything I need for me and Rebecca to disappear completely.

It's what I've always done to survive, to keep the monster from being caged. After Adrien is dead, even if no one is chasing me and Dante does let me go...my inner demon will always lurk beneath this innocent facade. One mistake is all it will take to send me down that dark hole of no return. Everyone and everything I touch turns to ash. Jude was sent to juvie, Lorcan was injured in a car crash, and Dino was ripped open by my own hands. And Dante will never stop hunting me.

I can't go through that again.

I won't.

I refuse to.

Before I head back to the rehearsal drinks, I check my phone for messages from Dante. *Nothing.* I sent him one earlier asking for a truce, which he's ignored. I need to kill Adrien tonight, but once I do, I open the game up to whatever Dante has planned for me. Savino may be my only answer...If he ever turns up.

Enough of this bullshit.

I scroll through my phone, looking for Polina's number. It's the one contact I have for the agency. After several rings, past the point where I think they might not care to talk to me, it connects.

"Viola, how's life?" It's Iskar.

"Put me through to him."

"Are you making demands? After what you did to my sweet Polly?"

"She was working for Adrien, not your boss," I say, taking a punt.

"My boss?"

"Savino," I hiss at him.

"You think the Barbaric Don owns this agency?" His voice is dripping in amusement.

"I know he does. Polina tried to have his son killed," I say, taking another stab. "She was using the agency for her own personal gain—taking out enemies for my father. That's why no one has come after me. I tidied up a loose end for you that would have started a war between the Camorra mafia and my father had you gotten rid of her personally. Savino owes me. Now put me through to him."

"I see. You've done your homework. And Savino is grateful, but he owes nothing to no one. Now, unless you have a job to bid for, I suggest you fuck off."

He hangs up just as my phone vibrates.

I glance down to see a message from Lorcan asking if I'm okay. No doubt, he's seen Jude come blazing back from our check-in. I scowl when I see it. I don't have time to babysit the boys tonight. Jude will just have to get over himself.

Breathe, Viola, breathe.

A few minutes later, my phone goes off again. This time it's Dino.

He's here.

Adrien.

Time to play happy families.

Adrien is talking to Sal and one of Dino's uncles when I return to the party. My father doesn't even acknowledge my entrance. He thinks that little of me. I'm used to being disregarded. I've had to endure his dismissal my entire life. And now, I use it to my advantage.

No matter how hard I push back against him, no matter how much I try to hurt him…my father doesn't think I'm a threat.

It's hilarious, but also perfect for what I have planned. When Dino gives me the signal, I will ask to speak to him alone. I have a hot shot in my pocket with his name on it and a draught of sedative ready to go in the beer his men are drinking. I've thought of a thousand ways to kill him, and the only way that makes sense is to end him on my killing table. It's a shame the cabin doesn't exist anymore. It would have been the perfect ending.

I walk to where Dino is, taking a drink off a nearby tray. Dino stiffly puts his arm around me, but that's to be expected. He's meant to hate me, according to what he told his family. His act is for them, not me. After we take my father somewhere we can be alone; Lorcan and Jude will help with that since I'm not strong enough to carry him. Dino will stay and keep his family occupied. I don't know what that entails, and I didn't ask. But his role is the most important. I glance into his eyes and see darkness lurking behind his perfect baby blues I never thought I would.

I did that.

He once told me he was the best partner I could want... willing to do what it takes. Out of all of them, Dino is the most broken. And that makes him similar to me in ways I can't explain.

I just had to almost kill him to get him there.

I should be glad of that.

But I'm not.

There's still a rawness inside me that mourns the boy who believed in love. Maybe he's still in there. Perhaps he can be saved.

But not by me. I need to let him go.

Quinn was wrong. It's not Dante who corrupts everything he touches.

It's me.

Drinks in the parlor turn into a sit-down dinner in the main hall. The staff has entwined fresh flowers all over the interior beams, making the house smell floral and fragrant for once. I never notice how the manor looks because my whole life has been spent hating it. But for once, it looks nice.

I check my phone for the hundredth time—still nothing from Dante, or Lorcan about when his father is supposed to be showing up.

"Edrei's fucking us over, isn't he?" Dino leans in to ask under his breath.

"We don't need him," I say dismissively. But the buzz under my skin tells a different story. I'm practically shaking.

Dino's hand settles on my knee under the table. "It's not the end of the world if we get married. We can still fuck shit up together."

Trapped. Trapped. Trapped.

I give him a loose smile, trying not to fucking bolt out of my seat. It's just a ceremony. It doesn't mean anything. And yet, I know it means fucking everything. *Why does everyone want to marry me all of a sudden?* My father married Rebecca and then locked her away. Even though I know, it's a formality. It's also a declaration. *I'll be owned. Someone will own me.*

This is why I need to disappear once this is over.

Being married is the final nail in the coffin.

"Viola," Dino calls my name softly, like a warning. I glance down to see my hand on his leg, digging my nails in. I purposely didn't wear my dagger because Adrien wouldn't allow it, and instantly I'm regretting it. I feel naked without it. I wish I'd taken Jude's knuckle duster when he offered me one earlier because at least that would be something to hold on to.

"Don't let your fear control you," Dino says, bringing me back to reality.

"I have no fear," I say offhandedly.

"You're such a fucking liar," he says with a harsh chuckle. "You're petrified." His bright blue eyes, the color of a summer sky, look deeply into mine as he squeezes my hand under the table. "Divorce is an option. I'm never going to keep you or trap you. You can go where you like and do what you want. You'll always be free with me, or be without me, if that's what you want."

I frown at him. "When did you turn into an adult?"

"When you didn't give up on me," he says, rubbing my thigh in a soothing way like one would with a feral cat.

My phone vibrates, making me jump. Fuck, I'm skittish tonight. Jumping at shadows all over the damn place. I reach to where it's strapped to my thigh and slip it into my palm. I don't have a purse or pockets, so the dagger holster has become helpful in other ways. It's a message from Lorcan telling me to get my shit together. I scowl his way, knowing he's right. I'm not composed enough.

I'm drawing attention.

But not as much as the two uninvited guests who have just walked in....

—Dante, in a striking blue suit that brings out the sky color eyes, hair razored short at the sides, and a girl with long honey blonde locks, pink lips, and striking cat-like eyes on his arm.

I can't help but stare.

What the actual fuck.

Dante nods at Adrien, who is sitting at the head of the table, and then scans the room until his twinkling eyes settle on me. The ends of his mouth curl up with a smirk as he walks over with languid grace to where we're seated.

"He loves to make an entrance, doesn't he?" Dino snaps next to me as Dante approaches with his date, all eyes in the room fixed on the stunning couple.

The girl Dante has brought with him nothing to write home about, but it's not lost on me that she's blonde too, whereas I'm hard and angular, she's soft and sweet.

Like a fattened calf.

"V," Dante says, cold blue eyes not leaving mine, even when his date reaches forward to hug me in my seat as though she knows me and we're old friends.

We're not.

"This is Lana," Dante adds.

"You must be V! I've heard so much about you," Lana says, her voice shrill in my ear as she envelopes me in a cloud of heady perfume. I resist the urge to stab her with the eating utensil that I still have clutched in my hand, and when she finally releases me, I don't give her another thought.

I only have eyes for Dante.

And he only has eyes for me.

"Lana Langfield? You're playing at our wedding tomorrow, right?" I hear Dino say, playing his role in this strange fucking game we all seem to be wrapped up in as she switches her attention to him, leaving the Devil for me to take on.

"How is your heart," I ask Dante casually, taking a sip of my drink from the table and glancing up at him.

He grins down at me, the smile not quite reaching his eyes. "How is the money I gave you? Did you get to put it to good use?"

A dark thrill of adrenaline surges through me. He knows about my plan to leave. Of course, he fucking does. Dante taught me everything—how to kill, how to disappear.

It's why I can never find him, and he'll always find me.

I dart a glance to Lorcan, who is watching us from the other side of the table, drinking his whiskey while sandwiched between Sorrow and an empty seat. Sorrow has a rabbit in headlights look on her face, angled toward Lorcan, her deep blue orbs fixated on Dante. I guess he does have that effect on people. Saskia, next to Sorrow, has Lola trapped in deep discussion and hasn't seen him come in. Quinn, further down, hasn't noticed either, or she's pretending not to. She's doing the role I asked of her, flirting with Sal, hand on his arm, staring intently into his eyes. And next to me, Dino asks Lana about her next album tour.

Everyone is doing their job.

Except me.

And Jude. The fucker is missing, no doubt sulking, but I can't do anything about that now. I need to fix this fuck up. Dante isn't meant to be here, but that doesn't mean I can't use him.

In Edrei's place.

Unless Edrei sent him to deal with me instead?

I gaze back at my mentor, watching me like a cat studying the plumpest mouse. It's a look that burns right through to my monster, waking it up from its slumber deep inside me. "Let's go to the terrace." I don't wait for him to respond. I get out of my seat, amid the staff bringing out the next course, and walk toward the external doors.

Adrien's eyes are on Dante and me the whole fucking time.

Outside, dusk has swept over the estate, softening the backdrop. I walk a bit toward the pavilion where hanging plants have taken over, out of view of the main dining room. I have no idea if Dante is following me until I smell his scent—chemicals, death, and smoke. His arm slides around my waist, dragging me back to him.

"You disappoint me. I taught you better than this," he says softly in my ear. "You should never turn your back on your enemy."

I lean into him, reaching up, looping my hand around the back of his neck as I turn my face up toward his. Our lips barely touch, and his breath…warm on my skin as I inhale deeply.

"So, you admit it. You are my enemy?" I grate at him.

"It depends," he says as the fingers of his other hand circle around my neck.

"On what?"

"On you," he muses. "Iskar thinks you've outlived your usefulness."

"Fuck, Iskar." I sneer. "The pussy hides behind a fucking corporate logo. I much prefer how you manage things. You get deep and personal with your agents."

He stills, and then I hear him snort. "Clever girl. I wondered when you'd work it out."

"You run the agency," I say to him, reaffirming what I already suspected the day I tortured Polina. She had no idea Dante was the one running the show. Neither did I until Quinn brought me the data proving Savino had another son. One older and placed with someone who Savino wanted to control. "For Savino, your father," I add.

Dante just chuckles. "Good for you," he says, tightening his hand around my throat. He sounds amused.

I'm not.

"You had me jumping through hoops to get this information when you could have just told me," I hiss.

"Now, why would I do that. It was much more fun to send you on Polina's wild goose chase missions."

"She didn't know you were her boss?"

"She suspected."

"And Adrien doesn't know?"

"He thinks the agency defers to him. It doesn't."

I slit my eyes. "Your real father came for you, didn't he?"

At that moment, the door to the interior opens, flooding the garden with music and chatter. We're hidden among the honey-suckle, but once glance over tells me Sal is outside smoking and on his phone.

"I'll tell you everything but not here," Dante says, releasing me from his grip enough to herd me deeper into the garden by my wrist. His grip is iron, and his pace is quick. But I keep up in my dress and heels. The rain has fallen recently, so the scent of the honeysuckle is heavy in the air as he steers me to a covered wooden seating area.

It's where we used to sit as kids and throw stones into the duck pond, making the fish dart every which way. There are no fish now.

Maybe they all died?

"Sit," he orders, but I just stand there, glaring at him as the rain starts to fall again. He sighs after a solid minute of me not sitting. Only then does he release his hold on me. He doesn't sit either. He stands in front of the wooden seating area where he's brought me, blocking my escape. If I don't mind swimming, only the duck pond has a clear exit.

"No more lies or games," I say, staring up at him. "Who are you?"

The light rain falls on him, coating him with a fine mist. It makes his blue eyes all the more clear and emotionless. "I couldn't tell you before," he says.

"But you can now?"

He shrugs. "Savino isn't open to sharing his private life with others."

"When did you find out that he was your birth father?"

He gives me a blank look. "The first time you ran away."

I nod at him. My mother and I first escaped when I was ten.

"I was already working for the agency then. I thought it was just another job for your father. When I got back after seeing him, you were gone."

And we would have stayed gone had Rebecca not broken down. She couldn't handle being on her own. Adrien had groomed her from the second they met to be dependent on him. She couldn't look after herself. She couldn't look after me. After she was committed, that was when Adrien found us.

"But you stayed," I say.

"I stayed for you. I knew Adrien was hunting you. You were supposed to have gotten out. I had to make sure you were able to survive."

I shrug. "Is that why you did eventually leave? Because you were sure?" Dante left pretty much as soon as he turned fifteen. Adrien didn't go after him. He just let him go. Now, I wonder if Savino had something to do with it.

"I had to. But I came back for you, didn't I?"

He did…when I turned the same age, fifteen. My father was the one who broke me, but Dante was the one who molded me. And then, he was the one who helped Rebecca escape the right way the second time. If it weren't for him, I would never have become what I am today.

But it wasn't me he did that for.

"Does Adrien know about Savino?"

Dante nods. "He's always known."

I nod at him as though all makes sense. Adrien's obsession with gathering power, using what pawns he finds. He sees Dante as just another pawn, like me. But he didn't train me for Adrien like he wanted me to think. No. Jude figured it out.

He did it for the mother he always wanted but never had....

"And your mother," I say, taking the necklace out from under the collar of my dress and playing with the locket like it's something I do every day. I don't. I just put it on this morning. But now I'm here waiting with bated breath, testing my theory to see if he knows who his mother is...

His blue orbs flare to life, tracking the necklace in my hand.

So he does recognize the locket. *Interesting.* And here I thought it was the picture of us as kids together looking like a family that he coveted the first time he took it from my hands. *A sick, twisted family, but there you go.*

And then... "I have no mother." He shrugs, eyes dead and empty again. "She's dead. She died in a suspicious house fire. You know this; you're the one who found the file."

Liar.

The file in my father's study was a decoy. The photograph of the woman on the other side of the locket says it all. She even looks like him. After I saw his birthdate next to Ophelia's name, I knew it was her in the picture with her blue eyes and blonde hair. The image is old and faded, so it's hard to tell, but it has to be her. If he doesn't know his mother, why would there be a picture of her inside this necklace?

And more importantly....

Why would Adrien have had it?

It's all in Dante's reaction to it. I just have to figure it out. I need to wait for the right time to bring it up. I also need to think of the best way to use the information.

So I say nothing, staring into his eyes as the drizzle sticks his new shorter haircut to his forehead. I know my hair is plastered to my face, just as my dress is stuck to every curve of my body.

As usual, Dante hasn't fucking noticed.

Because he's not motivated by lust at all.

What drives you, Dante, if it's not your dick or wallet. What the hell do you want?

"If you're not working for my father, what do you want?" I say, letting the necklace fall back against my shirt. Sometimes it's best just to ask outright.

He snorts, water flicking off him as he shakes his head. "I think that's obvious."

"No, it's not. All I can think is that this is entertainment for you."

The smile teases the corner of his lips. "V, I want what everyone else wants."

"And what's that?"

His eyes narrow, but he looks right at me, empty blue eyes pulling me into their depths like they always do. "I want you." He looks me up and down, wet curves and all. "And your name."

I blink at him. "My name? You said that before but I don't get it."

"I'll never be a Savino or a Harper Black. My father won't allow it unless…."

And there it is.

Dante wants to fucking marry me too.

TWENTY-EIGHT

VIOLA

I'M STILL REELING after leaving the pavilion.

Dante wants to marry me...since when? And why now? I already have a wedding tomorrow that was planned at supersonic speed without my actual consent or involvement. I once wanted a leafy London flat, proper running shoes with reflective strips, basil in a window box, and movies to watch with friends on weekends. And now I have one wedding and two proposals to contend with.

I still haven't gotten over Jude's declaration of undying love in the bathroom earlier.

Dino looks up at me when I return to the dinner table. Soaked through like me, Dante is already seated next to his date, arm around her, staring into her eyes like everything to him. *Is that how he looks when he's with me? Is it all an act?* I don't care if it is. If Dante is using me, then I'm using him too.

Dino sees me shivering and takes off his jacket and drapes it over my shoulders as I slip into my seat next to him. It's warm and smells of his cologne. I'm not cold. I'm burning up inside after Dante's offer.

"You're soaking wet," Dino murmurs, slipping a warm hand over the icy skin of my leg.

"It's raining outside," is all I say.

"Are we all good?"

I nod. "We made a deal," I say as I try to focus on my plate. Everyone is already eating around me.

"What kind of deal?"

"One that benefits us all." I will tell them about Dante running the agency, but not about his offer to marry me. I don't need that in the mix. One proposal is bad enough. The last thing I need is the boys getting jealous.

Because...

I agreed to marry Dante in return for one thing only—his agency to take out the entirety of the child prostitution network tonight. He has the means and the reach that I don't have. What would take me years, Dante could do in a matter of hours. I promised the boys that I would end this for them, and this is the only way to do it before I walk off into the sunset. And then, only then, will I hand over my father's business and officially give all the power to the blond, blue-eyed fucking Devil.

Still, marriage means nothing. Giving my name to Dante is just a formality. He won't be my husband in any way but on paper.

I *should* tell the boys. Lorcan would understand. But as soon as I think about how to say the words, they stick in my throat. I can't say it to Dino while he's sitting next to me with his baby blues fixed worriedly on me.

And what the fuck do I say to Jude after telling him I won't marry anyone.

There's a pause while Dino watches me eating or trying to. The slab of meat on my plate is cold now, so it's like trying to carve up leather. "How do you know you can trust him this time?"

"Because I have something he wants," I snap at him.

Me.

I focus on moving the blade back and forth, letting all the thoughts float inside my head so I can examine them individually. Dante...he *was* my blade. It's clear now that Dante has been playing my family just as much as my father has been playing him.

And all for what?

The Harper Black name.

Unless Savino wants both?

Lorcan.

A shiver runs down my spine as it hits me. Something Sorrow said to me earlier when she was snooping around the bridal guest wing...*jumping at shadows.* I stop cutting and look up. Lorcan is not at his seat anymore, and neither is Sorrow.

"Where the fuck did they go?" I hear myself say.

"Who?" Dino asks.

"Lorcan and Sorrow?" I croak.

Dino frowns at me. "Sorrow spilled her drink on him. Lorcan went to clean up. Why?"

"Fuck, she's the recruit. Lorcan knows where Byron is," I hiss at Dino, tossing my napkin onto the table.

Dino stiffens beside me. "What?"

But I'm out of my chair, shrugging his jacket off onto him, and walking quickly toward the double doors that lead to the main hallway. Dino is right behind me. The commotion we've caused has Dino's family watching, along with Adrien. But I don't fucking care.

If Sorrow has hurt Lorcan...

"Come in, don't fucking knock," Lorcan drawls as Dino, and I barge into his room. He's buttoning up a clean shirt and putting on a tie when we enter. Sorrow is nowhere to be seen.

"Where's Sorrow?" I ask, stalking into the bathroom to check.

"I've no idea. She fucked off the second she threw her drink on me."

Jude. I take out my phone and call him. It goes straight to voicemail.

I glare at Dino. "Call your fucking cousin."

He stares at me for a split second and then grimaces as he takes out his phone, dialing and pressing it to his ear. I fill Lorcan in on my suspicions while we wait. If she's not with Lorcan, then she's with Jude.

"Sor, where the fuck are you?" Dino snarls down the line. He pauses. "Do not. I repeat. Do not do fucking move until we get there." He hangs up and looks at me. "She's with Jude out the front of the house."

Sorrow has indeed got Jude. He's hanging over the bush in the central courtyard, emptying his guts. The outdoor covered seating area looks like a frat party hit it—empty bottles of beer litter every surface and a shit load of drugs on the table. Lorcan swears and goes over to help Jude get cleaned up.

"What the fuck happened?" Dino rounds on Sorrow.

"He said he wanted to get wasted," she hisses at him.

He sneers at her. "So you gave him Sal's stash of drugs. Are you out of your mind?"

I approach her from behind so she doesn't see me until it's too late, and then I twist her arm and shove her forward, quickly pinning her over the table.

Dino grimaces but doesn't interfere as I keep her there, calmy and securely, while she thrashes and seethes at me. I don't have my knife, but I don't need one. Sorrow isn't very well trained. She's so damn green. I'm surprised the agency let her out into the field. I trained for years before they took me on. They must be desperate.

Dante must be desperate.

"Now, tell me," I say, keeping my voice level. "Are you working for my father or Dante?"

"Fuck you," she grits out.

I yank her head back by her hair. "Do not try me. I'm not in the mood. Now I'll ask again, and you will answer. Though, if you lie to me, I will know, and then I will cut your vocal cords out so you can't lie to me again, got it?"

Breathing hard, she stills at that and then nods.

"Who are you working for?"

"Sal said the order came from some Italian mob guy."

Savino.

"I wasn't going to hurt him."

"Who?" I snap.

"The kid in the wheelchair. As soon as I saw his picture, I couldn't go through with it," she pants."

"Liar," I say softly. "You came out here to ply Jude with drugs to get information out of him." I glance at Dino. "Byron wasn't put in St Michael's to get him out of the way. He was put there for his protection," I say.

"You fucking bitch," scowls Dino from behind as the rage rips through me too. I twist her arm harder, making her cry out. She's petite like me. I could very easily break her arm.

"V, that's enough." It's Lorcan speaking, coming back to the seating area, talking me down.

"Viola, she's not worth it," Jude grits out, slurring his words as he leans against a low wall.

The buzzing is loud in my ears. It's been so long. They don't understand. I want to hurt her. I want this girl to feel what I feel right now...*absolute, suffocating darkness.*

A hand on my shoulder makes me tense up. "Let me deal with her," he says. I glance to my right and into his blue eyes. The same darkness I have lurks behind them. His dimple is twitching as his jaw clenches. "Trust me," Dino says. "I'll take care of this."

So I don't have to.

I let her go, and she falls into Dino's arms.

Lorcan and Jude are the ones who take me back to my room. I let them undress me to my underwear and bundle me into bed, treating me like glass. I'm shaking all over because I almost lost it again. Even though I didn't, the adrenaline is still shooting down my fucking veins, making every sense heightened and me painfully aware of everything.

I'm done.

I'm so fucking done.

It's dark when Dino joins us. Jude is holding me from behind, hand tucked between my legs, while Lorcan is where he usually is —the little spoon, his back to me, and my arms around his waist. I've no idea where Dino will fit until he eases in next to Lorcan, who shifts onto his back so I can put my head on his chest.

I'm drifting off to the sound of Lorcan's heartbeat in my ear and Jude snoring at the nape of my neck when Lorcan murmurs at Dino, "Touch me in my fucking sleep, Sin, and I'll castrate you."

"You can always come over this side and touch me if you get lonely," Jude says in a sleepy voice.

"Fuck off the both of you. I'm only letting you have her tonight because tomorrow she's all mine," Dino spouts.

"You know I have three holes, don't you?" I add. No one moves, no one says anything else. "Night, boys," I add, my lips curving up as I close my eyes because I know it will drive them crazy.

And because....

The buzzing has finally stopped.

"No, not fucking happening," Jude hisses, his lips searing the back of my neck as he rids me of my panties, hauling them off me. They're soaked through anyway. "You don't joke about that."

"I'm tired," I say with a sigh, wriggling away from him.

But Lorcan turns to me and runs a hand where the heat has pooled between my legs, where I'm dripping with desire for them. "You fucking tease," he whispers. "Don't lie. You fucking want it. You're already wet for us."

"Don't I get a say on who I get fucked by before my wedding?" I say, my mouth still curved into a dark smile.

"No, sweetheart. You don't," he smirks. I'm not wearing a bra, so he latches on to my breast, teasing his nipple with his tongue and teeth. As Lorcan's mouth pulls pleasure up from my core, tormenting me with slow lazy circles over each bud, I feel Jude kneading my ass.

The moans come without me meaning to.

"That's it, baby, submit to us," Jude says, voice tight with need as he presses his cock against me.

"Alright, my turn," Dino says. "I'm not being left out of this one. It's my fucking wedding tomorrow too."

"Make her come, Sin," Jude growls, biting my ear.

Cold air shivers over me as the sheets are pulled away, and I'm pushed onto my back. I open my eyes to see Dino standing over me, eyes dark, watching Lorcan and Jude tease the fuck out of me. Then he crouches down between my legs. Jude takes one thigh, fingers digging in, and Lorcan grips the other. They hold me open as Dino's mouth claims my soaking wet pussy,

Caught between the three of them, unable to escape, I can do nothing but lie there and take it. Every lick has me gripping the sheets, and every suck has me growling at them. Jude's teeth sink into the soft bend of my neck. Lorcan's tongue flicks across my bare breasts. Having them all at once, pleasuring me, stroking every part of me, is something I never expected or ever want to lose. It sends me spiraling over the edge, and I come hard, shaking, letting the darkness consume me.

I need to take back control.

"Fuck me," I grit out, panting, straining against their hands, pinning me down. I manage to slip a leg free and then an arm.

I reach for Jude first, pulling his mouth on mine. He tastes of toothpaste and the barest hints of the alcohol he drank earlier, but I don't care. This is Jude. His scent, his breath, is everything and more. I never want to not have him again. I bite down, tasting blood. He grunts as his tongue plunges into my mouth, lapping hard and hot, just as Dino's tongue eats the release between my legs and Lorcan's hands and kisses sweep down my entire body, lighting every nerve on fire.

I claw at Jude's shoulders, desperate for more. And more.

"Those fucking nails," Jude hisses, breaking the kiss to glare at me. He grabs my wrist and hauls it above my head, careful not to knock his splint. "Let's tie her up," he says. "So, we can abuse her holes in peace."

"Pass me her fucking panties," Lorcan says, sitting up, taking my other arm easily. I thrash against them, but Jude chucks my underwear at Lorcan. They flip me over, and one of them grabs both hands together, wrapping the wet lace around and around, tightly behind my back so I can't yank them free.

"You're all fucking dead," I seethe as I lie there, eyes glittering with rage, drinking in their scars and wounds as they look down at me. A possessive light flares behind their eyes as each one takes me in. Jude with his mischievous grin. Lorcan with his arrogant smirk. And Dino with his edible fucking dimple.

"If you're a good girl, we'll let you sleep in the bed with us after," Lorcan says as he lifts me onto my knees so my face isn't stuffed into the bedsheets anymore.

"So dead," I say with an amused scowl.

"You're lucky I brought lube," Jude says, sweeping a tongue over my lips as he kisses me, winking as he gets off the bed, presumably to go and get it.

Lorcan, still smirking with his penetrating green eyes, shucks off his boxers and positions himself off the bed to stand in front of me. It's not until his perfectly straight, beautiful cock is pointing right at me do I understand.

He bends down to kiss me first and then whispers. "Now open that beautiful mouth for my cock, sweetheart." He grips my hair, angling himself, his salty tip teasing my lips. Hungry for him, I open up, and he fills me completely.

"Fuck, that's it, beautiful," Lorcan says, coaxing my mouth up and down his shaft. The scent of him, and the velvet softness, driving me wild.

Dino chuckles, his hand pulling my hips up behind so he can resume his licking between my legs, He runs his tongue over my clit until the friction, and the feel of Lorcan gliding into my mouth has me desperate. I'm so soaked that I swallow him up when he finally eases his cock into me.

"Fuck, you feel so fucking tight," Dino pants, thrusting in deep, causing me to moan around Lorcan's cock, bucking between the two of them.

"I'm not even sure we need lube," Jude snorts when he returns and sees the boys spit roasting me. His eyes darken as he plays with himself, stroking his shaft until he's rigid in his hands. I let my eyes follow every pump, imagining Jude inside me too.

"She's fucking desperate for us. Look at her," Lorcan hisses, caressing my face as he fucks it. I look into his shattered green eyes and let him see I am.

I want every last drop.

"Sin, if you don't fucking move and give me her ass first, I'm going to abuse you instead," Jude says gruffly.

"Fuck, Jude, give me a fucking minute," Dino says, pulling out only to shift under me and drag me down onto his cock that way.

Jude chuckles and moves behind me. I can't see him but feel the cold, invading touch of his lubed fingers at my rear, and then his thumb slips into my hole. He massages. And I let out a moan, thrusting my hips back and then grinding onto Dino, all the while Lorcan slides his cock roughly over my tongue.

Jude leans forward, licking up my neck, stretching me in time to Dino's thrusting to speak in the shell of my ear. "I fucking promised you, babe, that I was going to own this ass."

I feel him then, hot at my hole. "Fuck, you're super tight. There's no way I'm going to last," he grunts. In answer to that, I push back. "Horny little thing," Jude laughs and spanks me hard. The pain and spine-ripping pleasure surge through me as Dino strokes out and Jude shoves in deep.

Then all three are fucking my mouth and pussy and rear, sliding in with deep, powerful strokes, using me, filling me, faster and harder…until I'm falling apart.

The orgasm explodes in ragged waves. I lose myself in the shattering of my release as Lorcan comes next, hitting the back of my throat with a groan. I swallow him down as Dino's hips thrust one last time, and he empties deep inside me.

"I'm going to fill this tight hole, " Jude promises as he shudders, holding me close, his cum spearing hot inside as he does just that.

I can't speak or move when he finally lets me go, except to collapse on top of Dino. I'm a mess from all of them, but I hardly care. There's nothing left inside me anymore. No pain. No hate. Not even desire. They drained me of every fucking thing.

With a sigh, Lorcan slips into bed on one side. Jude falls back on the other. And Dino cradles me in his arms.

"Are you bastards going to fucking untie me now?" I croak out after a few minutes of listening to them do nothing but breathe.

Dino snorts a laugh and kisses my forehead.

Someone tugs at my wrists—Lorcan, lazily trying to undo his handiwork, stroking my limbs to get the feeling back when he does.

Jude….is fucking snoring. Until I hit him. And then he's turning inward to hold me. Sleep comes at once, with my head on Dino's chest and my rear enveloped by Lorcan and his long legs.

And it's fucking dreamless.

TWENTY-NINE

DANTE

V'S WEDDING day is a busy one. I get up early and sit in the old kitchen with my laptop, drinking coffee until she wakes. I know she spent the night with the three of them. They're her shadows now, and I've accepted that they're not going away any time soon.

After she left the room with the Vice kid, I followed at a distance just to make sure she didn't do something she would regret. She didn't. Her boys stopped her, so I left them to it and returned to putting on a show for Adrien.

I never attend his parties. Me being there last night was the show of support he needed to disengage for one night. It gave me time to make good on my deal with V.

Her demand was simple enough, and I have the resources to pull it off. I'm just surprised that she didn't ask me sooner to take out the names on the list for her. But she's been distracted by Adrien and those fucking school boys for months. It was never the right time to guide her to her destiny.

Our destiny.

You see, we were always meant to be together.

Our lives are entwined.

I knew the moment I laid eyes on her.

She just didn't know it until last night, by the old pond, with the rain falling in her eyes. I let her see the truth in mine.

Telling V everything about me was a risk. It needed to be done. She's too clever and efficient not to have worked it all out for herself. I promised her she would know everything one day —I wasn't lying. I can never lie to V. All I can do is keep the truth from her. The truth that would hurt her.

Like the forged birth certificate and newspaper clippings, she found in her father's study...

I almost gave it away when she pulled the necklace out of her dress. But from her face, I could tell she didn't have all the facts. She was posturing, trying to get me to slip up.

I take the necklace with the pendant out of my pocket and look at it. I took it from around her neck last night when we were by the pavilion when she wasn't looking. I should burn it.

Just like I should have burned the file.

Instead, I slip it back into my pocket and work through the list V sent me the night before. Everyone on the list is now dead —one hundred and sixty-three, not including the victims or any of Savino's men. I can only use the agency so much without Adrien getting alerted. Yes, it's my agency, but for the role that I'm playing here...Adrien is the one who calls the shots. I've worked too long and hard to let him think otherwise and throw it away.

After I've confirmed the last kill, I finish my coffee and head to where the girls are getting ready on the west side of the house. Several rooms have been set aside for the bride and her party to prepare. I don't knock or hesitate. I just walk in.

Perfection doesn't begin to cut it.

My V is standing in front of the floor-to-ceiling windows on a stool, dressed all in white. One of the girls is fussing with the skirts, but V isn't in the room. She's staring off into the view, her eyes guarded and her mouth set in a grim line. I see her like this only when she's got her back up against it. I like seeing her struggle to survive.

It turns me the fuck on.

Suddenly, she jerks her head my way. Her eyes narrow when she sees it's me, and she motions to the girl at her hem to leave.

As soon as we're alone, she glares at me and flashes her thigh where knives upon knives are strapped. "If you're here to fight, I'm armed."

I don't smile at her words, but the corners of my lips twitch. "A deal is a deal," I say.

Her eyes widen. "So, it's done."

"You have to ask?" I cock my head. When she just stares, I add, "One hundred and sixty-three at the last count."

She lifts a brow. "You took that many out in one night? What *are* you? Fucking supernatural?"

"Don't insult me," I warn her, walking right up to her. "Preparation and hard work. Something you skirt around when it suits you. Now, my agency delivered, and I've done my part as I said I would. It's your serve. What's it going to be?"

There's no getting out of this deal, V.

Her eyes blaze, but she nods. Her whole body practically shakes as I pull her to me, tasting her because I can. She yields, briefly surrendering, moaning into my mouth. But it doesn't last very long; as voices resound through the open door, her fist thuds against my chest, where I still have an open wound, trying to push me off her. I don't let her go, not even when the voices get closer.

"I told you, you'd be mine," I say, in her ear, holding her close.

When I finally pull back, releasing her, V's brown eyes peer at me, peppered with hostility. Her lips are red where I kissed her raw. Her hair is mussed from where I threaded my fingers through it and yanked. It'll need to be redone.

Shame. She looks utterly fuckable.

"Don't mind me," Duke's sister cuts in, liquid green eyes

roaming the scene as she takes us in, clipboard propped up, of all things, in her hands. "Actually, do mind me because I'm obviously going to have to do Viola's hair and makeup again." She tosses her head with a sigh when I don't acknowledge her or leave and stands next to the dressing table. "Well?"

V scowls and shoves me away to get down off the stool. She gives me one last glance in the dresser's mirror as I lean against the doorframe to watch her get ready.

Saskia throws me a dark look. "If you're going to stay, pass me that veil."

I have to hand it to Duke's sister; she's no longer acting afraid of me. I do as she asks and take the veil over to her. Saskia starts fussing with it just as Viola crosses her legs and attaches more knives.

I've seen enough. I also know enough. The necklace is burning a hole in my pocket. She should have noticed by now that it's gone.

"The rest is up to you," I remind her as I walk out the door.

Vice is in the parlor with Duke and Marques. They stop talking when I enter. Marques looks like he's been hit by a bus.

"I'm going to the gym," I say to him. "You're coming too."

Then I walk out.

Viola will have her hands full today. The last thing she needs is one of her shadows fucking up. By some miracle, Jude turns up dressed in his shorts, followed by the other two giving me dark glares. They do a few rounds with me before we run it off.

There's potential there; I'll give them that. Duke has the better technique. At the same time, Jude relies on his brute strength too much. And Vice, well, he's entirely out of shape. But he doesn't back down, not even when I push him harder than the other two, physically and mentally.

Vice is seething, holding his side when we're finished. "I need to fucking sit down a minute," he says. I give him a look but say nothing. The wound in my chest is aching. If I can work through the pain, so can these three fucking clowns.

Jude grunts and sits down next to him. "I'm with you. I can't fucking take another step."

Duke, who hasn't spoken one word since he entered the gym, shakes his head at me. "Come on. We need to talk."

"Are we doing this now?" I ask as I dry the sweat off my face.

"Now," he says, turning away and walking to the running machines.

I casually walk over and step onto the one next to him. Only when we're at a good pace does he open his mouth.

"I told you I'd feed you to the fucking ducks if you hurt her," he snaps.

"V can take care of herself," is my answer. "And I haven't hurt her," I say. *Yet.*

Duke grunts a nod. "Not yet, but you're hiding something, and I don't fucking like it."

"We all have secrets," I say, exhaling, wishing I'd taken the scenic route so I could run in peace.

"Like your father? Viola told us," Duke grimaces, between intakes of breath. "You know that fucker, Savino, is my father too, so that makes us goddamn related."

"V talks too much."

Duke sneers. "I want to meet the fucker."

I grit my teeth and say nothing. I was being charitable, making them join me, and now I regret it.

Even more so when Quinn, hair in a tight ponytail and wearing all the gear, joins us and makes a beeline for the running machine next to mine.

"Viola told me, you know," Quinn says as soon as she gets into a rhythm and Duke walks off to take a call and is out of earshot. I have to admire her for getting straight down to business. "About your deal," she pants.

Are they fucking tag-teaming me today or what?

"Are you going to get in the way?" I ask her outright, keeping my voice level.

She gives a harsh laugh. "No, why would I? She's not going to stay put afterward. You know that, right? She always runs. How long have you known her?"

"A lot longer than you."

She rolls her eyes. "Oh my God, it's not a competition. You're just the same as those schoolboys. Infatuated beyond common sense."

"And you're not," I snort.

"Touche," she says with a smirk and then lapses into silence when Duke wanders back drinking water, staring at his phone.

"Why do I feel like this is the fucking storm before the shitshow?" he says to no one in particular.

"Because this is Viola, and she doesn't do calm," Quinn says, stopping her running to look at him, wiping her brow with her arm. "Why, what's the matter?"

"There's been a rampage of killings during the night throughout London." He looks over at the two others seated. "Have you seen this? It's fucking carnage. They think it's fucking gang-related."

Quinn looks at me while Duke carries on, but I've heard enough.

As Jude and Vice walk over, I grab my towel and leave them to it. I have things to do before the ceremony. I'm wasting time. Adrien will have seen the news by now.

Adrien's office is open when I walk into it. Gigi is on the far side of the room dressed in black—my usual signature color. Instead, I'm wearing royal blue. She practically bristles at me when I walk in.

Adrien does too. There's no love lost between us. And the look he gives me straight away is enough to tell me he knows. Adrien isn't stupid.

"When the fuck were you going to tell me? What kind of fucking fool do I look like? My own fucking agency, taking out the damned ring?" he booms.

I'm aware of Gigi pointing her weapon at me.

All this for the sake of Adrien's childhood sweetheart cheating on him.

It makes me sick.

"I gave the order," I admit. "Because it's my agency." I look him in the eyes, daring him to correct me. I earned it. I never asked for anything and got sweet fuck all from him. The agency is all I have.

It's mine.

Just like V.

"Give me one goddamn reason why I shouldn't gun you down where you fucking stand."

"Try it, Edrei," I say, using the name his Croatian-Serbian parents gave him at birth. The one he used to terrorize Italy with before coming to England and reinventing himself. "Just fucking try it."

I promised V I'd let her kill him.

She's going to be the one to pull the trigger, not me.

"If you weren't my fucking flesh and blood…" he grimaces.

I smirk at him. The secret has always been there, festering, hiding. V is not his daughter at all, but I am his son.

What's the best way to stay hidden from your enemies? Become someone else and lie to fucking everyone, including your own family.

"You hate that I am, don't you. That pretty blonde out there isn't even yours, and you'd much rather have her take your name than me because of who her mother is, isn't that right, Edrei Savino," I say, sticking the metaphorical knife right in.

"Never…*never* call me that name again," Adrien says in a dangerous tone. "Or I won't hesitate to put you down, boy."

That was his one rule when he revealed himself to me on my twelfth birthday—never to call him my father or Edrei Savino to his face, and he would give me the agency. I know now that was just a carrot he dangled to get me to do his dirty work for him all these years. I was never going to be his heir. He wanted a girl, especially a pretty one. He wanted someone he could manipulate.

Girls are highly malleable.

They are easily controlled.

Not V, though. You had your hands full when you killed her parents and took their daughter in as your own. In my pocket, I clutch the pendant. I know V planted a listening device inside of it. I had to prise it open to check. I hope she's listening to every single word.

"Just get the fuck out of here. Clean up the mess you made," he grits out.

"Gladly," I say to the man who disowned me at birth just for being born to a Croatian-Serbian woman. I walk out.

My work here is done.

All V has to do now is kill Adrien.

My fucking father....not hers.

THIRTY

VIOLA

I STARE at the windswept trees and the green and yellow rolling hills. I stare at the stagnant pond in the middle of a wild English garden, plagued with reeds and sacred floating lilies.

I stare and listen to the conversation between Dante and Adrien....

And nothing makes sense anymore.

Adrien is not my father.

The buzzing under my skin is back with a vengeance. Did it ever go away? *No, my love, I'm here. I've always been here. Keeping you safe, protecting you from everything....*

As long as you kill for me.

"Are you ready?" I glance over, ripping my gaze from the window. Saskia is standing there, in her bridesmaid dress, skirts in one hand, clipboard in the other, with one of those earpieces over her head. "The guests are waiting." She tilts her head, looking withdrawn. "So are the boys."

The boys.

"V, you know what needs to be done," Dante says in my ear,

speaking directly to the microphone in the necklace. "We have a deal," he reminds me.

You fucker, D. He knew I'd be listening. He knew telling me this would make me pause. That's why he left it so late. He waited until the moment before I was about to get fucking married to reveal everything in my fucking life to be a lie.

This whole thing…is a setup.

A betrayal.

A stab in the heart.

Just like you did to him.

Edrei Savino is Adrien Harper-Black. And he's not my father.

"Viola, are you coming?" Saskia asks me, her face pale as the white flowers adorned in her raven hair.

White.

So much white.

I should have worn red so you couldn't see the blood.

I drag in a breath and nod. "Let's just fucking get this over with." It has to be now. I'm primed for it. Everyone is here and exposed, just waiting to be plucked. They'll all go into hiding when Adrien, my so-called father, dies. Every fucker, whoever had any connection to him. I can't afford to lose the advantage.

I'll have to deal with him first.

Then I'll deal with Dante later.

Ave Maria begins to play the moment I step into the vestibule. Adrien is waiting with his hands folded, one over the other. His dark eyes sweep over me as he offers me his arm.

I stop and look at it, willing my body to take the last step.

But I'm frozen in place.

"Daughter, do not try me today," he grimaces, "I'm not in the mood."

I take his arm, and he grunts approval.

Then he turns to face the front and doesn't look at me again. I'm just a possession that he's selling off for a price.

A broodmare.

The music ramps up, and the doors open to the grand

orangery transformed for the day into a fairytale of white and green against a backdrop of gray brickwork.

Dino is standing at the far end with Lorcan and Jude beside him. They're in full morning suit attire—black morning coat, dark gray striped trousers, light blue double-breasted waistcoat, green and white flowers pinned to their lapels. Their faces are grim, like we're at a funeral, not a wedding. But all three are waiting to catch me. That much is clear.

If I fall, and I will as soon as I let the monster out…

They will catch me.

On the other side of the boys, Quinn and Saskia are standing, waiting, in soft, vintage green dresses with green and white flowers in their hair, with worried looks. Saskia looks like she's about to fucking cry. I don't know why. I'm not even getting married today.

As the guests on both sides get to their feet, eyes fixed on me, I finally force myself to walk down the aisle. And it dawns on me, like the bud of a bloom unfurling for the first time, that the man walking next to me—my tormentor, the monster who haunts my dreams, the demon who took me from my life and made me the way I am—is not my father.

He's nothing but a pathetic, weak old man…

Who stole me from my parents.

Rage, fresh and savage, suddenly chokes me up from the inside.

He's nothing like me. He didn't make me. He doesn't even own me. Not now, or ever again. He deserves to die.

Adrenaline surges as the wedding march begins.

"Breathe, V, breathe," Dante says in my ear. "You've got this."

My gaze sweeps the room to find D, but he's not there. He's in my ear, though, talking me through the kill like it's my first time. He's with me the entire time.

I almost snort at that. It's not my first fucking rodeo.

But it will be my last.

As we get to the end, I give one last look at the boys and nod at them. There are no guns here. Adrien's men made sure that everyone in the room left their weapons outside of it.

No one is getting in or out.

I was meant to drug him to fake a heart attack and then drag him off somewhere to kill him without an audience. But I can't be fucked with that.

I want him dead now.

"Kill him. I've got you," Dante says in a smooth whiskey voice right inside my head.

At least, I think it's Dante. It could also be my darkness.

I lift the bouquet I'm holding that contains a dagger in the middle of it, and with a smile, I yank the old man to me and ram it to the hilt into his fucking heart. I had plenty of training that day with Dante, so I didn't hit a rib. It slides through like fucking butter.

I cock my head at him and sneer. "That's for my parents."

Adrien's eyes widen as blood fills his mouth, coating his lips in bright, glorious red.

And then…amidst the chaos…

I relish the light leaving his eyes.

THIRTY-ONE

LORCAN

FUCKING carnage reigns after Viola stabs Adrien.

As she turns and starts slashing and stabbing Adrien's guys, one by one, a devious look on her face, everyone runs fucking screaming in the opposite direction. At the same time, the doors burst open, and Dante enters, calmly walking through, taking several of them out with a swift bullet to the head.

When he gets closer to us, he indicates to Dino. A dark look flashes across his face. "Tell your fucking family to back off, or we'll have a war on our hands. They're firing at my men outside."

"Fucking Sal," Dino spits and goes off to sort him out.

Jude chuckles, slipping metal spikes over the fist of his good hand. "Looks like we're fucking doing this," he says, launching himself at the first guy to look at Viola funny.

Saskia is just fucking standing there, blood spraying over her in an arc. So I grab her and drag her out of the way, shoving her at Quinn. "Get her away from here," I snap. Quinn shouts something back to me, but I'm too busy seeing it in slow fucking motion...

Gigi, aiming her fucking gun at Viola.

Dante shouts my name.

I have seconds to react, snatching the gun he chucks at me out of the air, and shooting the bitch in the chest.

Dante nods at me. "Block the exit," he orders, disappearing into the fray.

You've got to be fucking kidding me?

I shoot a look at Viola to make sure she's okay. Of course, she fucking is...and then haul my sister and a grim-faced Quinn to where people are piling up, past Adrien's men dead on the floor. As I shove them both through the doors, I turn back to the chaos running rampant through the room.

Dino, gun in hand, is back shooting down anyone who tries to get close to Viola as she storms through the wedding with her blades. Jude is fucking Jude, hitting anything that moves and loving it. I've no idea how this became the fucking plan. It was supposed to be a fake fucking heart attack. But now there's blood and death everywhere I look. Everything is fucked.

But Viola....

She's a vision—all in white and covered in blood.

An absolute fucking demoness.

God, I fucking love her.

THIRTY-TWO

VIOLA

ADRIEN and his men are dead in a matter of minutes. Dino's family, not wanting to start a war with Ed Savino's son, leave as soon as everything goes to the dogs. And then Dante and his agency take care of the rest, even the cleanup.

It's a family matter, after all.

There's blood all over me and my wedding dress when I finally get to my room. My body feels light and my mind blissfully empty as I strip out of the sticky, wet lace. I hate getting blood on my clothes, but I don't mind today at all.

The dress was hideous.

I crank the shower down to freezing and immerse myself in the cascade of icy water. My senses are heightened as I lather up, enjoying how the suds feel against my skin. For the first time in a long time, nothing is tethering me to this earth.

I'm fucking free.

A knock at the door draws me back to reality.

I don't rush to answer it. I take my time, savoring the last remnants of rapture that comes with a kill. Even if it wasn't exactly what I wanted—the isolation, the loss of control, and the need to destroy are gone.

For now.

Ths knock is more insistent this time. "Come in," I shout, sighing as I step out from under the shower, wrapping a towel around myself.

Dante is in the bedroom, waiting when I come back through. He stands there, stock still, hands in pockets, cold eyes roaming over my body as I head to my closet. There's the briefest flare of heat in his icy blue orbs as I drop the towel and start to get dressed. The window is open, so the cool air teases soft shivers down my spine while his look penetrates through to my bones.

I'll never get over how much I want him.

"You lied to me," I say as I reluctantly drag on a pair of jeans and throw a t-shirt over.

"You needed one last push," he says, tilting his head. "The shock of the truth gave you the edge and focus required to get the job done. You can't deny that."

I shoot him a dark look through the mirror as I tease my wet hair into some sort of loose style. "You used me to kill him."

"He was still the man who took everything from you. Not being related by blood doesn't change that, V. I promised that you would get to end him, and I delivered. You deserved that, at least."

I drag in a lungful of air as I turn to face him, shoving my hands in my pockets to match him. "So Adrien was Edrei, and he was your father?" I say. "That's got to fucking suck."

Dante smirks, the humor reaching his eyes for once. "I've known for a long time. I got over it."

"And Ophelia?" I say, plucking the name out of the recesses of my mind.

"I wasn't lying. She's dead."

"But she was your birth mother?"

He nods, watching me like he's waiting for something else.

What else?

"So what now? We get married, is that the deal you wanted?" I dig at him, glancing away.

He chuckles. "No guy could ever cage you, V. Why would I want to clip your wings?"

I frown, recatching his gaze. "But you said—"

"I never asked to marry you. You assumed that's what I meant. All I want is his name, as his biological son. I prefer to take over his empire without anyone challenging me. You're the only one who can do that."

I look around my room, and nothing about it feels like mine. "Take it. It's all yours. I don't want it."

He shakes his head. "It's *ours*. Adrien didn't leave a will, but you were officially adopted. You have just as much right to his estate as I do."

I shake my head. "I don't want any of it."

"I'm not going to give you any more money, so you should at least keep half."

I grit my teeth at him. "Fine, we'll share. Happy now?"

"Almost." He shifts in his stance. Head cocked. "I'm opening a training arm of the agency at Sacred Heart. I'd like you to head it up."

I stare at him. "Fuck, no."

"It won't be for a while. Think about it. I could use someone like you. And it pays well."

I roll my eyes. "I'll think about it."

"Good. Otherwise, the academy is your home, regardless. If you don't want to stay here, that is."

I don't ever want to come back here, ever again. "Is that all?"

He shifts his attention to a file on my dressing table. It's one I recognize. My bloody prints all over it are a silent beacon reminding me of when I fucked up the most. The file wasn't on the dresser before. Dante must have put it there.

"Just...I came to give you that. It's the file you found on me in your father's office. It's yours. The agency changed the dates and names to protect you. Everything, who you are, who your real parents are, is in there."

I stare at it blankly, but deep down feel as though it might come alive and bite me.

Do I really want to know who I am?

"What about Rebecca? How does she fit into all this?"

"It's all in the file, V," he says, giving me a cryptic look. He doesn't want to tell me—OK. I dart a glance at it. I'll read it in the car.

After a pause, I exhale and look directly at him. "So, us inheriting equally, does this officially mean you're my stepbrother?" I ask.

Dante shrugs, blue orbs searing into my soul. "I'll be whatever you need me to be. I've always been yours," he says casually. "Just as you've always been mine."

I slit my eyes at him. "Have I?"

"You have. Although now, I'm willing to share you," he says matter-of-factly.

My mind flies to indecent places and all the things I might just have to look forward to. "We're going to need a bigger bed," I say. "At the academy."

My ex-mentor doesn't say anything else; he just smiles—a cold empty one, but a smile nonetheless.

I'll consider that means an Alaskan King is on order then.

Lorcan, Dino, and Jude are waiting outside with their cars as I'm finally able to leave. As the three of them look at me, coming down the stone steps, suitcase in hand, I know something is up.

"What?" I ask, coming to a stop in the courtyard.

"We've made a decision," Lorcan says, taking off his shades, so his cut-grass green eyes immediately spear me. He's wearing his usual black t-shirt and ripped jeans, looking undeniably edible. "We're coming with you."

"Are you now?" I say, jutting my hip out as I look at him, all off them.

Dino, wearing his biker jacket and rings all over his fingers, runs a hand through his hair. "You're more important to us than any fucking family obligation."

"You *are* our family, babe." Jude grins, threading a hand around my waist. The hunter-green shirt he's got on brings out the hazel of his eyes as he slips a hand into his pocket and pulls out a lone knuckle duster in a silver-white metal, glinting in the sun.

It's not Jude's usual weapon. This one is small, elegant where the metal tapers, with the barbs much more discreet hidden beneath a line of diamonds set into the curves. He pushes it into my hands. "I think you'll agree this is much better than a fucking ring," he says.

"What is this? Why are you giving me this?" I ask, furrowing my brow, adrenaline spiking through me.

"It's from us all," Lorcan says, shifting his stance, hands in pockets.

Dino gives a sheepish look. "Four rings in one."

"Or a hole for each of us," Jude says with a smirk, kissing me on the forehead.

"For each of you...you mean Dante too?" I ask. I almost choke on my words.

Lorcan's gaze slides to Dino, the hardness behind his eyes about to set. "The fucker chipped in, but he said you'd just throw it in the pond if we gave it to you," he grits out.

Dino's jaw tightens as he looks away. "If you don't like it...."

"What's not to like?" Jude stares right at me.

You've got to be fucking kidding me?

I give them all an incredulous look as they stand there, unable to look me in the eye. Well, except for fucking Jude, who looks like he would rather fight me or anyone right now than have me give the knuckle duster back.

I look at it, running my fingers over the warm white metal. It's pretty but also deadly. Interestingly, my monster likes it.

But…

"You really want me to wear this?" I ask, looking at each of them.

"Or just keep it," Jude says quickly. "Until you're ready."

"Even if you never are," Dino adds, baby blue eyes focused on mine.

Lorcan is looking at me, too, waiting.

"You're all fucking ridiculous," I say, meaning it.

"Yeah, well, you won't fucking marry any of us, will you, sweetheart," Lorcan chides.

"I'll see if it goes with anything I wear," I say, slipping it into my pocket.

There's a collective sigh of relief, and then Jude claims my lips. As Dino brushes his lips to my forehead, Lorcan steps in behind to kiss the back of my neck.

"Well, we chose the fucking wrong time to leave," says a grating voice while someone else clears their throat. It's Saskia and Quinn.

"Don't mind us," Quinn says, grinning at me.

I roll my eyes and extract myself from the three boys. Lorcan takes my case and loads it into his car while Jude and Dino help the girls with theirs.

"So where are we going?" Lorcan asks me once everything is packed away.

I've no idea where we're going now that I don't have to run. "I need food," is all I can say to that.

"Is he coming?" Lorcan asks, glancing up at the house. I presume he means Dante.

I shake my head. "He's got some family business to take care of. He'll find us later." I do not doubt that Dante *will* find us later.

I get into the front seat of the disgusting yellow Mclaren, slipping on a pair of shades. Saskia and Quinn are already in the backseat.

"Are we going back to the academy?" Saskia asks.

"I think we're going to get waffles first," Quinn says in answer, looking up from her phone. "It's tradition."

In the wing mirror, Jude gets into his car behind, and Dino slips his helmet on and straddles his bike. And then Lorcan leads the convoy out of the estate. We're the last cars here. Everyone else has already left, apart from a hideous brown Mustang with one window missing out the back and bullet holes all over the hood.

He should really get a new car now he's a Harper Black.

The dogs are barking, throwing themselves at the wire mesh surrounding the gatehouse when we get to the gate.

"Those poor puppies," Saskia says, pressing her nose to the glass.

"Wait," I say to Lorcan. "Stop."

He frowns at me but pulls over, making the other vehicles behind us do the same. I unclip my belt just as the gull-wing doors open. At the side of the gatehouse is a pen full of my father's hunting dogs. A couple of the dogs are barking, and the rest are just watching me.

"We're taking them with us, right?" Quinn asks, suddenly next to me.

"What am I going to do with five dogs?"

Quinn raises a brow. "What are you going to do with four men?"

She's got me there.

It takes several minutes to load the dogs into Jude's car, much to his annoyance.

"They're going to fucking destroy my car," he moans after the last one is tethered to the front seat.

"It's a heap of trash anyway," Dino snorts, ruffling the ear of one of the dogs before closing the passenger side door.

"You're a heap of trash," Jude bitches back, heading to the

driver's side and getting in. Through the windshield, the dog in the front seat can be seen trying to get onto his lap while he shoves it back.

"I hope you know what you're doing," Lorcan says as we walk back to the Mclaren.

"Oh, she does." Quinn grins at him as we get back in the car. "Finally, I've been telling you for years to get yourself a dog," she says to me.

"There's considerably more to handle than just one," Lorcan frowns, glancing behind as the convoy restarts.

"I'm sure Viola can multi-task," Quinn says.

And Lorcan snorts as if reliving the night before.

I close my eyes, hoping they'll all just go away.

"Do they have names?" Saskia asks.

I shake my head, eyes still closed. *Why the fuck would they have names? I don't even know my name.*

Then I remember the file.

It's inside the backpack I brought with me, still stained in Dino's blood. Only now, it's heavier, filled with much more information that Dante has been collecting about me. Real documentation instead of forged ones. I take it out and read through it, occasionally stopping to take it all in.

"All alright?" Lorcan asks, placing a hand on my thigh after I close it shut and stuff it back into the bag. When I don't answer, he adds, "We can talk about it later."

I say nothing at first and just look out the window at the passing foliage, dark in places where the light can't reach, like me.

Saskia has fallen asleep in the back, and Quinn is deep into her work on her laptop. It's just me and Lorcan and the world outside of it.

Like when we left Sacred Heart the first time, and it was just us.

But now, when I reach inside, I come up with a tangled mess of all sorts of jagged emotions. Not full, blinding ones. Just bits, scattered pieces of what was my lost soul, coming back to life. Curiosity. Satisfaction. Desire.

Is this what living feels like?

"My real mother was called Viola too," I say, breaking the silence. "He named me after her."

Lorcan nods at me. "She was Adrien's childhood sweetheart?"

"He was her stalker. She had a restraining order against him in Italy. He tracked her down and killed her when my mother tried to start a new life in England." Lorcan's hand on my thigh tenses. He opens his mouth to say something soothing, but now I've started, I can't stop. "She met my father when she was an exchange student here. He was Rebecca's brother," I continue.

"So Rebecca is your aunt?"

"Adrien married her after he killed my parents." I wait a few seconds before adding, "He burned them in a fire."

Lorcan takes my hand as he drives, squeezing it as I let him. "So Hawkes is your real name?" he asks when the silence between us drags on.

"It is. And this is my mother," I say, opening the pendant that was stuffed into the file. A note attached to it said as much in Dante's handwriting. On one side is a picture of two chubby toddlers, one older and fairer, the other darker and more sullen looking. A photograph of a woman with blonde hair and blue eyes is on the other side.

Lorcan glances at the open pendant in my hand before turning his eyes back to the empty road ahead. "She's beautiful."

"I take after my father," I snort.

"Who wasn't a psychotic monster," Lorcan reminds me.

"No, no, he wasn't," I say after a few minutes while that sinks in.

"And neither are you," he adds with surety.

I look at Lorcan then, knowing he's got me and that I also have him, Dino, and Jude. Even Dante has a place in my heart. I used to not want to get caught. I used to be careful. I trusted no one. But now, with them beside me, it's like my heart has started beating again. Hot, rich blood has started pulsing through me, opening me up to the light, chasing the cold and dark from my veins.

I wouldn't say it's love.

But it feels....warm, like the smooth metal on the sleek weapon in my pocket when I close my fingers around it.

Maybe one day, I'll know what love is.

And just maybe…

I'll wear all four rings for them.

And finally, admit what's carved into my stained, monstrous stone-cold heart.

———

ALSO BY MALLORY FOX

WICKED HEARTS AT WAR

A Dark Stepbrother Bully Romance

War Of Hearts

Wicked Hearts

Hearts Break

A VIOLENT AGENDA

A Dark Serial Killer Romance

A History of Violence

A Legacy of Sorrow

A Promise of Torment

MARKED

A Dark Capture Romance

Marked for Death

DIE FOR YOU

A Dark Mystery Romance

You Consume Me

STANDALONES

A Dark Teacher Student Romance

Sinful

A Dark Monster Romance

Gods May Cry (writing as Lea Jade)

ABOUT THE AUTHOR

Mallory Fox is addicted to reading, chocolate-covered pretzels, and looking deep into heart-melting, big brown eyes... the canine kind.

She loves to write deliciously dark romance with wicked, twisty plots about forbidden love, unhinged FMCs, jealous possessive harems, and all kinds of angsty smut.

Mallory currently lives in London with her bean-shaped dog and the rest of her non-furry family.

Find more Mallory on Facebook or sign away your soul at malloryfoxauthor.com/newsletter.

#wickedwordswithheart

Printed in Great Britain
by Amazon

19488438R00180